The Maes
Wore Mohair

A Liturgical Mystery

by Mark Schweizer

SJMPBOOKS

Liturgical Mysteries
by Mark Schweizer

Why do people keep dying in the little town of St. Germaine, North Carolina? It's hard to say. Maybe there's something in the water. Whatever the reason, it certainly has *nothing* to do with St. Barnabas Episcopal Church!

Murder in the choirloft. A choir-director detective.
They're not what you expect...they're even funnier!

The Alto Wore Tweed
The Baritone Wore Chiffon
The Tenor Wore Tapshoes
The Soprano Wore Falsettos
The Bass Wore Scales
The Mezzo Wore Mink
The Diva Wore Diamonds
The Organist Wore Pumps
The Countertenor Wore Garlic
The Christmas Cantata
The Treble Wore Trouble
The Cantor Wore Crinolines
The Maestro Wore Mohair

ALL the books now available at
your favorite mystery bookseller or sjmpbooks.com.

"It's like Mitford meets Jurassic Park, only without the wisteria and the dinosaurs..."

Advance Praise for *The Maestro Wore Mohair*

"This book is so good that it should win some kind of award or prize or something, if only they gave out awards and prizes for books."
Jeff Byrd, real estate mogul

"A great many people now writing would be better employed raising chickens."
Alex Schweizer, brother

"The only mystery is why did I keep reading after page one?"
Beverly Easterling, incidental character

"Whenever God closes a door, somewhere he opens a window. The author should find that window and jump out."
Maggie Michaud, ex-bookclub member

"Some books should be tasted, some devoured, but only a few should be chewed and digested thoroughly. Luckily, my dog took care of that last part."
Monica Jones, jewelry designer

"With his thirteenth book, Schweizer has shown amazing perseverance, a virtue whereby mediocrity achieves a certain inglorious success."
Dr. Richard Shephard, consultant

"I've had a perfectly wonderful evening reading a book. Not this book, though."
Caroline Rollins, choir member

"Schweizer has Van Gogh's ear for dialogue."
John S. Dixon, peanut broker and organist

"A Templar unmasked. A legendary virus. Tabitha, a microbiologist and swimsuit model, finds herself haunted by her past when terror strikes anew. Now she must join forces with the meddling Dr. Winkie to unlock the puzzle. The journey takes them from a Turkish bazaar to a private spacestation and finally to the gateway of hell itself. But the prize for victory may prove to be a threat to all life on Earth ... Wait, what book is this again?"
Beth Brand, ghostwriter

"I am returning this otherwise good paper to you because someone has printed gibberish all over it and put your name at the top."
Robert Lehman, composer and church musician

For Mollie and Bob Rich
who taught me to sing,
and introduced me to the wonderful, wonderful
World of Liturgy.

The Maestro Wore Mohair

A Liturgical Mystery

Copyright ©2015 by Mark Schweizer

Illustrations by Jim Hunt
www.jimhuntillustration.com

All rights reserved. No part of this publication may be reproduced, stored in a retrieval system or transmitted in any form or by any means electronic, mechanical, photocopying, recording or otherwise, without the prior written permission of the publisher.

Published by
SJMPBOOKS
www.sjmpbooks.com
P.O. Box 249
Tryon, NC 28782

ISBN 978-0-9844846-8-3

July, 2015

Acknowledgements
John and Karen Dixon, Betsy and Jay Goree,
Beverly Easterling, Chris Schweizer, Donis Schweizer

Prelude

"You know that you're going to be an old man by the time that baby gets into high school."

Pete was sitting on the back deck, joining me for a late Friday afternoon beer and cigar. My Romeo y Julieta indulgence had been relegated to Friday afternoons. Beer was okay anytime. For now.

"I know," I said, "but there's nothing I can do about it. By the time graduation rolls around, I'll be in my sixties."

"Maybe you'll be lucky and she'll drop out and become a rock-star or something. Then you won't have to endure the ignominy of pretending to be her grandfather."

"How do you know it's a she?" I said.

"I just assumed," said Pete.

"Well, it's a thought," I said. "I'll speak to the kid about it in fourteen years or so."

"You really should quit smoking cigars," said Pete. He took a hard pull on the Cuban, then watched his slow exhale catch the light summer breeze and disappear against the river view. "With a new baby and all, you need to think about your health. These things will kill you."

"That's why I'm down to Friday afternoons, outside on the deck. One cigar per week."

Pete leaned back in the wooden Adirondack and put his feet up on the deck rail. He took the cigar out of his mouth and looked at it, rolling it lovingly back and forth between his thumb and index finger. "I can take some of these off your hands if you want. We wouldn't want them to go bad."

"Not a problem. They're in a fancy humidor." I looked at my own cigar, resting between two fingers, then put it back between my teeth and gave it a puff. "They should be good for a couple of years anyway."

"Mmph," grunted Pete. He looked out across the river at the hawk we'd been watching for the past twenty minutes. It was circling, maybe tracking some small animal, maybe eyeing some carrion. Whatever held the hawk's attention was on the other side of the water and, although we tromped through that pasture regularly, our crossing was downstream several hundred yards. The bird seemed to know that neither Pete nor I would be bothering him, nor would the dog who was busy sniffing out whatever he could find in the woods further up the hill.

The hawk dropped out of the air and vanished into the tall grass.

"Got it," said Pete, pointing the lit end of his cigar at the bird flouncing around in the foliage. The hawk struggled, flapped hard for a few beats, then rose into the air carrying an unfortunate rodent to its inevitable doom. "Red-shouldered hawk," Pete said. "Female, I think. I couldn't tell till she popped back up. Big one, too. She probably has a nest somewhere up there." He nodded toward a grove of mature walnut trees up river, the hawk making a beeline for the canopy. We watched until the hawk disappeared into the trees.

"Meg's still in Charleston?"

"Until tomorrow," I answered. "Her conference ends tonight, but she's staying over and driving back in the morning."

Pete nodded, took a sip from his bottle of beer, then followed it with another draw on the cigar.

"Mmph," he grunted again. It was a grunt of contentment and I was happy to follow his lead.

"Uhmph," I replied.

We sat quietly for about ten minutes, listening to the sounds of the meadow, grunting occasionally, and considerably diminishing our cheroots. I heard a vehicle drive up to the front of the house and, although I couldn't see it from my chair on the deck, I knew who it was. We didn't get many visitors out here in the middle of two hundred acres.

"Another beer?" I asked Pete. My own bottle had been empty since the hawk left. "I think Nancy and Dave just drove up."

"Well, why not?" said Pete.

I got up and walked to the door leading into the garage. The good beer was in the beer fridge in the garage. The regular kitchen fridge had a small supply of okay beer for guests who wouldn't appreciate the good stuff. Dave usually drank the okay beer, but Nancy knew there was good beer available and so, wouldn't be mollified with a bottle of Heineken. Good beer for everyone. I felt magnanimous. I *was* magnanimous.

Magnanimous because the beer in the beer fridge was something special. I had moved from being a beer enjoyer to being a beer enthusiast. I was able to do this because of Meg's prowess in financial management and the fact that our fortune was now such that we didn't have to worry about spending twenty dollars on a bottle of beer — black-market prices to be sure, but it didn't matter because I wasn't going to tell her anyway. I retrieved

6

four bottles of Pliny the Elder, a brew of exceptional rarity and deliciousness, and headed back onto the deck.

"What's this?" said Dave, looking askance at the long narrow bottle I handed him, dark brown with a green and red label.

"Beer, Dave," said Nancy. "It's beer. Good beer."

"Not Heineken?"

Nancy rolled her eyes. "Give him a Heineken, Hayden."

"Refrigerator in the kitchen," I said to Dave, and he left to fetch it.

"I'll take that one home with me, if you want," said Nancy, reaching for Dave's bottle. "It'd be a shame for you to have to walk it all the way back into the garage. I'll give it a good home and raise it as if it were my own."

"You're lying," said Pete, his feet still propped up on the deck rail. He popped the cap off his own beer and took a long swallow, then passed the church key to Nancy. "That poor thing doesn't stand a chance at your house. Probably wouldn't last till sunset."

"I guess not," admitted Nancy. "Still ..."

"Take it with you," I said. "You want a cigar?"

"I wouldn't mind."

Lt. Nancy Parsky was still in her uniform, a cop with attitude: trousers, shirt, badge, and gun. Her brown hair was pulled back into a no-nonsense ponytail. Dave Vance was in his uniform, which was to say, tan chinos and a button-down blue shirt. Since he did most of his work in the office, he didn't bother with the state-approved option. My uniform was jeans and a polo shirt, although on this particular afternoon I was also wearing a light poplin jacket against the cool edge of weather coming through. My own gun was in the pickup. My other gun was in the organ bench. I had a badge somewhere. It said, "Police Chief, St. Germaine, North Carolina."

I reached into the breast pocket of my jacket and pulled out a cigar for Nancy. Dave wouldn't want one, I knew. Dave was a nonsmoker.

"Cuban! Nice! Thanks, Hayden."

"You're welcome. Anything happening in the Village of St. Germaine on this lovely afternoon?"

Nancy reached into her breast pocket and retrieved a notebook, then flipped it open.

"Traffic ticket to Lena Carver. She wasn't happy. You should be hearing from her next week. A couple of parking warnings to out-of-towners. I stopped by Helen Pigeon's house and heard about Sue Clark's dog scaring her goats again."

"You know," I said, "I don't really want to hear about those goats anymore."

"You're not kidding. Why would anybody want to raise Tennessee Fainting Goats anyway? The whole concept is stupid."

"So what'd you do?" asked Pete.

"Shot Sue's dog," said Nancy, without a blink. She tucked the notebook away, then took her beer and parked herself next to Pete. I walked over and lit her cigar.

"She did not," said Dave, walking back onto the deck, Heineken in hand.

"I thought about it," said Nancy. "Then I thought about shooting Helen. Maybe I need a vacation."

"All of us have thought about shooting Helen," Dave said.

"What kind of dog is it?" asked Pete.

"Some kind of schnitzley wiener thingy with long hair," said Nancy between puffs. "I don't like those designer dogs. Gimme a big ol' mutt any day."

As if on cue, Baxter the Swiss Mountain Dog made his appearance onto the deck and headed straight for Nancy. Not a mutt by any stretch, Baxter was, nevertheless, big.

"There he is!" she said, giving him a hug, then rubbing his head vigorously. Baxter was a favorite of hers and the feeling seemed to be mutual. He sat down beside her wooden chair and rested his head on her lap.

"I like a big dog, too," said Pete. "Maybe I'll get a dog."

"You have a pig, Pete," said Dave. "A truffle pig."

"I could have a dog. I could have both. The world's my oyster."

"It is," I agreed. "As long as Cynthia doesn't find out. A big dog is hard to hide."

"It'll be a puppy when I get it," said Pete. "Then, by the time it gets big, she'll love it."

"Maybe you should just get one of those oysters," said Dave. "Then when it gets too big you can eat it or feed it to the pig."

"You can't play fetch with an oyster," said Pete, "and they're not cuddly. Oh, sure, when it's a cute little baby mollusk squirting around the bathtub, you think, 'I can grow to love this bivalve,' but sooner or later, you sit down on it in the tub. Then, bam! Oyster stew."

"I can see the drawbacks," I said, and tried the beer. Delicious.

"On the upside," said Nancy, "you might get a pearl out of the deal."

"We were discussing," said Pete, "before you arrived, the fact that Hayden would be in his sixties by the time his daughter is out of high school."

"You're having a daughter?" said Dave. Then, "Wow. I never thought about how old you'd be."

"Ancient, and it's fifty-fifty on the daughter."

"As for your decrepitude," said Nancy, "there's nothing you can do."

"My feeling exactly," I said.

Nancy angled her head and gave me a long look. "At least Meg is younger than you."

"Not that much younger," I said. "We'll probably be so infirm we'll have to send the child to a fancy French boarding school."

"It's what all the rich people do," agreed Pete.

"Yep," said Dave, then took a long swig from his Heineken.

"When I get my new dog," said Pete, "I'm going to send it to boarding school."

"Have you chosen a name yet?" asked Nancy.

"I think maybe Fritz," said Pete, "or Fritzi if it's a bitch."

"Not the dog," said Nancy in disgust. "The baby."

I nodded. "If it's a boy, Lord Remington. If it's a girl, I'm leaning toward Cornelia — after my great-great aunt — or maybe Abishag. That one's very Old Testament."

"Old Aunt Corny," said Pete. "She'd be so pleased."

Nancy snorted. "This is why you won't be naming the baby," she said.

"Of course I won't. I have no delusions."

"Does Meg have any thoughts?"

"I'm sure she does, but I am not at liberty to say. She says you have to actually meet the baby before you name it. That way you know if the name fits. I say, if the baby throws up when you say its name, that means you'd better think of another one."

"Not the same with a dog," said Pete. "I'm calling it Fritz or Fritzi, so don't you go stealing my dog's name for your baby."

"Fritzi Cornelia Konig if it's a girl," said Dave. "I like it."

"Me, too," I said. "I'll put it on my list."

Pete growled. Baxter pricked up his ears at the sound and glanced over, but his head remained on Nancy's lap, his eyebrows going up and down as his gaze shifted. Nancy rubbed him between the ears.

"There's the hawk," I said, pointing across the river at the big bird we'd seen earlier, now circling again. "Back for another snack."

We smoked our cigars, drank our beers, and watched the hawk, and it was good.

The late afternoon sun was warm enough, but the breeze coming off the river gave a chill to the air as the sun began to drop behind the mountain and the shadows lengthened across the far meadow. Pete, Nancy, and Dave said their goodbyes and left me to feed the dog and make myself some dinner.

Baxter was happy with a can of dog food poured over his chow. I was happy with the last two pizza slices left over from a lunch run to the Bear and Brew on Wednesday. Meg had been gone since Wednesday morning and I'd been surviving on this pizza for three days now — for supper anyway, breakfasts being taken at the Slab Café and generally large enough to hold me well into the dinner hour.

I carried the pizza into the den and sat down at the typewriter desk, setting the plate off to the side. This was an old typewriter, Raymond Chandler's typewriter, now mine, thanks to the aforementioned fortune. Money could buy typewriters, but not talent — this was Meg's assertion as she read the stories I continued to produce on the old machine and pass out to the choir for their amusement or, as she put it, their amazement. I had quite a pile of them now, some better than others, but all, in my opinion, reeking of genius. Reeking. Yes, that was the word Meg used as well.

I took a bite of the mushroom and sausage slice, then opened the drawer of the desk and pulled out the large manila folder containing these masterworks of detective choral fiction. There they were, my darlings: *The Alto Wore Tweed, The Baritone Wore Chiffon, The Soprano Wore Falsettos, The Cantor Wore Crinolines.* Eleven all together, containing some of the most brilliant prose ever penned. I picked up a page and read it again.

Lilith was dead, as dead as her dream of becoming the head maid in a high-rise leper condo that was permanently unclean.

What was Meg thinking? This was brilliant. The only problem I could see was that I'd already made my way through the choir and used every singer and voice part I could think of: bass, baritone, tenor, countertenor, alto, mezzo, soprano, treble, diva, and cantor — even squeezing in the organist. Still, this was Raymond Chandler's typewriter after all, and if it couldn't provide inspiration, nothing could.

I put a piece of paper into the typewriter and rolled it behind the platen. Fortifying myself with another bite of pizza, I clicked on the green-shaded banker's lamp and placed my fingers on the old glass keys. The digits seemed to move with a will of their own.

The Maestro Wore Mohair

Baxter, from the kitchen, looked up from his dog bowl and gave a mournful howl.

But what does a dog know?

Chapter 1

Saturdays at the Slab Café were always busy and this one was no exception. I'd talked to Meg and she was on her way home from Charleston, planning to arrive in the early afternoon. Plenty of time for breakfast.

Noylene was waiting tables, looking harried as usual. She didn't open the Beautifery on Saturdays and even during the week didn't take any appointments before eleven. She'd gotten her start as a waitress and enjoyed the work. As the wife of Brother Hog McTavish, international tent revivalist, and the mother of Rahab McTavish, toddler evangelist, she didn't need the job. The money seemed to flow over them in Showers of Blessings.

"Morning, Chief," she called, when I walked in.

"Morning, Chief," echoed about twenty patrons, all of whom I knew. The only ones who didn't sound the greeting were the visitors to town, the ones not sure of just how friendly they should be.

"Good morning," I called back. "Beautiful morning." I saw Cynthia Johnsson sitting at a table with Georgia Wester, their heads close together. The Mayor of St. Germaine and the Sr. Warden of St. Barnabas — a high level meeting, no doubt. Cynthia's gaze came up and she motioned me over to the table.

"Sit here," she said, pulling out a chair.

"Something up?"

"Nah," said Cynthia. "Just chatting."

"Where's Pete?" I asked. Pete Moss owned the diner and was usually to be found, if not behind the counter or in the kitchen, at least holding court at one of the back tables.

"He said something about picking up a guy named Fritz," said Cynthia. "I didn't get the whole story. He was on his way out the door."

"Ah."

"We were discussing the dead body," said Georgia.

Noylene appeared at the table with a coffee pot, turned a coffee cup right-side-up, and filled it. "The usual?" she asked.

"What usual?" I replied. "I never get the same thing."

"Exactly," said Noylene, moving to the next table. "Coming right up."

Cynthia laughed at my confused look. "She's been that way all morning. Don't fight it. You might get something good."

"I *might* get a liver and chive omelette," I said. "Pete had that on the menu last week."

"Yeah," said Georgia, unimpressed. "That's a good point. Now about that dead body."

Georgia owned Eden Books, the bookstore on one corner of the town square. St. Germaine had about fifteen shops and eateries on the square, all looking out across Sterling Park. The two largest buildings in town were also on the square: the courthouse and St. Barnabas Episcopal Church. The library and the police station, Noylene's Beautifery, the Slab, a flower store, a jeweler, a hardware store, the Ginger Cat, the Bear and Brew, these, and a few more, made up the downtown retail district.

"Who's minding the store?" I asked.

"I don't open till ten," said Georgia.

"Really? Ten?"

"Or whenever I finish breakfast," she said, shrugging. "No one wants a book before ten. Anyway, most of my business is internet now. But, back to the body."

"That body was in the woods for thirty years at least," I said. "Maybe more. That's the verdict from Dr. Murphee. A skeleton, and not much left of that."

The body under discussion had been found by two young teen-aged boys tramping around Coondog Holler just after school let out in June. They had slid down a wash and one of them kicked up the skull, half-buried in the silt, and covered with leaves. The skull came home with the boy and, after he put it through the dishwasher, ended up on the bookshelf of his bedroom. His parents never noticed it and nothing would have been said if his partner in crime hadn't been convicted by the Holy Spirit during the prayer circle at the St. Barnabas Youth meeting. He tearfully confessed their transgression to the group. Linda Whitman, current sponsor of the youth group, called me, and I visited young Jack Tinkler's room with his mother in tow.

"But I didn't kill him!" protested Jack as his mother loudly pronounced a perpetual grounding on the boy.

"You put a skull in my new dishwasher!" screamed Mrs. Tinkler. "It still has hair on it!"

A dejected Jack showed us the gully and we found the rest of the bones tout de suite.

"So it's not PeeDee McCollough?" said Georgia. "I thought maybe it would be. That's right down the mountain from Ardine's trailer."

The tale in the wind was that Ardine had fed PeeDee, her abusive husband, a cup of oleander tea when her three children were small. PeeDee had been a fixture around town as recently as twelve years ago. According to Ardine, PeeDee just decided one day he'd had enough of family life and left for the Florida panhandle, leaving his three children, Bud, Pauli Girl, and Moosey, fatherless but better off.

"It appears not to be PeeDee," I said. "It's a woman's skeleton."

"Are y'all going to do a DNA test?" asked Cynthia.

"I suppose we will," I said with a sigh. I hadn't gotten the entire report back from Kent Murphee yet. The Watauga County Medical Examiner was scheduled to take a rare vacation, a three week tour of Peru but, although he offered to postpone the trip, his wife, Jennifer, was less accommodating. There was no hurry, I assured him, and they took off for the glories of Machu Picchu.

"I saw on the Discovery channel that you can trace your ancestry through a DNA test," said Georgia. "I'll bet that it's someone from around here. You can probably narrow down the family anyway."

"I doubt it. Unless they're newcomers like me, everyone here is related at some level. Plus, that would be very expensive doing all those tests."

"Hmm," said Georgia, thinking. "I guess you'll just have to use your detective prowess to figure out the murder."

"First of all, we don't know that it *was* a murder. It may have been some hiker that had an accident. Thirty years ago, there wasn't anything out there."

"Maybe a bear got him," suggested Cynthia.

"Quite possibly," I said brightly, although there was no evidence of a bear attack. Kent would have spotted that immediately. Bears are not delicate eaters. "Yes, a bear," I said. "Possibly a bear. Let's go with that."

"No, it was murder," said Georgia. "I can feel it in my bones. Besides, we haven't had a murder for at least six months. It's getting too quiet around here."

"Well, you still have the church to worry about," I suggested. "Surely there are dastardly doings afoot."

"It's been pretty quiet," Georgia said.

I knew it had been quiet. I'm the organist and choirmaster, my part-time job. We'd gotten a new interim priest following Father Dressler's hasty departure after the Blessing of the

Groundhog on Candlemas. Father Dressler had been our interim when the Rev. Rosemary Pepperpot-Cohosh and St. Barnabas parted ways over a small matter of one hundred thousand dollars, a one-way ticket to Nicaragua, and a yoga instructor named Enrique.

I'd been the musician at the church, off and on, since I moved to St. Germaine twenty-three years ago. I'd seen the clergy come and go and I enjoyed working with many of them.

Some of them.

Okay, two of them ... but those two had the longest tenure and counted for seventeen of the twenty-three years. Our current rector seemed like a nice enough and competent fellow and he made his living as an interim priest, smoothing over the rough spots and acting as a mediator for those parishes in turmoil. I'm not sure ours was one of those, but St. Barnabas certainly had its problems finding and keeping clergy.

Thomas Walmsley was married with two grown children. His wife, Mallary, was a tenured university professor and, we were informed, would continue to teach and make the long commute from Northern Virginia to the Blue Ridge Mountains of North Carolina on school vacations and holidays. We hadn't met her yet, even though Thomas had now been serving St. Barnabas for a few months. If he had any quirk, it was his penchant for wearing his alb barelegged, his bare feet covered only by sandals, giving him the look of an affluent monk. This was only during services. On a normal day, he'd dress like any other middle-aged priest.

"I don't know if he has shorts on or not," Carol Sterling, one of the communion servers told me. "I'm pretty sure not, but I'm not asking. At least he changes in his office."

"Even Kimberly Walnut is behaving," said Georgia. "Now that she's a deacon, she wants to change her title again and revisit her job description. Apparently 'Christian Formation Director' has given way to 'Minister of Christian Development and Ministry.' These things are very important to Kimberly Walnut."

"I thought sure she was going to get the sack after the groundhog incident," Cynthia said, "but Father Dressler resigned so fast, she escaped. I swear, she's got more lives than a cat."

Georgia nodded her agreement. "Maybe the whole thing taught her a lesson."

"Nope," I said. "Not a chance."

"This week she's at her yearly touchy-feely Uni-luther-presby-metho-lopian conference. I just can't wait to see what she comes back with. Not only that, but she's doing some degree study on-line that we're paying for."

"How is the search committee doing? Any consensus?"

"As a matter of fact, yes," said Georgia. "We have two recommendations to present to the vestry. The plan is to invite these two to come in for interviews, stay the weekend, meet folks, and maybe celebrate during a service. The bishop is good with that."

"Sounds like a plan," I said. "Make sure they preach while they're here."

"Of course."

"Didn't we do that before?" asked Cynthia.

"It's a long story," Georgia said, with a heavy sigh.

We heard the old cowbell bang against the glass of the front door as it swung open, then Pete's voice booming across the room.

"Big news!" he announced to no one in particular. He saw the three of us sitting in the back and decided we would be the first to hear his news. He wove his way between the tables, glad-handing most of the customers, then grabbed the last chair and sat down.

"Big news," he said again.

"Well, what is it?" asked Cynthia. "What's the big news? The whole restaurant is waiting to hear."

Pete looked around. Cynthia was right. Everyone had stopped eating and talking, and was waiting on Pete's announcement.

"Huh," said Pete. "Well, it *is* big news. Camp Possumtickle has been sold again."

"Really?" said Cynthia.

Camp Possumtickle had been the summer camp of choice for many of the kids within a couple of hundred miles, Cynthia included. When it was bought by the Christian Nudists, there had been a sense of melancholy among those who had fond memories of their camping experience. Renamed *Camp Daystar*, the Daystar Naturists of God and Love (DaNGL) had kept the camp going for several years. But eventually even naked Christian Karaoke loses its appeal, and we'd heard the nudists were strapped for cash. Our hope was that a nonprofit group, or rather a *non-prophet* group, would buy it and restore it to its former glory — cabins, canoes, counselors, campfires ... the whole kit and caboodle. We'd seen it advertised on the internet, but hadn't heard any news.

16

"Well, don't keep us on tenderhooks," said Noylene. "Who bought it?"

"A consortium out of Texas. They specialize in entertainment venues."

Everyone looked at Pete, waiting.

"We're getting a Renaissance Fair!"

Chapter 2

The Maestro Wore Mohair

It was a dark and stormy night — "dark" in this context meaning having little light, rather than being evil or wicked (which is definition No. 2 on dictionary.com), and although the night might not be evil per se, it was most certainly No. 8: gloomy; cheerless; dismal — and the rain fluttered down like an orphan's tears on Christmas. I heard the metallic clank of the mail flap, glanced at the office door, and pondered the unexpected delivery that was the size of a shoebox, but much thinner and longer, as if the person wore shoes that were size eighteen, extra-flat.

"You might as well come in," I called into the dark (No. 1 again.)

The door opened darkly (No. 16b: acoustically damped) and there she stood: a dark and stormy dame (No. 4: swarthy; not pale or fair — stormy: characterized by violent passions.)

She gestured to the three-day old pot of joe bubbling on the hotplate and exclaimed violently and passionately, thus fulfilling her "stormy" epithet, "Gimme a coffee and make it dark!" (No. 7: containing only a small amount of milk or cream.) I reached for a cup, spit in it and wiped it out with my pocket handkerchief, then poured a dose and set it on the edge of my desk.

She didn't come in, but tossed her dark (No. 6: brunette) hair and considered me darkly (No. 9a: sullenly). "Pedro sent me," she said, her voice dark (No. 16a: having a back-vowel resonance), "I'm in trouble and I need a shoofly I can trust."

"You can trust me, Doll-face," I said, "for two yards a day plus expenses. You can trust anybody for two yards a day. What's your moniker?"

"Monika. Monika Knight, but you probably know me as Stormy."

I could hear Meg in the kitchen, a pot or pan clanging occasionally against this or that. I had Leonard Bernstein's *Chichester Psalms* on the stereo. It was a fine piece, music to write to, beginning by gathering energy, dissonant sevenths sounding in every chord like church bells. Then, in a jubilant 7/8 meter, a festive acclamation in Hebrew, "Make a joyful noise unto the Lord, all ye lands."

"Supper will be ready in a little while," Meg called, "so finish up, and wash your hands. You've been playing on that typewriter all evening and Lord knows who had their fingers all over those keys."

"Raymond Chandler," I called back. "That's who."

The delicate voice of a boy soprano came over the speakers singing a tranquil melody: the second movement, "The Lord is my shepherd." I kept typing.

"I've heard of you," I said. "The opening act down at Buxtehooters. You and your cousin. You've got a singing duo."

"You've heard of us?" She sounded pleased, but her expression was dark (No. 9b: frowning.)

I nodded. Dirk and Stormy Knight, the hottest ticket on the strip, dark on Sunday (No. 15: offering no performances.) What I'd heard was that the act was dark (No. 11: destitute of culture), but in this town, that was no reason not to cash in.

"He's not really my cousin," she went on. "Dirk is more like an unrelated uncle. You know, the kind that used to live in the basement, but has now moved into the den and put up a bed sheet to define his space."

I nodded again. I had such an uncle. Everyone did.

"Hey, you," called Meg. "Don't make me come in there. We're having lobster."

"Lobster?" I called back.

"Lobster and steak. I picked up some spiny lobsters in Charleston. They're fresh."

"Give me just a couple more minutes," I said. "I'm on a roll here."

x

I looked at the package, still on the floor, and queried interrogatively, "Wassa?" She followed my gaze, then bent down and picked up the envelope with all the grace of a spiny lobster, one of the most graceful and delicious crustaceans in the animal kingdom, and I should know, I've eaten enough of them. She swayed up to the desk, her hips grinding like a garbage disposal stuffed with lobster shells, then suddenly became dark as the aforementioned decapod (No. 14a: silent; reticent), then stormy, then dark again (this time No. 12: hard to understand; obscure), then whimpered darkly (No. 8), "Pictures. Terrible pictures."

x

"Dinner is served," came the call. "I'm giving yours to Baxter if you don't hurry up."

I clicked off the lamp and went into the kitchen where, as promised, there were two reddish-orange lobsters eyeing me accusingly from a serving platter. The steak, at least, wasn't trying to stare me down.

"These things are huge," I said, pulling out Meg's chair for her.

"I had a crazy craving for lobster this morning, so I picked them up at the fresh market before I left Charleston."

"So your cravings are finally paying off for me."

"I'm not having steak," Meg said, sitting down. "No rice either." She made a face at the bowl of rice pilaf. "I'm having a corn dog with mine, and a slice of mango. Do you want a corn dog?"

"Nope. The steak will be just fine."

"Then I'll save the other one for a midnight snack." She brushed away a strand of black hair that had gotten loose from

20

her ponytail, then pushed the two lobsters across the table. "Would you crack mine for me? The thought of all that lobster juice just makes me sick."

"But the meat doesn't?"

"Not a bit. In fact, I'm dying to have at it."

"Sure." I spent a few minutes breaking open the shells and plucking out the edible bits while Meg filled the plates, mine with rice and steak, hers with sliced mango and a corn dog.

"Now, tell me about your adventures in Charleston."

Meg sighed. "Terribly boring. I sat through two classes, then decided I knew more than the presenters, so I took off to do some shopping."

"So, pretty much like the last conference you went to," I said.

"Pretty much," she agreed.

Now four months pregnant, Meg looked terrific, but then, she always looked terrific.

She took a bite of the corn dog and, after two chews, spit the wad back on her plate, a soggy lump of cornmeal and hotdog. "I didn't know they tasted like that," she said, wiping her tongue with her napkin.

"What did you think they tasted like?"

"I don't know. I've never eaten a corn dog." She sighed again, put down her fork and looked at me from across the table with her big blue-gray eyes.

"I feel like a water buffalo," she said.

"Well, you don't look like one," I said, happy to reassure her. "Not yet anyway."

"Some women glow when they're pregnant."

"I heard that."

"Am I glowing yet?"

"Umm ... Not yet." I knew I was on shaky ground here, but still felt that honesty was the best policy.

"I'm either going to start glowing soon or turn into a giant moist cow."

"I vote for glowing," I said, "but moist cow is all right, too."

Tears sprang to her eyes. She didn't say anything, just got up, dropped her napkin on her plate, and went back into the bedroom. I looked at Baxter lying on his rug in the corner, head resting on his two paws, his ears perked.

"You can have the corn dog," I said. "The lobster is mine."

Chapter 3

Thursday night was choir rehearsal night. It had moved over the years, from Thursdays to Wednesdays and back again, at the whims of the clergy and staff. I prefer Thursdays — a day closer to Sunday and one less day the choir has to forget everything they've rehearsed. As was our tradition, the choir had taken the summer off. That is, we didn't have our Thursday night rehearsals, and we sang easy anthems on Sunday with whomever happened to show up. On this Thursday in August, though, summer was over, and the choir was ready to come back.

On rehearsal nights, I usually arrive at the church a good hour before the choir to get some practicing done on the organ. Today was no different. I'd gone through the upcoming hymns, a few anthems, and was well into the postlude for Sunday, Arthur Baynon's *Festal Toccata,* when the choir began to arrive.

The choir loft in St. Barnabas Episcopal Church was situated in the back balcony and had always been so. When the church had burned a few years back, there was some rumbling about putting the choir in the front where people could see them, but the idea gave way to tradition and we ended up in the back where we'd always been. The church was a good size, not too big, not too small, acoustically brilliant, with a fine new pipe organ. St. Barnabas also had an endowment that would choke a moose. All good things.

Marjorie, usually the first to show up, found her seat in the tenor section. She had sung in the St. Barnabas choir since she was a young girl, first as a soprano, then an alto, and now, in her seventies, a tenor. She kept a flask in the book holder of her choir chair. "For emergencies," she claimed.

"Nice playing, Hayden," said Marjorie, "and I really mean it this time. Not like last week when I said it just to be polite. Man, you really stunk it up that day."

"Thank you," I said, "but in my defense, that's how the piece was written. A Max Reger *Capriccio* is not for the faint of heart."

"Ah, well," said Marjorie, "that would be me, the faint of heart. Give me a good ol' hymn anytime." She picked up her choir folder and immediately found my new detective yarn on the back of the psalm for Sunday. "Oh, goody," she said. "A new story."

I'm a private eye, a gumshoe, a shamus, a snooper: a
Liturgy Detective, duly appointed by the bishop, pre-
absolved for all venial sins, with a license to carry a
concealed aspergillum and the guts to use it. Business
had been good, too good, almost. What's good for me is
usually bad for the Church Triumphant, but what did I
care? My 401K was growing like the hair on a six-month-
old piece of baloney stuck to the bottom of the
refrigerator crisper, the one you don't clean out because
the handle is broken and besides, it doesn't smell that
bad anymore. Thanks to the shenanigans of ministers,
priests, fathers, padres, pastors, organists, clerics,
deacons, praise-team leaders, bishops, and the rest, I was
just a hop, skip, and liturgical twirl away from
retirement. Holy Laughter retreats, nude Christian
Karaoke, "Cat in the Hat" Eucharists, these were all part
of my bindle.

"Is Meg coming to choir tonight?" asked Bev Greene, the next
to arrive. "I need to ask her something."

"I think so."

The sound of shoes clomping up the wooden steps to the loft
signaled the arrival of the rest of the choir. They were prompt,
but, of course, this was our first rehearsal since June. They were
bound to be prompt. Next week it might be a different story.

"Hello, Hayden," said Rhiza, appearing at the top of the steps.
She made her way down the three risers to the front row where
the sopranos sat. Rhiza Walker had a degree in vocal music. We
had studied in the same music department once upon a time.
After a Master's degree, I passed on a career in music and went
into law enforcement. Rhiza passed as well and married rich. Very
rich. She could still sing beautifully.

"We've got a new story," called Marjorie, still engrossed and
not bothering to look up from her paper.

"I'm not sure that's an enticement," said Rhiza, finding her
seat next to Bev. "I've read Hayden's best work, you see, and it's
not terribly better than his worst."

"Hey," I said. "This one's different. New. Fresh."

"No, it's not," said Marjorie. "I still don't get it."

"Why come to me?" I asked, but the question was moot as a cow with a speech impediment. I already knew. Following the news of normalized relations with Cuba, the word had hit the street. Castrati. Hundreds of them, maybe millions, grown on a castrato farm down in Cuba, and just coming of age. They were marshaled by their leaders, Fidel Castrato and his brother Raúl, the singing Castrato Brothers. I'd never heard them in person, but as warblers, they were legendary. Their singing school was legendary, too. Guaranteed fame and fortune for the best and worst of them, but there was just one little catch ...

℗

"You see," I said. "I'm taking my prose to a whole new level. By rejecting an objective truth and global cultural narratives, I'm creating an unprecedented situation in which the reader is confronted with the conditioning of his own perception and has to reconsider his biased position."

"Horse dookey," said Marjorie. "Pardon my French."

"Agreed," said Meg, filing in with the others. She, Rhiza, Elaine Hixon, Bev, and Georgia made up the soprano section. "I already read it and I'm not reconsidering my biased position. It's horse dookey."

Nineteen singers currently sang in the St. Barnabas Episcopal Church choir. Like most church choirs, they sounded good on most Sundays, very good on some occasions, less than stellar on others, but all the singers enjoyed it. The five sopranos in the front row were joined by three altos: Goldi Fawn Birtwhistle, Tiff St. James, and Dr. Ian Burch, PhD. Goldi Fawn was a Christian astrologer and hairdresser, Tiff, our scholarship singer from Appalachian State, and Dr. Ian Burch, PhD ... well ... he was our countertenor — a male alto — with a cherished doctorate in early music burnished by a specialty in the French Chanson (1413-1467), and all the personality disorders that suggests. He was a fine singer, though, and principally joined the choir so he could sit beside Tiff and "breathe in her musical essence." Tiff didn't seem to mind the attention too much and kept the unfortunate man's advances at bay.

The other three altos, Marty Hatteberg, Sheila DeMoss, and Rebecca Watts, the town librarian, sat behind them. Back Row Altos — BRAs, and proud of it.

"What's a castrato?" asked Marjorie, putting the story back into her choir folder. "I never heard of such a thing."

Dr. Ian Burch, PhD was more than happy to elucidate. He stood, raised one hand into the air, trying to still the general hubbub, and when that didn't work, gave an enormous "ahem," which sounded like a goose honking, thanks to his magnificent, glowing proboscis. Bob Solomon, in the bass section, answered with a belly laugh.

"Is it duck season already?" said Mark Wells. "I don't even have my decoys out."

Dr. Ian Burch, PhD ignored him. "The castrati," he began, "were surgically altered male singers principally employed in the Baroque era. Castrati, plural. Castrato, singular. The voice is produced by castrating the boy singer before puberty. As a result, his voice never changes and the effect is equivalent to the soprano or mezzo soprano of today, but with much more power, expressiveness, and flexibility."

"Yowch," said Phil Camp from the bass section. "That's a high price to pay for art."

"Is that what happened to you, Ian?" asked Tiff, sweetly.

"You know perfectly well it is not," sniffed Dr. Burch. "I am a countertenor. A falsettist, if you must classify my gift." His head bobbed angrily on the end of his long neck, and his large ears reddened. "Castration, as a way of producing high voices, was made illegal in 1870 and banned by the church even before that. You can read about the castrato and countertenor voices in a paper I submitted to the American Choral Directors Association for their journal."

"Good for you," I said. "I get that journal. When did it appear?"

"Well," said Dr. Burch, "it hasn't been accepted yet, but I published it on-line. I'll be happy to send you the link." He sat down and smiled at Tiff, showing his uneven and slightly greenish teeth. She pretended not to notice.

"Hang on," said Marjorie. "You mean they ..." Her voice trailed off. "They actually ..."

"Indeed they did," said Bert Coley. "Snip-snap! *Viva il coltello!*" Bert was a tenor and an officer with the Sheriff's Department in Boone. He'd been with the PD, but recently changed jobs due to the better hours, he said. He'd been singing with the choir since he was a student at the university. "Long live the knife!"

Randy Hatteberg, the other tenor, made a sour face. "Let's change the subject," he said. "What about that skeleton you guys found in the woods?"

"Yes," said Georgia, smirking. "Tell us about that skeleton."

"We don't know anything about that skeleton," I said, "except it is that of an unfortunate woman. Kent will be back on Monday and he'll give us his verdict."

"I'll bet it was murder," said Goldi Fawn.

"Of course it was," agreed Sheila.

"Probably a love affair gone horribly wrong," Goldi Fawn said.

"A lover scorned," Sheila said. "Hot blood and cold lead."

"Exactly my thinking," agreed Goldi Fawn.

"Nope," said Mark Wells. "I bet it was a bear attack. Back then, there were bears everywhere."

"Well, then," I interrupted, "now that we're all here, let's get started. Why don't we sing through the hymns for Sunday just to warm up? Then, on to the psalm."

Chapter 4

"I'm contesting this ticket," said Lena Carver angrily, barging into the police station in a snit. She smacked the piece of paper down on the counter. "This is an outrage. I claim police malfeasance and ... and ... corruption, or something."

I looked up from my desk where I'd been going through the week's reports. My small office was set back from the main reception area, but the door was always open.

"You got that ticket last week," said Nancy. "I'm sorry, but the statute of limitations has expired on contesting it."

Lena looked confused. "Huh?"

"Yes," Nancy said, picking up the ticket and looking at it. "You see, if you'd only brought this in by yesterday, we could have taken care of it for you, but now it's too late."

"I was out of town!" wailed Lena. "Well, I was out of town on Monday, but I didn't know I had to come in by yesterday. It doesn't say that anywhere on the ticket!"

"No, it doesn't," said Nancy, sympathetically. "It just says you have to appear in court on the 15th of September, or mail in the fine."

"I want to talk to the chief!"

"Morning, Lena," I said, coming out of the office.

Dave Vance appeared outside the glass door to the police station and pushed it open with his foot, his two hands busy with coffees and a box of donuts from the bakery across the square.

"Hi, Lena," he said. "Want a donut?" He put the box down on the counter and held out the cardboard Holy Grounds coffee caddy to Nancy and me. We happily took our cups.

"No, I do not want a donut!"

"This is good coffee," I said, taking a sip. "Do you ever get coffee over at Holy Grounds?"

"Of course I do," said Lena. "Now about this ticket ..."

"I like a dark roast. Lately they've had a Kenyan extra-dark that I really enjoy."

"I like that one, too," said Dave, but they didn't brew it today. This is an Ethiopian blend."

"It's nice," I said, taking another sip. "Piquant and savory."

"This ticket," said Lena.

I picked it up and gave it a look. "Forty-five in a twenty, failure to use a turn signal, and an expired license tag. Sounds bad, Lena."

"The turn signal wasn't my fault. That bulb's been broken for months."

"Ah," I said.

"That license plate sticker is good till my birthday."

"Your birthday *last* year," said Nancy.

"I was on my way to an emergency hair coloring. Noylene said she had a cancellation and could take me at three o'clock. She told me I couldn't be late or she'd take Waynett Stubbs instead."

"If you'd only come in yesterday," said Nancy.

"What happened yesterday?" asked Dave.

"Quiet, Dave," said Nancy.

"Hayden, the ticket is four hundred seventy-five dollars! And *then* my insurance will go up."

"Yeah," I said, "that's tough. You sure you don't want a donut?"

Lena sniffed. "Well ... okay. Maybe one." She took a Bavarian Creme and gave it a nibble.

"You take this ticket down to Caroline Rollins," I said. "She's a good lawyer. She can probably get you some relief on the turn signal, maybe even on the tag. That is, if you haven't had any other tickets in the last couple of years."

"Not that were my fault," said Lena.

"You were in a school zone. You can't do forty-five in a school zone. Not during school hours."

"If only you'd come in by yesterday," Nancy said again, shaking her head sadly.

"How about if I come sing in your choir?" Lena asked me. "I'm a good alto."

"Well, I certainly would be glad to have you," I said, "but I don't know if it will save you from traffic court."

"I'm sure Jesus would appreciate it," said Nancy. "Maybe you'd get some points against all those kids you almost ran down."

Lena glared at her and snatched her ticket back off the counter. "I'll take this to Caroline and see what she can do for me. I was going to come sing in the choir anyway. Hollie is going to come with me. We need to get our voices back in shape. We're going to sing duets at the new Renaissance Fair. They're already advertising for performers on the website."

28

"It won't be open for a year," said Dave. "Next fall, they said."

"We'll be ready," said Lena.

"That's great," I said. "The choir meets Thursdays at seven."

"I know when you meet," said Lena, then turned and stomped out the door into the summer morning.

Sunday morning was a gloomy mess: heavy fog, a misting of rain, and general pre-fall chill in the air with a storm forecast for later in the morning. Typical for the mountains, but not welcomed. Not in late August. Meg and I drove the ten miles into town in my pickup, an old Chevy, now updated and restored to a splendor it never knew when it was on the showroom floor in 1962. Gone were the old springs and shocks, the ancient transmission, worn out vinyl upholstery, and rusted out floor. Even the old engine was gone, replaced by a 5.3 liter V8 EcoTec3 and a fancy computer to run it. The new sound system included satellite radio and an mp3 port. I liked my old truck, but I wasn't a purist. I liked comfort better. The outside had been refurbished as well, now sporting a new blue and white paint job, brightly polished chrome, and an oaken truck bed. The chrome and the wooden truck bed did not come standard on the original, but it was a nice touch I thought. Meg drove a Lexus, and we took that into town on Sundays, but with the weather looking iffy, four-wheel drive was usually a good option to have, especially once we left the paved roads on the way home.

"What's this we're listening to?" she asked.

"*Fantasia on a theme by Thomas Tallis*. Ralph Vaughan Williams."

"I've heard it before."

"Sure," I said. "It was used in *Master and Commander*. That movie with Russell Crowe."

"I remember. It sounds different though, without waves crashing all around."

"Well, give this weather a few hours and you might be surprised."

We arrived downtown. I dropped Meg off at the front doors of St. Barnabas, then drove around the square and parked in front of the police station. I walked across Sterling Park to the church, umbrella at the ready, and headed up to the loft a few minutes before I knew the rest of the choir would show up for the 10:15 rehearsal. Our service was at eleven o'clock.

Meg was already in her choir chair, as was Marjorie, and most everyone else.

"What's going on?" I asked.

"Nothing's going on," said Marty. "We just like to be early."

"Since when?"

"Since the rector is introducing his wife this morning," said Georgia. "Didn't you get the email yesterday?"

"No, I did not."

"Hayden never checks his email," said Meg. "I made sure we were here on time."

As if on cue, Father Tom Walmsley opened the door connecting the sacristy with the nave and entered the sanctuary followed by a tall woman with short dark hair. From the back balcony, we couldn't get a good look, although the entire choir stood and craned to get a peek. Father Walmsley was already in his robe but not yet in his vestments. His bare legs flashed, and his sandals made a flapping sound as he walked down the aisle.

"May we come up, Hayden?" he called.

"Absolutely. Come on up."

The choir quieted immediately and went into their "best behavior" mode. Most of them.

"I don't like this anthem," said Marjorie loudly. "We shouldn't be singing about turtles anyway. I don't even know what a turtle sounds like."

"Shhh!" said Georgia. "Save it for later."

"What's this voice of the turtle? Turtles don't have voices!"

"You should have brought this up last Thursday night," hissed Rebecca.

"I tried to, but nobody would listen to me!"

"Hush up!" whispered Elaine. "Best behavior."

"If a turtle had a voice, it would probably just go 'aaaaack!' I think I heard one do that when I hit it with a lawn mower."

"Oh, my Lord," said Bev, hiding her face in her hands.

Father Walmsley appeared at the top of the steps, then came into the loft followed by the woman. She was just over six feet tall in her black heels, thin, and dressed in *New York Professional:* a dark blue pantsuit, cream-colored blouse, and a patterned scarf. Her hair was short, stylish, and dark, with a smart smattering of gray at the temples. She wore little makeup, or else it was so well done so as not to be noticed. Her reading glasses hung from a thin gold chain around her neck. A small, tight smile played on her lips.

"Don't get up," said Father Walmsley. "I'd just like to introduce my wife. I know I've been here a while now and you've all been wondering if she was real or just imaginary." He waited for laughter to follow his joke, but was disappointed. "Anyway," he continued, "this is Mallary. Dr. Mallary Clochette." He paused for a second, then said, a little sheepishly, "Maestro Clochette. I thought I'd come up and introduce you because she's also a choral musician. A conductor."

That got everyone's attention.

"What do you think about turtles in church?" asked Marjorie. "This turtle anthem is driving me crazy!"

"Oh, no," muttered Bev.

"*My Beloved Spake*?" Mallary asked. "Henry Purcell or Patrick Hadley?"

"Purcell," I said, "but not all of it. We're doing an abbreviated version."

"You know," said Mallary, "though Mr. Purcell takes the lyrics from the Song of Solomon, it really feels more like a celebration of spring and young love than anything else, with its talk of the time of the singing of birds, and the rain being over and gone. I love verse anthems anyway. My favorite part in this one is when the voice of the turtle is heard in the land."

"Really?" said Marjorie.

"Absolutely. Purcell wrote this piece when he was only eighteen, and he had clearly never seen a turtle in his life. Of course, the turtle in question is most certainly a turtledove, but with translations being what they were, scholars are not sure if Purcell knew that or not. At any rate, the music changes dramatically and he writes in a rather exotic, mythical-beast vein. It's quite wonderful really — a moment of delightful strangeness in the middle of a Baroque gem."

I looked over at Dr. Ian Burch, Phd. He was frowning and staring down at his music.

"You're welcome to sing with us," I said. "We'd be happy to have you."

"Thank you, no. I need to be down front on display."

That did bring a laugh.

"I'd love to chat after the service," she said, looking at me, but including everyone in the choir.

31

"We have coffee after the service in the Parish Hall," said Father Walmsley to his wife. Then to us, "We'll see you there."

They disappeared into the stairwell. "Well," said Marjorie, "it all makes sense now. I'm happy to have turtles in church. Why didn't you explain that to us, Dr. Ian Burch, PhD?"

"My expertise is not in the Baroque verse anthem," said Dr. Burch, still scrutinizing his score. "Hayden should have made it plainer."

"My mistake," I said, cheerfully. "Now that we all agree that turtles can be included, let's sing through this one.

"I like to be inclusive," said Marjorie.

ρ

By the time the service began, the storm that had been building all morning had come over the mountains and slammed down on the town in full force. Thunder crashed around us and the rain was coming down in sheets. Most of the congregation that had decided to chance the weather had already arrived and found their seats. The ones that were planning on coming in late probably turned around and went back home rather than brave the onslaught.

We listened to the announcements, sang the processional hymn, heard the opening sentences, and launched into the *Gloria*. "Glory be to God on high," the congregation sang. We hadn't had good congregational singing for a while, but lately they'd stepped up their game. The lights flickered once, but our backup generator kicked on immediately and we continued.

The Old Testament Lesson was from the *Song of Solomon*, the text we'd be singing later in the service. Kimberly Walnut was the reader.

"The voice of my beloved! Look, he comes, leaping upon the mountains, bounding over the hills ..."

Kimberly Walnut was of the opinion that Holy Scripture should be read as though it was Reader's Theater, acted out, with dynamic inflection and different character voices if need be. Her vision of her beloved leaping over the mountains was disconcerting, to say the least.

"My beloved is like a gazelle or a young stag. Look, there he stands behind our wall, gazing in at the windows, looking through the lattice." Kimberly Walnut bit her lip slightly, half-closed her eyelids, and looked positively wanton, relishing the thought of her Biblical Peeping Tom. Her voice became low and sultry. "My beloved speaks and says to me: Arise, my love, my fair one, and come away ..."

Now, the *Song of Solomon* is a fine text. As young teenagers, given the assignment of memorizing a few Bible verses, who amongst us has not chosen Chapter 7: 7-8?

Your stature is like that of the palm,
and your breasts like clusters of fruit.
I said, "I will climb the palm tree;
I will take hold of its fruit."

So I say, let him who is without sin cast the first coconut. However, the licentiousness with which Kimberly Walnut was now reading made every male in the congregation from the ages of twelve to fifty squirm uncomfortably. It was terribly intimate. "My beloved speaks," she continued, "and says to me: Arise, my love, my fair one, and come away: for now the winter is past, the rain is over and gone."

It was at this precise moment that we heard a tremendous crack followed instantaneously by the explosion of thunder, a lightning strike either on the church or somewhere very near. There were some frightened screams from the congregation, the sound being so startlingly loud and so close, and Kimberly Walnut's microphone crackled for several moments. The generator, still running, kept all the lights on. St. Barnabas itself, being relatively new, was equipped with all the necessary precautions for lightning strikes: air terminals for discharge, conductor cables, grounding rods, and whatever else the insurance company had suggested. It didn't help us against what came next.

The lightning hadn't found the church, but instead hit the huge oak tree standing behind the building. The decision had been made to keep the tree when the new building was going up, chiefly because it marked the year that St. Barnabas had been founded. The Founders Oak, we called it, planted in 1842, had survived the fires that had taken the last two church buildings. We couldn't bring ourselves to cut it down and so it remained, in the back garden, shading the entire area.

It was in the silence a moment later that we all heard the tearing sound of wood splitting and coming apart and following

33

that, another crash, less loud but just as terrifying, as a limb came crashing through the image of St. Barnabas himself. The eight-foot-tall stained glass window at the back of the choir loft depicted the mature apostle, our "Son of Encouragement" as the window proclaimed, with his bald pate and curly white beard, his scarlet robes and gold embroidered cope, looking every ounce the bishop. This is a romantic era depiction of the saint that we all realize has very little to do with what Barnabas might have looked like, but it is a good copy of the old window that had been destroyed in the last fire, and we were very happy to have had it replicated.

Now there was a branch jutting from St. Barnabas' midsection. The window had stayed mostly intact, probably due to the lead and solder, and the clear glass UV panel that protected it from the outside. The glass that had broken loose was confined to the top tier of the loft. Thankfully, the singers were all sitting further down. The branch that had punched through our namesake saint, the end of a much larger limb that had broken away from the tree, was about as big around as a baseball bat and had several twigs sprouting from it. Some of the leaves had been stripped away by the impact and littered the floor, but there were plenty left, waving ominously as the wind whipped against the part of the limb that remained outside. Then, suddenly, there was quiet, a dead quiet, and the storm was gone. It was still dark outside, we could tell that by the shadows against the windows, but the wind was stilled, the rain stopped, and the lightning ceased.

Most of the congregation were on their feet and heading toward the front of the nave, wanting to assess the damage for themselves, having heard the crash and the breaking of glass, but not able to see from where they were sitting.

"We're all okay," I called down. "A branch came through the stained glass window, but everyone is fine. Not even a scratch."

"Thank heaven!" said Father Walmsley. He had come to the lectern when Kimberly Walnut had collapsed in a heap on the steps following the crash of thunder. "Everyone, let's take a seat. I think the worst is over. Anyway, if it's not, we're far safer in here than if we run outdoors."

The parishioners seemed to consider that for a moment, then decided that the priest was probably right. They returned to their pews and Father Walmsley went straight into his sermon, this one obviously improvised on the spot, heartfelt and well-timed. He

34

talked about God's grace and our Christian community, and offered several prayers along the way, thanking God for his protection and mercy. By the time he was finished, his flock had calmed considerably, and we continued with the service.

There were many visitors to the choir loft after the final hymn, all wanting to view the carnage and attest to the fact that it was a miracle that no one had been hurt. I'd never seen the loft so full during the postlude, and the crowd didn't seem to notice that I was still playing. They chatted gaily among themselves, pointing at the offending branch and offering suggestions as to how to proceed with the cleanup.

"Duct tape, that's what we need," said one man. I couldn't see who it was from where I was sitting. "We'll just cover this with a tarp."

"It doesn't look that bad," said a woman. "It sure was scary though."

Another: "We should get a broom and sweep this up at least."

"It looks like there's a tree growing out of his stomach," said a kid's voice.

I finished the piece and turned the instrument off.

"That was lovely, Hayden." It was the first woman, Joyce Cooper. "Sorry if we disturbed you."

"Nah," I said with a smile. "I'm not used to anyone listening to the postlude anyway."

Minutes later, Meg and I wandered down to the Parish Hall for coffee and fellowship and spotted a new parishioner right away. I'd met Susan Sievert earlier in the summer when she'd been looking for a house. I didn't know she was one of the Frozen Chosen.

"Hi, Susan," I said, and introduced myself again. "Hayden Konig, itinerant organist. This is Meg, my much better half."

"So nice to meet you," said Meg.

"Some service, huh?" I said. "It's not often we get to experience God's wrath during a worship service."

"Kinda terrifying," agreed Susan.

"I blame Kimberly Walnut," I said. "I expect it was her risqué interpretation of the *Song of Songs* that was to blame. God is not mocked."

"Hush," said Meg. "It wasn't that, and you know it."

"Susan's the new trumpet teacher at the university."

"Welcome! How's school going?"

"Great," said Susan. "We're already in the second week of classes. I'm getting the hang of it."

"Are you a singer?" asked Meg, always on the lookout. "We'd love to have you in the choir."

"I'm not," said Susan, apologetically. "If you need a trumpet player, though ..."

"Hmm," I said. "How about that bass aria and chorus from the *Dettingen Te Deum?* We could have it ready in a couple of weeks."

"I don't know it, but I'm happy to give it a try. Handel, right?"

"Right. I'll email you the music if you like."

"That would be great."

"To tell you the truth, we practiced it last Wednesday," said Meg, giving me the eyebrow. "I think Hayden's been planning on it since he met you in June."

Susan laughed. "Just let me know when. I don't have any weekends booked yet."

A few short conversations later, I found Mallary Clochette, cup of coffee in hand, talking to the matriarchs of St. Barnabas. Wynette Winslow and Mattie Lou Entriken were a pair of apple-cheeked grandmothers, both in their seventies, that had been best friends since they were in the first grade together.

"Morning, Hayden," said Mattie Lou, as I walked up. "That was quite an event, wasn't it? I'm so glad no one was hurt."

"Good morning, ladies," I said. "I'm just as thankful."

"It was a frightening two minutes," agreed Mallary.

"We've just been chatting," said Mattie Lou. "Did you know that Maestro Clochette is the Director of Choral Studies at Mt. Basil University?"

"I'd heard something like that," I said.

"Before that," added Wynette, "she was an assistant professor at Temple. She's going to be taking a sabbatical this semester to work on her conducting book."

"Starting in a few weeks, right, dear?" said Mattie Lou.

Wynette said, "Father Walmsley has two children by a previous marriage, but he and the Maestro have only been married for four years. Clochette isn't her maiden name, though. That was the name of her first husband."

I was always amazed at the information these two women could extract from a victim in under three minutes.

"I'm sorry," Wynette said to Mallary, "I didn't get your maiden name." Maiden names were very important to women of a certain age in St. Germaine. It was who you were.

"Maestro Clochette says that she doesn't have any children," interrupted Mattie Lou, then added, "I suspect that she placed her career over family concerns. Not that there's anything wrong with that, mind you. Sometimes I wish I'd followed my original career path and become a professional fan dancer. There was some real money in that, I can tell you."

"You weren't that good," said Wynette. "I saw you dance at the Purple Pussycat Lounge in Asheville back in '47. Or was it '48?"

"It was '49, dear, and don't tell me I wasn't good. I had men almost crawling up on that stage to get a peek behind that fan."

"They didn't need to," said Wynette. "You were flashing them right and left. I'm amazed you weren't hauled downtown. Then again, you always were a mite friendly to the Asheville Sheriff's Department."

"Oh, she's just jealous," Mattie Lou said, turning her attention back to us. "Just between us, Dr. Clochette, Wynette's still miffed that the Purple Pussycat wouldn't take her. She was a little too plump."

"Plump?" said Wynette. "Balderdash! They offered me a job. I told them I wasn't interested."

"The choir did a good job on that anthem," Mallary said, the smile frozen on her face. "Especially considering the circumstances. One of the men told me that you'd only had them back for one rehearsal since their summer hiatus."

"Well, we have sung that anthem before. The abridged version, anyway."

"Still, they acquitted themselves well."

"You'll be here full time then, in a couple of weeks?" I asked.

"Sooner, maybe. I have a few more things to wrap up at school, then I'll be moving down. I'll be working on the project until Thanksgiving. Then I'm due to go back for a few weeks and conduct the Christmas concert. My associate is preparing the choirs, but I'll need to make the final adjustments."

"We can't wait for you to come down," said Mattie Lou. "You'll fit right in."

"Thomas told me about the skeleton you found in the woods, then about some other ... how shall I put it ... past improprieties that have happened in St. Germaine."

"Oh, yes," said Wynette, brightly. "We're well known for our murders."

"Does this sort of thing happen often?" Mallary asked.

"Pretty much every week," said Mattie Lou.

Chapter 5

Fidel Castrato and his brother Raúl, the singing Castrato Brothers. I'd have this case wrapped up by lunchtime.

"It's not the Castrato Brothers," Stormy Knight said, as if reading my mind like one of those people who makes a living reading people's minds, or at least tells them what they weigh within three pounds. "I know you really want to work that case, but forget it. You don't have the cojones."

"Ouch," I said, my voice rising.

"People will think you've lost your marbles, but the seminal fact is that there is a vas deferens between the Castrato Brothers and the Countertenor League.

"Ouch, ouch!" I squeaked.

She smiled cruelly yet wanly. "It's a common ... misconception."

"Ouch, ouch, ouch."

"Not to mention the eunuch aspect to the case. But, as a detective, let's face it: you're a cut above the others."

"All finished," said the voice of Dr. Kent Murphee over my cell phone. "That skeleton. You want to come down and take a look?"

"Sure," I said. "I'll bring Nancy with me. How was gay Peru?"

"Not so gay," said Kent. "I presume you're speaking in the context of Peru being a country full of mirth, which in my recent experience, it was not."

"I was," I said. "Another bad pun. I think this writing is beginning to affect me."

"Beginning to affect you?" said Kent. "Beginning, you say?"

"Yes. Anyway, we'll be there in an hour."

"See you then."

I wiped a tear from my eye and contemplated the compliment. "So, Sweetheart," I said, crossing my legs, chomping down on a stogy, and collating her curves through the cigar smoke, "if that's not it, then fill me in."

She tossed the envelope onto my desk and snaps spilled across the escritoirish expanse like Pictures at an Exhibition, or rather like Pictures of an Exhibitionist, the one marked "Little Hut with Chicken Legs," particularly disturbing.

I gave them a look-over. "A real professional job," I said, scooting them back into a pile and sliding them into the envelope. "Blackmail, eh?"

"Yes." Her eyes flashed angrily, not so much like a lightning flash, but more like a spark you'd get from touching the cat after walking across a shag carpet, so they really "sparked" angrily, but that doesn't convey the exact amount of anger which was somewhere in between lightning and sparks. "I don't know who's behind this, but they want ten thousand clams to keep them under wraps."

"Is it worth it to you?"

"Sure."

"You have ten thousand?"

"No, that's why I called you."

I took a long pull of my stogy and adjusted my shorts. I knew the case would come up sooner or later, and come up it had. The pictures said it all. Liturgical codpieces. It was only a matter of time.

Kent Murphee's office was a jumble of books, strange antique medical instruments, stacks of papers, half-smoked cigars, and mostly-empty bourbon bottles. Nancy and I made ourselves right at home in the two old leather chairs facing his cluttered desk.

Kent was dressed in his usual tweed coat with the worn elbow patches, matching vest, a stained tie, and corduroy trousers. The shirt might have been clean, it was hard to tell, but the jacket hadn't seen a dry-cleaner since Ronald Reagan was president. He kept his pipe in the breast pocket when it wasn't clenched between his teeth and, usually, he kept it lit. This morning, though, it didn't seem to be, as his pocket wasn't smoking. "Can I get you guys a drink?" he asked.

"Holy smokes, Kent!" said Nancy. "It's ten in the morning."

"Yeah?"

"So, just a little one."

"Me, too," I said. "Bourbon. Some of that good stuff."

Kent poured us both two fingers in what passed for clean glasses, then pushed them across his desk toward us.

"How's Meg?" he asked. "Everything going well?"

"I suppose," I said. "She's hoping to start glowing soon."

Kent shook his head. "Jeeze. I remember those days. Jennifer never did start glowing." He shrugged. "Well, maybe she did, but I was too scared to say anything."

"You two should just clam up," said Nancy. "No good can come of this conversation."

"That's true enough," agreed Kent.

"Skeleton," said Nancy.

"Ah, yes, the skeleton." Kent downed what was left in his glass, adjusted his reading spectacles, and lifted a sheaf of papers from the top of his desk. "Female Caucasian, approximately seventeen to nineteen years old, five feet, ten inches tall. Let's go give her a look."

We finished our drinks, then followed Kent down the hall and into his examining room. It wasn't fancy: shelves and counters, an autopsy table, a large sink. There were no tools lying about. A bright white light illuminated the stainless steel table in the center of the room, where the bones of the woman were laid out, more or less in an order we could recognize as human.

"That skeleton's been in the woods for a long while," said Kent. "Between thirty and forty years I'd say, but there's no way to tell for sure. She *probably* died from a traumatic brain injury. At least she has quite a hole in her skull. The edges of the injury have degraded over the years, so I can't tell what kind of instrument was used to do the deed. Maybe something jagged — that's what the hole looks like — but it could have been almost anything."

"What do you mean, '*probably* died from a brain injury?'" asked Nancy.

"There's a hole in her head, certainly," said Kent. He poked his pencil into a hole on the left side above where her ear would have been. "But she might have died from exposure, or heart failure, or something else entirely. In fact, the hole might have been caused post mortem, although I don't think that was the case."

"Murder?" I asked.

"Maybe, maybe not. Could have been a hiker who fell and smashed her head. Could have been murder, or an accident, or anything, really."

"How much of the skeleton do we have?" I asked.

"Maybe eighty percent. We're missing a lot of the smaller bones. It's been picked clean by insects, time, and different smaller mammals. There are teeth marks evident on almost every major bone. Rats, possums, raccoons, maybe. No bears or coyotes. There wouldn't be many bones left if one of those had gotten to the remains."

"Any chance of DNA?" Nancy asked.

"We can get some DNA, but we'd have to have something to compare it to," said Kent. "Not much chance of that. Not on a thirty-year-old case."

"Dental records?" I said.

"Probably," said Kent. "There are a few good teeth left. Of course, again, you have to have something to match them to."

"We don't even have a missing person," said Nancy. She pulled her pad from her breast pocket and flipped through some pages, then said, "I went back forty years looking for a missing person report. There were a few, but no young women."

"What about over at Appalachian State?" Kent said.

"Oh, sure," said Nancy. "Students always take off for home or parts unknown without telling anyone, but there was nothing unsolved. I checked the whole county, Appalachian State included."

"Hang on," said Kent. "Here's a thought." He walked over to one of the counters, opened a drawer and, after rifling for a few moments, came up with a business card. "Why don't you get one of those forensic artists to take the skull and reconstruct what she looked like? If she was from around these parts, someone might recognize her."

"Good idea," I said. "That might be our only option if nothing else turns up."

Kent handed me the card. "I know a guy. Dr. James Peterman. He works over at the body farm in Cullowhee."

I looked at the card. "I thought the body farm was in Knoxville."

"That's the original one, but they opened one at Western Carolina University in 2006. I'm on the board. It's not nearly as famous, of course, but they do good work. It's known as the Forest." He took the card out of my hand, squinted hard to read it. "Umm ... Forensic Osteology Research Station. FOReST."

The Body Farm in Knoxville, Tennessee is the University of Tennessee Anthropological Research Facility located a few miles from downtown on Alcoa Highway, behind the Medical Center. It was started in the early '80s by a man named Bass to study the decomposition of human remains. Dr. Bass was the head of the university's anthropology department, and as official state forensic anthropologist for Tennessee he was frequently consulted in police cases involving decomposed human remains. Since no one at that point specifically studied decomposition, he opened the first body farm and it had since become quite famous.

The UT farm consists of a two-acre wooded plot, surrounded by a razor wire fence. At any one time there will be a number of bodies placed in different settings and left to decompose, exposed in a number of ways in order to provide insights into decomposition under varying conditions. I hadn't ever been there, but it was famous. Ruby, Meg's mother, had threatened to leave her body to the place, much to Meg's dismay. Of course, according to Meg, Ruby still had years left to contemplate the decision.

Meg: Bugs will eat you. They put you naked in the woods. You will bloat and rot. Then bugs and worms will eat you.

Ruby: Sure, but I'll already be in heaven, safe in the arms of Jesus. That's just my used-up shell. My corporeal carapace.

Meg: Are you listening? Bugs ... will ... eat ... you.

Ruby: Oh, don't be such a baby. Besides, maybe it'll do some good for the world. Just think, you can visit me on Mother's Day. I'll keep an eye out for you."

Meg: *Mother!*

"Let me give Jim a call," said Kent. "Can you give me an hour?"

"Sure. We'll go get a cup of coffee or something. Anything else we should know about our Jane Doe?"

"Nothing I can tell you."

An hour later, the three of us were back in the autopsy room, this time with Kent's iPad.

"Hi, Jim," said Kent, looking at the tablet. "The connection is good. This is Hayden Konig and Nancy Parsky of the St. Germaine

Police Department." Kent turned the tablet to face us and the spectacled face of Dr. Peterman appeared.

"Good morning," Dr. Peterman said.

"A pleasure," I said. "I hope you can help us."

"I'll certainly try."

"Here's what we have," said Ken, and clicked the view on the camera so both he and Jim could view the skeletal remains. "Caucasian woman, aged twenty, five foot, ten. Cause of death is probably a blow to the head."

"Seems about right," came the voice from the iPad. "You have quite a bit of the skeleton. That's rare for a body that wasn't buried."

"The bones were scattered," said Nancy, "but not too far. A radius of maybe twenty feet. There are teeth marks on the larger ones. Raccoons, maybe, or possums."

"You might be right about possums. They'll eat anything. Raccoons will hang around a dead body, not to eat it, but to snack on the bugs, hence scattering bones all over the place. We do see that and it can mislead investigators. Long after the rest of the skeleton has been lost, skulls can still be found because animals have trouble dragging them away."

"Why is that?" Nancy asked.

"Too big to fit in their mouths and they have no thumbs."

"Here's the problem," I said. "We have no missing persons listed, nor do we have any way of finding out who this might be."

"Ah," said Jim. "You're thinking facial reconstruction."

"That's what we were thinking, yes."

"We don't have a facial reconstruction program here," said Jim. "Not at the present time. But I do have a grad student who is working in that area, a gifted artist as well as a forensic scientist. He doesn't do the clay reconstruction like you've seen on TV. He works in high resolution 3D computer animation. Understand, this is highly subjective. Still, it might provide some help."

"How long will it take?" asked Nancy.

"A day or two," said Jim. "He's very clever and he's trying out a new program that does the imaging very quickly."

"Sounds great," I said. "What do we need to do?"

"Send the skull down. FedEx will be fine. Kent has the address. We'll do a CT scan, then return the skull and get started."

"How much does something like this cost?" asked Nancy.

"How about three hundred bucks?" said Jim.

"Deal," I said.

Chapter 6

Staff meetings at the church happened on Wednesday mornings, and I attempted to schedule police business on Wednesdays as much as possible. As a part-time musician at the Episcopal church, I didn't have much to say during these meetings anyway. I chose the music for the services, including the hymns, and was happy to leave everything else to the rest of the staff. This Wednesday, though, I hadn't found anything pressing to do and decided to make an appearance. According to Georgia, Kimberly Walnut, now our newly crowned Minister of Christian Development and Ministry, had returned from her week at warm and fuzzy church camp and was just aching to fill us all in on the newest ministries blossoming on the cusp of the contemporary and more relevant church.

I walked into the meeting room, took a coffee mug from the side table and poured myself a cupful. Community Coffee, good and always available at St. Barnabas in one pot or another. Marilyn, the church secretary was already sitting at the head of the table. She didn't drink coffee, but had a glass of water sitting beside her legal pad.

"Morning, Hayden."

"Good morning," I said. "How are things?"

She gave me a thin smile and a shrug.

The rest of the group came in behind me from different directions: Georgia Wester, Bev Greene, Joyce Cooper, Kimberly Walnut, Father Walmsley, and Billy Hixon.

"Isn't this a staff meeting?" I asked. Billy and Bev weren't on the staff, although Bev had been the church administrator for a time. One of the previous rectors had done away with her job — made her redundant, as the English are fond of putting it. Billy had a lawn service and took care of the grounds. Both he and Bev had taken their turns as Senior and Junior wardens over the years, but Georgia and Mark Wells were currently in those positions. Joyce was the head of the altar guild.

"Combination staff and worship committee meeting," said Marilyn. "Didn't you read your email?"

"Nope," I said.

"Why am I here?" said Billy, settling his six-foot-four frame into a chair. "I ain't on either one of those committees. Pass those cinnamon buns over here, will you?" Joyce pushed a platter of huge rolls across the table: giant confections bigger than

45

grapefruits with dark cinnamon and white opaque frosting oozing from every swirl.

Marilyn looked at her pad, then at Billy. "Sorry. My mistake."

"I'll just take one of these buns then, and be on my way." He took two, wrapped them up in a couple of napkins and stuck them in pockets on both sides of his jacket. "Pleasure doing business with you," he said with a grin.

"I see the scaffolding is going up," said Marilyn. "I'm sorry I missed Sunday, but I looked at the weather and thought I might just as well worship at home. I heard it was very exciting."

"Too exciting," said Bev. "I don't need that kind of excitement."

"What's the verdict on the damage?" I asked Billy. "Did you hear anything yet?"

"Yeah. Mark Wells and me met with the insurance guy yesterday. The stained glass window is busted, of course, and will have to be sent back to St. Louis for repair. That's gonna take about six weeks, but they say they'll work us in as quickly as they can. That big limb that came off the oak tore part of the roof off, broke the slate and most of the gutters on that side. Best case scenario, four weeks, then we wait for the window. We'll put up the scaffolding and leave it till the whole thing is fixed. No sense taking it up and down. The insurance guy agreed to that."

"We're covered for everything?"

"Everything," said Billy, not smiling. "That tree's coming down though. We'll have to pay for that. It was split pert near in half, top to bottom. It's a shame, but we can't leave it."

"That is a shame," I said.

"We'll plant another one and they can worry about it in another hundred and fifty years," said Billy. He tipped his baseball cap. "Y'all have a good day."

Lena Carver came in just as he was exiting and took her seat at the table. "Is this the worship committee meeting?" Lena was a new parishioner at St. Barnabas, although she'd been in town for a few years. She gave me a scowl, no doubt still smarting from the traffic ticket.

"Yes, it is," said Father Walmsley, then turned to Marilyn. "Is everyone here?"

As if in answer to his question, two more people entered the room, Pam McNeil and Marty Hatteberg, Pam being another new member to the church. Kimberly Walnut liked to include new members on committees where she could. It was a policy I didn't disagree with, not that I'd been asked.

"Good morning, all," piped Pam. "What a lovely morning! Thanks for inviting me."

"Coffee," mumbled Marty. "Black."

"That's everyone," Marilyn said to Father Walmsley.

"Great," said the priest. "Let's get started."

After our opening prayer, Kimberly Walnut presented a short devotion, which she started by asking us all if we were Silly Putty.

"What?" said Bev. "What on earth are you talking about?" Bev had just about had enough of Kimberly Walnut over the years. Now, according to Bev, it was war.

"Do not conform any longer to the pattern of this world, but be transformed by the renewing of your mind," said Kimberly Walnut, reading off her notes. "Romans, chapter 12, verse 2."

"Fine," snapped Bev, "but what does that have to do with Silly Putty?"

"I think I see," said Father Walmsley, trying to gentle the conversation. "The verse gives the idea of being pressed into a mold. Like Silly Putty." He paused for a moment, then added, "Well, if you pressed it into a mold or something."

"You mean like clay, or bread dough, or mud, or cement, or jello salad, or a hundred other things?" said Bev. "Why Silly Putty?"

Lena said, "Back when I was a kid, we used to stick Silly Putty onto newspapers and pick up the impression. Usually the Sunday comics. Seems to me you could bounce it, too. Maybe we should be impressionable and bouncy."

"And stretchy," said Georgia.

"Hang on," Pam said. "Are we supposed to be Silly Putty or to *not* be Silly Putty?"

"We're not," said Joyce.

"We are," said Marty. "See? Silly Putty always goes back to its original shape — the shape that God created — no matter how much it's stretched. Like us."

"God didn't create Silly Putty," said Bev. "I think it was DuPont or maybe General Electric. Anyway, it doesn't go back to its old shape. Not that I recall, anyway. It sort of just lays there."

"It does when you stuff it back in the egg," said Joyce. "Is God the egg?"

"Probably," said Marty.

I shook my head. "In this instance, I think that God is the comics page, the egg is the New Testament, jello salad is the Lambeth Quadrilateral, and the Silly Putty is the Doctrine of Transubstantiation."

Pam laughed. Kimberly Walnut looked confused and didn't answer, then flipped a couple of pages, and went straight to the wrap-up. "Uh ... Here we go. We can't afford to conform. We need to *trans*form. If we don't let God transform us, we'll be like putty in the world's hands — and that's worse than silly." Kimberly Walnut looked around the table with a smug smile on her face.

"That's the worst analogy I've ever heard," said Bev. "Pathetic and trite. Is this what you learn at those retreats?"

"Now, now," said Father Walmsley. "I'm sure Dr. Walnut was just looking for a way to make the scripture relevant to us here today ..."

"*What?*" said Bev, horrified.

"I mean that maybe this scripture could be illuminated a little more clearly, but even so, Silly Putty ..."

"Not that!" said Bev. "The other thing."

"What other thing?" said the priest.

"*Dr.* Walnut!" said Bev. She stared at Kimberly Walnut with contempt.

"Dr. Walnut has completed her Doctor of Ministry in Spiritual Formation," said Father Walmsley, smiling broadly. "I'm sure we're all very proud of her accomplishment."

"You're kidding!" said Bev. "She never left here to go do a doctorate. We would have noticed that."

"I did it all on-line," said Kimberly Walnut. "Liberty University. Thirty credit hours, and I just finished up my dissertation. They gave me thirteen hours credit toward my degree because of my life experience."

"Your dissertation?" said Bev. "You didn't do a dissertation."

"Well, my thesis project."

"I'd like to see *that* transcript," muttered Bev.

"Congratulations, Dr. Walnut," I said. "What was the title of your project?"

"*Fifty Nifty Thrifty Ministries for Growing Your Congregation,*" she said excitedly. "I already have a book deal with Archangel

Publishing. It will be available to every church in the country. Maybe the world!"

Bev put her head into her hands and laid it on the table. "Oh, my Jesus, it rhymes," she groaned. "I know what *this* means."

"Dr. Walnut has some ideas she'd like to share with us all," said Father Walmsley. "She's been working very hard, and many of these, I'm sure, will be included in her book. St. Barnabas is going to be Dr. Walnut's ministry laboratory. I'm very excited about the possibilities!"

"Like the Blessing of the Groundhog?" Georgia said. "That was great! I hope that's in Chapter One."

"The glow sticks on Christmas Eve?" said Marty. "The Great Crack? That was special."

The Great Crack hadn't gone so well. *Someone* had decided that glow sticks were preferable to candles on Christmas Eve, at least for the 5:00 PM service when the most children were present. Everyone was to take a glow stick, snap it on cue, and wave it aloft during the singing of *Silent Night*, bathing the sanctuary in a warm, nuclear green glow. Unfortunately, this same someone had left all the sticks outside on the steps until five minutes before she needed them, and since the temperature was hovering just above zero, the goo had gone quite solid. The sticks did crack — "exploded" would be a better description — and green chunks of glowing ice sprayed across the congregation. Several parents took their kids over to the ER in Boone, not sure if they'd ingested any of the chemicals or not. No one showed any lasting effects though.

Kimberly Walnut ignored both Marty and Georgia. She opened the thick notebook in front of her. "The first thing I'd like to talk about is the formation of our new Cuddling Ministry."

"She's insane, of course," said Bev.

Georgia nodded her head. "Last week at the vestry meeting, she brought a newspaper article explaining how Kentucky had passed a law saying that it was legal for ministers and church officers to carry weapons inside houses of worship."

"Why on earth would she care about that?"

"One of her Christian Development friends told her about how her congregation was held up during a church service."

"Really?"

"I guess," said Georgia.

"Doesn't she know that Hayden has a gun in the organ bench?" said Bev. "We've got the police chief in the choir loft, for heaven's sake."

"She *is* insane," said Georgia. "Anyway, she's gotten herself a gun permit."

"Who's insane?" said Meg, walking up to the table. After the meeting, I'd called Meg and arranged for lunch at the Ginger Cat. Bev and Georgia were more than happy to come along.

The Ginger Cat, an upscale eatery owned and run by Annie Cooke, sat on the northwest corner of the town square, prime real estate in St. Germaine. Next to the Ginger Cat, on the other side of Main Street, was Noylene's Beautifery (an Oasis of Beauty), and Eden Books. The Bear and Brew was just a block down Main and featured beer and pizza. St. Barnabas Church dominated the west side of the square, the courthouse, the east. The library and various shops filled in the space along Main Street.

I stood and pulled Meg's chair out for her, then scooted it in as she sat down. "Kimberly Walnut," I said. "Kimberly Walnut's insane."

"*Dr.* Walnut," said Georgia.

"Oh, my," said Meg. "Dr. Walnut. When did this happen?"

"She got some on-line doctorate at Liberty University," said Bev. "Now she's apparently weaseled herself a book deal."

"And we're the guinea pigs," added Georgia.

"Can't Father Walmsley stop her?" Meg asked.

"He could," I said, "but he won't. He drank the Kool-Aid. She won't be corralled until we get a new full-time priest."

"How about you, Georgia? Can you stop her?"

Georgia shook her head. "I have nothing to do with programming or staff. I'm just the Senior Warden. If I could fire her, I would, but I can't."

"So there's no help for it?" Meg asked.

"Not yet," I said. "I must confess, I'm very interested in this Cuddling Ministry."

"What?"

"Oh, yes," said Bev. "Kimberley Walnut's idea of the moment is to start a Cuddling Ministry. According to her research," — Bev put *research* in fingerquotes — "people don't get the amount of human touch they need on a daily basis, and a cuddling ministry is the solution. She's going to train the cuddlers, then let people sign up for one."

"Sort of like a Stephen Minister?" said Meg.

"Nothing like that," said Bev. "This is weird. Very weird and creepy."

"We all need to experience the healing power of human touch," I said. "All strictly platonic, of course. She's calling it *Sarah's Snuggles*."

"Who's Sarah?" asked Meg.

"Old Testament Sarah," I said. "I think Kimberly Walnut views all women in the Bible as snuggly. Personally, I didn't ever think of Sarah as being all that snuggly. She did send Hagar and Ishmael out into the desert to die horribly."

"Maybe she snuggled them first," said Georgia.

"If Kimberly Walnut was going for alliteration, she might just as well have chosen Salome's Snuggles, or even Sapphira's Snuggles."

"Salome was a bad girl," said Bev. "I know that much. Her kind of snuggling might not be what Kimberly Walnut is after. I don't know about Sapphira."

"God killed her for lying about money," I said.

"Really?"

"I think I'm going to be sick," said Meg.

"I know how you feel," said Georgia.

"No, seriously," said Meg, getting to her feet. "I'm going to be sick. It's the smell of oysters."

"I don't smell anything," said Bev, but Meg was already racing for the bathroom.

A second later, our waiter appeared and filled our water glasses.

"Good morning, Wallace," said Bev.

"Morning, Wallace," said Georgia.

"Good morning, ladies. Chief. Did I see Mrs. Konig a moment ago?"

"You did," I said. "She excused herself momentarily. Something about oysters."

"Speaking of oysters," said Wallace, "that's our lunch special. Oysters Rockefeller. It looks wonderful."

"Ooh," said Bev. "Tell us about it."

"Six fresh oysters topped with a mixture of finely chopped spinach, watercress, green onions, fennel seeds, and grated Parmesan, broiled in their shells with copious amounts of butter. These are going to be served with a small pear and pomegranate salad." He lowered his voice. "The secret ingredient is absinthe, drizzled over the oysters just before they go into the oven." Wallace

51

made a gesture toward an adjacent table. Jeff and Helen Pigeon had both ordered the Oysters Rockefeller which had just been delivered. Wallace was right. The special looked delicious.

"I'll have that," said Georgia.

"Might I suggest a Blanc de blanc Champagne? Bud recommends our Franck Bonville Grand Cru. Forty-one dollars for the bottle. Fifteen dollars a glass. Bud says it's light and elegant: the chalk in the soil sings through the nose and offers a backbone that frames the entire wine with white flowers, golden apples, and a hint of spice cake."

"Sounds delightful," said Georgia. "If Bud recommends it, I'm happy to give it a try."

"Same for me," said Bev. "Just a glass."

"Yes, just a glass," said Georgia.

Wallace smiled and nodded, and wrote the order on his pad.

"How's Bud doing, by the way?" asked Bev.

Bud McCollough, oldest of the McCollough children had turned twenty-one last year, and opened a wine shop. I was a silent partner in the firm. Bud was a wine savant, and the youngest master sommelier in the country. He could walk the walk and talk the talk and when he told you that a wine had "enormous coarse bubbles as though a hippo farted in the fermentation tank," or that it tasted like "Chanel No. 5 in gladiator shorts," you'd better listen. The Wine Press was doing very well, both with the walk-in clientele and with internet sales. If you wanted a wine — cheap, expensive, or in between — Bud would steer you in the right direction. He also had a deal with the Ginger Cat, pairing various wines (that he supplied) with their daily specials and signature dishes. He was never wrong and most of the customers took his suggestions.

"How about you, Hayden?" asked Bev. "What are you having?"

I looked over toward the bathrooms and saw Meg stagger out, looking as green as the pear and pomegranate salad.

"Sadly, I don't think Meg and I will be staying for lunch after all," I said.

"You are still paying for it, though, aren't you?" asked Georgia. "Otherwise we're splitting the watercress sandwich and a glass of lemon-water."

I nodded and got to my feet. Meg was already heading for the front door. "Put it on my tab, will you?"

"Sure thing, Chief."

"Now, Wallace," said Bev, "about dessert ..."

Chapter 7

"We have a picture from our forensic artist," said Nancy. "It came in on my email this morning."

"Well, let's see it," I said.

Dave, sitting at the front desk reading a vampire novel, got up to look as well.

Nancy produced a piece of paper from the color printer in the office. She pushed it across the desk and said, "We can get better quality printing from the Office Max in Boone."

I looked at the drawing. It was good — that is, it looked professional — but I had no idea if it resembled the victim or not. Time would tell. The girl in the drawing looked to me to be somewhere between fifteen and twenty years old. In this drawing she had mousy brown, straight hair, framing a high forehead. Her nose was small and straight, her eyes, large and blue. Prominent cheekbones, a full lower lip, a round chin. Her eyebrows were set high and it gave her a distinctive look. She had a slight smile.

"She was pretty," said Dave.

"I talked to Max Dunlap," Nancy said. "He's the artist." She pulled out her pad, flipped a few pages, and consulted her notes. "He thinks she might have been blonde, but doesn't know for sure, so he went with a nondescript light brown. The hair is straight, because almost every teenaged girl in the seventies had straight hair. Blue eyes, because if she was from this part of North Carolina, there is a 56.7% chance she'd have blue eyes."

"I guess they know their stuff," I said. "Let's get some flyers made at Office Max and take them around town, then send this picture over to the *Tattler* and the *Watauga Democrat*. We might get lucky and someone will recognize her."

"I heard about the Cuddling Ministry," said Mark Wells. "Where do I sign up?"

The singers filed into the choir loft and made their way to their seats. Wednesday night suppers had resumed in the parish hall and most of the choir attended, then topped the evening off with choir rehearsal.

"Do you want to be a cuddler, or be cuddled?" asked Steve DeMoss.

"Cuddler," said Mark. "No, wait ... cuddled. No, wait ..."

"How do you think Jane is going to take to all of this?" said Meg.

"Oh, she don't care. As long as she don't have to do it."

"You're going to have to shave, you know," said Rebecca. "No one wants to be cuddled by a three-day growth of boar bristles."

"And take a bath," said Phil Camp.

"And take off your baseball cap," added Sheila.

"Hang on! I bathe semi-regularly. Who came up with all these cuddle rules anyway?"

"How does everyone know about this?" I asked. "Kimberly Walnut just ran this past the Worship Committee yesterday."

"She announced it at dinner," answered Fred May. "Complete with a rather lengthy introduction by Father Walmsley."

"Well, I'm taking the class to be a cuddler," said Goldi Fawn. "As a purveyor of beauty over at Noylene's Beautifery, I hear all the stories. Most of these people just need a good cuddle."

"I'm not signing up," said Marjorie, with a sniff. "I had enough of that in the war."

"Which war was that?" asked Tiff. "The Civil War?"

Marjorie gave Tiff a look of disdain. "The Great War, dear. The war to end all wars. Dubya Dubya Two. I was a sixteen-year-old nurse's aide in France, and there was plenty of cuddling, I can tell you."

"I'm pretty sure that wasn't cuddling," said Bob Solomon.

"That's what we called it," said Marjorie. "We weren't as crass back then. I remember this one time, Henri and I went back into the general's supply room ..."

She was interrupted by Lena Carver, appearing at the top of the stairs. "We'd like to join the choir," she said, coming into the loft with Hollie Swofford right behind her. "Where do we audition? I brought my copy of *Cantique de Jean Racine.*"

"I just have a hymn, if that's okay," said Hollie.

"No audition necessary," I said. "We're happy to have you both."

"We need to get our voices in shape," Lena announced to everyone. "Hollie and I are going to audition to sing duets over at the Renaissance Fair when it opens. We're calling ourselves *Sapphire Lily.*"

"Really?" said Sheila. "They're already auditioning performers? It's not even going to be open for a year."

"Check out their website," said Lena. "It's all right there."

"How about you, Ian?" said Tiff. "What about your Raucous Flute Compost thingy?"

"The Rauschpfeife Consort," said Dr. Burch, PhD, "does not audition for Renaissance Fairs. I suspect we'll be contacted once the park is up and running and we shall be happy to go over and give a concert or two."

"I sing alto and Hollie sings soprano," Lena informed us.

"Hollie can sit here," said Meg, scooting over one seat, vacating a chair between herself and Rhiza.

"Can I sit back here?" asked Lena, moving toward a chair beside Marty.

"Better not," said Marty, putting her folder in the empty chair. "We're Back Row Altos. It's like a club. You should go ahead and sit in the front row."

Lena looked confused but didn't say anything, stood for a moment, then moved up a row and took the seat next to Goldi Fawn Birtwhistle.

"Don't mind them," whispered Elaine. "They're choir snobs."

"You know what I like about these choir stories?" said Marjorie. "You always get to learn new stuff." Marjorie had found the latest installment and had dived right in. I was always grateful for an appreciative audience.

"No, you don't," said Meg. "You don't learn anything. He makes it all up."

I knew this skizzle would come up sooner or later. The dirty snaps said it all. Liturgical codpieces. It was only a matter of time.

"Liturgical codpieces?" I asked. It was the obvious question, a question as common as a spare tire on the roof of a mobile home. It was usually the first question out of a priest's mouth as he prepared for his ordination, followed by, "What's this wafer thingy?"

"No, that's not it at all," she mewed whimperously, with still a little angriness thrown in, like that sparky cat.

I nodded and smiled like a South Carolina congressman being handed an envelope full of twenties at that Waffle House on I26, the one that had the one-legged waitress with the missing eye and just the two teeth: Pirate Jenny, they called her, but not to her face. Liturgical codpieces are an accepted part of the priestly tradition, a tradition going back all the way to Melchizedek the Unsupported. They were available in all the liturgical colors, from midnight-blue to cranberry, from seafoam to the brightly bedazzled flamingo and gold of Septuagesima. They were made of mohair and every priest I knew had a closet full.

☙

"What's a codpiece?" asked Goldi Fawn, looking up from her paper.

"Ian?" I said. "This is your area of expertise, is it not?"

"Well, certainly I have a few in my collection," said Dr. Ian Burch, PhD, "since it was popular in the fifteenth and sixteenth centuries. The codpiece is a pouch that is positioned at the crotch of a man's breeches and used to envelope and accentuate the area. They could either be relatively plain or extremely ornate. I have both."

☙

The snaps featured Stormy Knight, of course, and some fledgeling clerics, most of whom I knew. I'd seen these types of pictures before, taken at the after-ordination parties at almost every seminary in the country. Baby priests flaunting their new codpieces, sucking on smoldering hookahs, slurping raw oysters, and drinking absinthe out of plastic communion cups.

"Old news," I said. "There isn't a male priest in the diocese that doesn't have a codpiece glamour photo stashed somewhere. Some of the female ones, too."

"Tis not the codpieces," sobbed Stormy, braying unhappily into her hanky. "Look closer."

I pulled out one of the snaps and gave it another going over. It was grainy with bad lighting, but it wasn't hard to make out what was going on.

"There," said Stormy. "In the back." She extended a long digit and tapped a shadowy figure.

"O ... M ... G ..." I muttered tweetly.

"I heard that in medieval times a codpiece was a handy container for storing one's lunch," said Mark Wells. "A cross between the modern lunch box and the fanny pack. Right there in front where you could get at it."

"You don't say," said Marty.

"Yep. Because of the working man's fondness for fish, it became known as a codpiece."

"*Absolutely false!*" said Dr. Ian Burch, PhD, angrily. "*Cod* is Middle English, meaning *scrotum*. The codpiece is strictly a decorative element for covering the male genitalia!"

"Ahh," cried Tiff, making a face and covering her ears. "Too much information!"

"I'm sure Mark was just kidding, Ian," said Meg.

"Indeed I was," said Mark. "I would never keep a fish in my codpiece. Maybe a liverwurst sandwich, though."

"Time to sing," I said. "Handel first, then Robert Lehman's *Simple Gifts*. Codpiece discussion after."

Chapter 8

August had yet to turn to September, but fall was definitely in the air. Up here in the mountains, we felt the change a bit earlier than the rest of North Carolina. The leaves wouldn't start changing for a few more weeks, not reaching their peak until late October, but cool weather was in the forecast and I, for one, always looked forward to it.

Meg was drinking her morning cup of herbal tea when I left the house. I took the truck into town, windows rolled down, enjoying the crisp morning and a Prokofiev piano concerto on the stereo, Number 3 in C Major. Of his five concertos, the third has garnered the greatest popularity, but I had finally decided that was no reason not to like it. The concerto radiated a crisp vitality that echoed the September morning perfectly — lyrical passages punctuated with clever dissonances. Just the thing for an autumn drive.

It was ten miles into town, ten miles of winding byways, roadside waterfalls, blooming rhododendron and mountain laurel, wildflowers; goldenrod, aster, coneflower, and Queen Anne's lace, and all of it enhanced by Prokofiev's masterwork. I slowed for a doe beside the road, unafraid of the truck, scarcely looking up from her feeding as I passed. The second movement began in E minor, a theme and five variations, each remarkably different and each a dazzling example of Prokofiev expressing his sarcastic wit in musical terms. I took my time, pulling into my parking place in front of the station just as the third movement finished. I checked the station door — locked — then walked up the sidewalk to the Slab Café where I found Nancy waiting for me.

The Slab had customers. All four red vinyl-covered stools at the counter were occupied by workmen. There were another dozen patrons scattered around the tables in twos, threes, and fours, chatting amongst themselves, most probably enjoying a leisurely breakfast.

Nancy had staked out our usual table in the back, a four top. Officer Dave was bound to join us momentarily, never one to miss a free meal. Pete still comped the members of the local constabulary their breakfasts. He started the practice when he was the mayor and wanted to keep tabs on the goings on in the town. Now that he wasn't, neither Nancy, Dave, nor I saw any reason for him to curtail the practice. Of course, since Cynthia was now mayor, and Pete's significant other, he viewed himself as the power behind the throne, a puppet ruler, his Rasputin to Cynthia's Alexandra. Cynthia saw it quite differently.

"Good morning, Chief," said Nancy.

"Morning. How's the coffee this morning?"

"Better than last week."

Noylene put a cup down in front of me and filled it. "Last week Pete was trying to cut corners. He bought that restaurant blend that sort of smells like roach powder." She made a face. "I threw it out. This is the regular stuff."

Cynthia came out of the kitchen, saw us, and came up to the table. "Morning, Hayden."

"Good morning, Madame Mayor. I see you're waiting tables this morning."

"Until something better comes along. Maybe a governorship. Or a run for the presidency."

"What's the special this morning?"

"Corned beef hash and two eggs, grits and a biscuit. Now to city business. How's the murder investigation coming? I heard you have a picture of the victim."

"No one said anything about murder," I said.

"We do have a sketch," said Nancy, "done by a forensic artist. I'm going over to the newspapers this morning to give it to them. Maybe we'll get lucky and someone will recognize her."

"From thirty years ago?" said Cynthia.

"Yes," said Nancy. "Approximately."

"I heard you have a picture," called Pete, who'd just come out of the kitchen wiping his hands on a towel. He tossed it into a sink behind the counter and came around to join us. He plopped into the chair beside Nancy.

The cowbell hanging on the door of the Slab clanged against the glass and Dave walked in carrying a stack of flyers.

"Speaking of pictures," said Nancy, "here they are. Hot off the press."

"Morning, all," said Dave and handed us each a flyer. It featured the color sketch of the unknown girl with a caption:

Do You Know This Girl?
Missing since the late 1970s (approximately)
17 to 19 years old — 5' 10" tall

— followed by the St. Germain Police Department contact information.

"Nobody I know," said Pete, "and I grew up here."

"She might have been around during your 'hazy' days, dear," said Cynthia. "As I recall, there are several years in the late '70s and early '80s that you have no recollection of."

"Well ... that's true enough," agreed Pete. "All of 1978 is just about gone. June of '76 is pretty stable."

"We'll put them up around town for a few weeks," I said. "Admittedly, it's a long shot."

"What's the breakfast special?" asked Dave, pulling out the last empty chair at the table and sitting down. "Oh, never mind, just bring it to me."

"Me, too," I said.

"I'll have my usual," said Nancy, referring to her two soft-boiled eggs and fried potatoes.

"Sorry, this isn't my table," said Cynthia, with a haughty sniff.

"Where's Noylene?" I asked.

"She's on her break."

"Then how do we get breakfast?" asked Dave, his voice rising in panic.

"Jeeze, Dave. Relax. I'll get it," said Cynthia.

"Good help is so hard to find these days," said Pete.

"How's your new dog, by the way?" asked Dave. "Frisky or something like that."

"Whose new dog?" said Cynthia. Her voice was menacing.

"Not Frisky," said Pete. "Fritzi. And no, I didn't get her. She had a wild look in her eyes."

"It was a puppy," I said. "It probably just needed to go out."

"It's a good thing you didn't get it," said Cynthia. "I have enough to do taking care of that truffle pig. I'm always the one to go out and feed her."

"Yes, my darling, but you're the one who wanted to put her all the way out on Cutoff Road."

"It was the only place for her. You know what that pig sty smelled like after six months. The neighbors were threatening to call the health department."

"Now, c'mon," said Pete. "You know that Portia has more than paid for herself. I'd say ten times over at this point."

"Seems about right," said Nancy. She and I were the other two investors in Pete's Pig Project. Dave could have gotten in on the ground floor, but he'd declined our invitation.

"You own that pig out by Tinkler's Knob?" asked one of the burly men at the counter. "The one that looks like a sheep?"

"Yep," said Pete. "She's a full-blooded Mangalitsa, highly trained in the art of truffle hunting."

"That's a fancy pig, sure enough," said a second man. He had on a ball cap and, having finished his breakfast, was now digging around his gums with a toothpick.

Our pig was a little over three feet long, nose to tail and stood two feet high at the shoulder. She had large jowls that framed her short face and snout. Her ears were large, shading eyes that were the most startling blue, and she was covered with long, gray, curly hair. Pete had fenced in most of the two acres that he owned on Tinkler's Knob, complete with a lovely stream, and Portia ran free when she wasn't digging truffles for us. Cynthia went by every day and supplemented her free-range diet. In the winter, we packed her up to a barn in Boone and boarded her.

"You might want to move yer pig," said the third man. "We won't bother it, but the noise of the machinery might make it skittish."

"What noise?" asked Cynthia.

"Bulldozers, chainsaws, and a couple of excavators. That property backs up to a camp, and we're tearing it down."

Nancy looked across the table at me, her mouth open. "Why didn't we think of that?"

"Moving the pig?" said Cynthia.

"Oh, man!" I said. "It's what? A mile and a half as the crow flies?"

"Maybe," Nancy said. "More like five if you have to take the roads, but you're probably right, tromping through the woods."

"Never thought about it," I said. "Camp Possumtickle's been closed to campers for so long, it didn't occur to me."

"Me either."

"What on earth are you talking about?" said Cynthia.

"The girl," I said, tapping the picture in front of me. "What if the girl came from the camp?"

The work crew had been demolishing the camp all week. By the time Dave, Nancy, and I arrived, only the main office, the outdoor pavilion, three cabins, and half of the dining hall were still standing. Gone were the lodge, the storage buildings, the camp store, the barn, most of the old camper's cabins, the basketball and tennis courts, the communal restrooms, the old dock by the lake, the swimming pool — almost everything else.

"Wow," said Dave. "Just ... wow."

"That's sad," said Nancy.

"It is," I agreed. "I wasn't a big fan of the Christian nudists, but at least the camp was still here."

Dave said, "I was out here last spring on a bear call and it didn't look like the same place. Those nudists didn't do any upkeep at all. The volleyball game was fun to watch, though."

"Did you join in?" Nancy asked.

"Nah. One guy dove for a low ball. I heard the crunch and had to leave. But from what I saw, the camp was kind of a mess: rails on the lodge were falling off, there was a big tree lying across one of the cabins, the grass hadn't been mown, half the dock was gone."

"The nudists never had any money," said Nancy. "I wonder why."

"No pockets," said Dave.

I laughed. "I don't know the reason, but the DaNGLs had financial problems from the beginning."

We went over to the office. A white commercial pickup truck was parked outside and a sign nailed to the wooden door said *Deerfield Entertainment, Inc., Tyler, Texas.* Nancy didn't knock, but opened the door and we saw a man seated at a desk facing us, busy scribbling in a notebook. The desktop was littered with papers, some in stacks, some not. He was in his thirties, probably, but looked older due to a receding hairline, jowls, and a pallid, splotchy complexion. He smiled and stood when he saw us.

"Come on in," he said, extending a hand. "I'm Jerry Jarman."

"Chief Hayden Konig." I shook his hand. "This is Nancy Parsky and Dave Vance. We're from the Police Department in St. Germaine." This was obvious, in Nancy's case, but she was the only one in uniform.

"I can assure you that all our permits are in order," said Jerry, suddenly looking nervous. "As for any complaints ..."

"There haven't been any," I said. "Nor problems, either. We're here on a totally different matter."

"Oh." Jerry sat back down, relief evident on his face. "Well, what can I do for you?"

"I wonder if we could see the old Camp Possumtickle records? Specifically, we're looking for ..." I paused and looked at Nancy. "What do you think?"

"Probably 1975 to 1985," she said. "That should cover it."

He shook his head. "Nope. Sorry. We got rid of all that stuff first thing. Made a heck of a bonfire, I can tell you. Boxes and boxes of that stuff, probably going all the way back to the '50s."

"Dadgummit," I said to Nancy. "We should have thought of this earlier."

"Are you tearing down the whole camp?" asked Dave.

"We're leaving what we can use," said Jerry, "but it's not much. The pavilion, this office, one of the cabins. We'll redo them of course, and build everything else from scratch. We'll be constructing a whole sixteenth-century English town — twenty-two acres including the jousting ring. It'll be as authentic as we can make it."

"With bathrooms?" asked Dave. "Authenticity is one thing, but I like a bathroom."

"We call them Jakes," said Jerry, grinning. "Jakes and Jills. Electricity, too, of course. Propane lines, an infirmary, food preparation, costume rooms, storage, break rooms for the performers and associates ... the usual stuff. That's the infrastructure. Hopefully, if we do our job right, it won't take away from the experience."

"From what I've read on-line about your group, you're very good at this," I said.

"We are," said Jerry. "This is our seventh Renaissance park. It's a great location." He paused, thought for a moment, then said, "Hey, does this have anything to do with that missing girl? I saw her picture in the paper this morning."

"It does," I said. "I'm sorry we couldn't get those records. It would have helped us a lot."

"Yeah, I'm sorry, too. The only thing I saved were the old camp pictures. You know, those panoramic shots of all the campers. I thought they were sort of neat."

"Really?" said Nancy. "You saved the pictures?"

"Yeah. They're in the back. Will they help?"

"Maybe," I said. "How many do you have?"

"All of them, I guess. Hundreds. I didn't put them in order, but I bet they're all there. Four or five per summer, some of the girls camp, some of the boy's camp."

"May we take them with us?" I said. "We'll bring them back if you want."

"Sure. I was going to make a wall of them. Sort of a nostalgic tribute, you know? To the old camp."

"Sounds like a fine idea," I said. "We'll return them when we're finished."

Chapter 9

"Sue Clark's stupid dog is scaring my goats!" Helen Pigeon said. "I want you to put a stop to it!"

Helen caught us on the sidewalk as we were heading back to the Slab. Dave and I each had an armful of photographs, each about two feet long and eight inches high.

"Helen," I said, "we're in the middle of something right now."

Helen blocked our way, her hands on her hips. "Nancy said she was going to shoot that thing." She turned to Nancy. "Didn't you? Didn't you tell me that?"

"She didn't mean it," I said. "We can't go around shooting every dog that barks at goats."

"These are not ordinary goats. They're fainting goats. They are an investment. Jeff and I are going to enjoy a comfortable retirement thanks to these goats."

"Really, Helen? That's your retirement? Fainting goats?" I didn't try to hide my amusement.

Helen sighed with exasperation at having, once again, to explain. "It's not funny. Fainting goats have been around for a long time, sure, but this is a new breed. The first *angora* breed of fainting goat. When we get it established, we can start selling the breeding stock for a lot of money, I can tell you. These are rare goats! What if a dog started barking at your prize pig?"

"I'd have to shoot it," I admitted. "The dog, not the pig."

"Exactly!"

"I don't even know what a fainting goat is," said Dave.

"*Tennessee* Fainting Goats," said Helen. "Stiff-leg goats, nervous goats, whatever. They have a muscle condition called myotonia something-or-other. Jeff knows the actual term. When the poor things get startled, their muscles lock up and they fall over."

"Really?" said Dave. "I'd like to see that."

"Fine," said Helen angrily. "Just come over anytime that terrible dog is out. It starts barking and all the goats faint."

"They actually faint?" asked Nancy.

"They're fully conscious, but they can't move."

"Is this harmful to the goat?" I asked.

"Well," admitted Helen, "not so far as we know. But it's very irritating to look out your window and see eleven goats lying in the yard with their feet sticking straight up in the air. I tell you what ..." She was fuming now. "You'd better take care of this, or I will."

"Take it easy," I said. "You had two dogs of your own. Those bloodhounds. When they ate that passel of kittens down the street from you, I didn't shoot them."

"Not the same thing at all," said Helen. "Those kittens were dangerous."

"I'll have another word with Sue."

Helen spun on her heel and began her march across the park.

"Don't we have some sort of anti-goat ordinance on the books?" asked Nancy, as we continued down the sidewalk.

"We do have a livestock restriction, but you know we hardly ever enforce it. Anyway, the Pigeons live just about ten feet outside of town and all our restrictions. They can raise walruses if they want."

Nancy held the front door to the Slab open for us. We found a table in the back, and dumped the photos.

"What's all this?" asked Cynthia. The breakfast crowd had gone, and the only customers left were Diana Evarts, the owner of the Bun in the Oven bakery, and Pam McNeil.

"All that's left of Camp Possumtickle's records," I said. "Let's pull some tables together."

"What's up?" asked Diana, seeing the commotion.

"Detective work," said Dave. "High-level detective work."

"Can we help?" asked Diana. She and Pam were already on their feet and walking over, coffee cups in hand.

"Sure," I said. "Who's minding the bakery?"

"Jacki's got it. I'm just meeting with Pam about the Music Club's next meeting. Cupcakes are on the menu. Cupcakes and Rachmaninov."

"Sounds great," I said, then, "Here's what we have. Camp pictures from the 1950s through the '80s. The date is printed down at the bottom. The first thing we need to do is get them in order."

"Sounds fun," said Pam. "I love old pictures."

"Let's get this wrapped up," said Nancy. "I'm off to Charlotte when we're finished. I have tickets for the Hornets game tomorrow."

Pete came out of the kitchen. "What's up?"

"The game is afoot," I said.

"Oh, goody," said Pete, with a grin.

It took us only about ten minutes to arrange the photos in chronological order. We stacked the early photos neatly, 1950s, '60s, and early '70s vintage, and placed them aside on another table. We decided to begin with 1975 and work from there.

"So, here's the plan," I said, handing a flyer to everyone. "We're looking for this girl. Her hair may not be the same color, but these are black and white photos anyway. If you see someone who looks like our mystery girl, set the photo aside and we'll go back to it. My feeling is that she'll be a counselor, but let's look at the older campers as well. Let's start in the early eighties and work backwards."

"I don't think she'll be a camper," said Nancy. "A missing camper would have thrown up all kinds of red flags."

"I agree, but let's look anyway."

"Wouldn't a missing counselor have thrown up just as many flags?" asked Pam.

"Probably," I said, "but not necessarily. I worked at a camp when I was in college. Sometimes, near the end of the summer, college and high school students just disappeared, especially if the campers had gone home. It drove the director crazy. They were supposed to stay all the way through the season to help close up, but some just took off and headed home."

"What about their final paychecks?"

I shrugged. "It wasn't like we were making much money back then. They still had to mail us our final checks."

"I get it," said Pam. "Let's get started."

There were two hundred people in each picture, and after looking for a half-hour, we'd had no luck.

"These pictures are really big," said Cynthia, "but the faces are really small. I need a magnifying glass."

"How about some reading glasses," said Diana. "I saw some over at the Ginger Cat, in their knickknacks by the cash register. You want me to go borrow some from Annie?"

"The highest strength she's got," Nancy said, and Diana was on her way out.

Five minutes later, Dave said, "I've got a maybe." He pointed to a girl looking back at us from 1979. I looked hard at the face.

"That's a maybe," I agreed.

Pete said, "You know, a lot of these girls look alike."

"That's for sure," said Cynthia. "Long, straight hair. Skinny. Shorts and a T-shirt."

The door opened, the cowbell clanged, and Diana came back into the restaurant. "Mission accomplished," she said. "I got the plus-threes."

We all put on the readers, and began again.

A couple of minutes later, the bell announced another visitor. We all looked up as Helen Pigeon called from the front door, "Come quick! That dog is at it again!"

I sighed. "We're busy right now, Helen. Your goats will be fine until we finish up."

"I want you to catch him in the act. Make him do the perp walk or something."

"We don't need to," said Nancy, peering down at her photo. "We know he's the one." Then she stopped her search and looked back up at Helen. "Do you even know what a perp walk is?"

"No," Helen harrumphed. "No, I don't, but he needs to do one."

"Later, Helen," I said, going back to my own photograph.

"What's everyone doing?" Helen asked, her upside-down goats now seemingly forgotten. "Why are you all wearing reading glasses? You look like a bunch of grandmothers." Then, "Can I look, too?"

I ignored the question, and Helen made herself comfortable standing behind my chair and peeking over my shoulder.

"Here's an idea," I said. "Pay close attention to the girls standing up near the back or near the edges. She was five feet ten — pretty tall for a girl. I'll bet the photographer would have put her in the back row, and standing up. Short girls were usually seated in the front."

"Good point," said Dave.

"We're looking for a girl?" asked Helen. "Ooo, the dead one? Is that her picture?"

No one bothered to answer.

Five minutes later, Pete said, "Hang on ... hang on ..."

"What?" said Cynthia.

"I got her!"

We all stopped what we were doing, got up, and crowded around Pete.

"Where?" Pam said.

"Right there." He tapped his finger on an image at the far right of a photo labeled "Camp Possumtickle, July 17-30, 1977."

"If that ain't her, I'm a goat roper."

"Hey," said Helen, indignant.

"Right there. Look at her eyebrows. See how high they are? Straight hair. And she's a good four inches taller than any of the other girls near her."

We all peered at the black and white photo.

"Could be," Nancy said. "It sure looks like her."

"She might not be a counselor," I said, squinting hard at the image. "She might work in the kitchen, or the office. Maybe in Arts and Crafts, or something like that."

"If that's her, how do we find out who she is?" asked Cynthia.

"Maybe someone will remember her," I said. "I guess that's our best hope. Perhaps the camp director knows who she is."

"Do you know who the director was back then?" Diana asked.

"I have no idea, but that information shouldn't be hard to find," I said. "That guy, probably." I pointed out another figure in the picture, a man in his fifties, fit and well-tanned, wearing shorts, a T-shirt, and a ball cap. "But this was over thirty years ago. I'll bet he's deceased."

"Look at this one," said Dave. He put a photo in front of us with the dates July 31 - August 13, 1977. The girl was in this photo, in the back, on the right, but this time there was a boy next to her, his arm draped around her neck, her arm encircling his waist.

"Huh," said Nancy. "How about that? Is he one of the counselors?"

"Summer romance," Pete said. "Happened all the time at camp."

"Still doesn't help us," said Nancy, unless we can locate the director. Or even the assistant."

"Or a counselor," added Dave. "Even a camper might remember." He paused, then, "If we can find one."

"Oh, my God!" gasped Helen.

"What?" Nancy said. "Did you see a goat or something?"

"That boy with his arm around the girl. I think that's Ron. Lemme see your glasses."

"Ron who?" I asked, and handed her my pair of readers.

"Ron Pigeon. Jeff's brother." Helen put on the readers, bent down, and put her face within three inches of the photo. "Yep. Ron."

"Really?" I knew Ron Pigeon and this looked nothing like him. Ron was a big guy, overweight, with a big mustache. His brown hair was cut short and he wore thick glasses. This boy looked as though he barely weighed one hundred sixty pounds soaking wet, had long blond hair that drifted onto his shoulders, clean shaven, no glasses.

"I think so," said Helen. "I didn't know him then, but I've seen family pictures. I met him when he was in his early twenties and he hadn't changed that much. It sure looks like him."

"Did Ron ever mention working at the camp?" I asked.

"Nope."

"Did Jeff work there?"

"Not that I know of, and I'm sure he would have told me. Jeff is six years older than Ron."

"Hey," said Dave. He'd been quickly scanning the other '77 photos. "The same kid's in all of them, but he's in the middle of the picture. He's not with the girl in this first photo."

"So, a *late* summer romance," said Pete. "The best kind."

"Let's talk to Ron," I said.

"He's on a cruise," said Helen. "I think he'll be back at the end of the week."

"Helen," I warned, "don't you say one word to him about this. Jeff either."

"Oh, I wouldn't," said Helen, shaking her head and smiling sweetly. "Now about my goats ..."

Chapter 10

I pulled out one of the snaps and gave it another going over.

"There," said Stormy. "In the back." Her finger hovered lingeringly over the photo, then dropped sadly into her forlorn lap.

I peered closely at the figure. She was beautiful with large brown eyes and flowing golden locks: a long-necked beauty making love to the camera, her lips slightly parted, the tip of her tongue tantalizingly visible behind straight white teeth, her ample udders shimmering in the moonlight.

"Maaaa," she seemed to say.

"Adeline Angora," said Stormy Night. "A Tennessee Kissing Goat and the belle of the ball. Now gimme a shot of that eel juice."

Meg had my typed pages in front of her as she reclined on the overstuffed leather sofa in front of the fireplace. I'd built a fire, even though, in my opinion, the evening wasn't quite cold enough to justify it. Still, Meg loved a fire, and it was September in the mountains. Baxter liked a fire, too, and was lying at Meg's feet, his nose poked toward the flames. I sat at my old desk, Raymond Chandler's hat on my head, my fingers dancing across the keys of his old Underwood No. 5. Bach was on the stereo. Good ol' Bach. Cantata 180: *Schmücke dich, o liebe Seele.* Just the thing for an early autumn evening.

"Have you seen Archimedes lately?" she asked, looking up from her reading.

"I haven't. Not for a couple of weeks."

Archimedes was an owl. Our owl. Well, not really. He was his own owl and came and went as he liked. We had an electric window for him in the kitchen, but he spent most of his time outdoors in the summer when the weather was good. We fed him in the winter, but this summer he seemed to prefer being outside on his own. He was eight or nine years old by my reckoning, old for this type of owl, but the county agent said a barn owl could live for twenty years or more, especially if it didn't have to forage on its own.

"This is excellent imagery," said Meg. "I like how her finger hovers lingeringly, then drops sadly into her forlorn lap."

"I'm an artist painting with words."

"My lap is becoming forlorn."

"Hmmm," I replied thoughtfully, giving my now standard reply to statements I dare not comment on.

"I can't explain it," she said, "but I am strangely entranced by this story."

"I expect it's hormonal. You're feeling very maternal and vulnerable, yet anxious and somewhat excited," I said, quoting something I'd seen on the Lifetime channel quite by accident.

"Yes, that's it exactly," Meg said, the unobserved eye roll evident in her voice.

"It's a love story," I said. "You're probably identifying with Adeline's ample udders shimmering in the moonlight."

I ducked the pillow just in time.

<p>

"Bad news," said Dave, when I answered the phone.

"It's late, Dave," I said, looking at the clock. It was blinking 1:47 AM. "Or early. I don't know which."

"Tell Dave to call back in the morning," muttered Meg. She turned her back and buried her head in her pillow.

"Meg says ..."

"I heard her," said Dave. "It's Savannah Jean Butts and a couple of the ladies from one of the Holy Word of God Pentecostal Church prayer circles."

"Oh, Jeeze."

"You should get down to the emergency room. Watauga Medical Center."

"Where's Nancy? Can't she take it?"

"She's in Charlotte, remember? Hornets game tomorrow."

"All right, fine," I grumbled, then hung up the phone, climbed out of bed, and got dressed.

"Drive carefully," mumbled Meg, not looking over.

It took me forty-five minutes to get to the hospital. An ambulance, running all its lights, might make it in forty, but not much quicker than that, the roads consisting of switchbacks, hairpin curves, and steep grades. I parked and found my way to the emergency room entrance, went in, and saw Larlene and Harmony Hickey sitting in the waiting area. Across from them was Rich Newport. He was thumbing through a National Geographic, circa 1994. The Hickey twins were members of Holy Word of God Pentecostal Church. Rich was a godless heathen. In an area where everyone is known by their religious affiliation, an avowed atheist was an anomaly.

"Hi, Chief," said Rich when he saw me. He sounded tired or maybe just disgusted.

"Morning, Rich. What's the deal?"

"I'll tell you the deal," spat Larlene.

The Hickey twins were identical as far as looks went. Not so much in personalities. Larlene was the outgoing twin. Her sister, Harmony, rarely said a word, just looked at the world through huge, pale blue eyes. They both had thin yellow hair, pasty skin coupled with a blotchy complexion, and both wore shapeless, matching, sack-like dresses that hit them well below the knees.

"I'll tell you the dang deal," she said again. "Savannah Jean is back there lying on a table and we don't know if she's gonna live or die. She's been tore apart by a beast from the pits of Hell!"

"Luger," said Rich. Luger was a German shepherd. He'd been a bomb dog, sniffing out armaments in the middle east, but was now retired, and Rich had adopted him about a year ago. There'd been a big article in the paper. "He bit Savannah Jean on the leg. Broke the skin I'm afraid."

"Dang near tore her leg off!" sputtered Larlene. Harmony nodded angrily. "We want that dog put down."

"It was just after midnight," said Rich. "I let Luger out and was getting ready for bed. It's not fenced, but Luger knows to stay home. He doesn't leave the property unless I'm with him. Then I hear these screams from the back yard."

"Screams of horrible pain," said Larlene. Harmony nodded.

"I still don't know what they were doing in my backyard. I can't get a straight answer."

I looked at the Hickeys. "Ladies," I said, "what were you doing in Rich's back yard?"

"We was doing the Lord's work." Larlene wiggled her back straight and sat as tall as she could in her righteous indignation. Harmony followed suit. There they sat, ramrod straight, ready for the next question.

"And what did the Lord require of you at midnight on a Saturday in someone else's yard?" I asked.

"We was *lookin'* for four-leaf clovers."

That caught me by surprise. I shot Rich a questioning glance. He just shrugged his shoulders.

"Savannah Jean says that four-leaf clovers are evil and must be uprooted. They're demonic."

"Demonic," said Harmony, finally entering the conversation.

I didn't comment, so Larlene continued. "God told Savannah Jean in a dream to get rid of all the four-leaf clovers in the neighborhood. God told Savannah Jean that three leaves are perfect, just like the Trinity — Father, Son, and Holy Ghost. God told Savannah Jean that he never intended for clovers to have more than three leaves. God told Savannah Jean that Satan was responsible for the extra leaf, and that we should rid the neighborhood of the works of the devil."

"Devil," added Harmony.

"God told Savannah Jean that he don't want superstition cutting in on his territory. He wants everyone to stop believing that four-leaf clovers or rabbit feet are good luck. Feet belong on rabbits, or in the stew pot, not in somebody's pocket."

"Pocket," said Harmony, with a decisive nod.

"So why were you in my yard?" asked Rich.

"You got a whole patch of four-leaf clovers in your back yard. We heard that girl Bernadette and those other boys talking about them. They collected a bunch and are gonna sell them for a dollar a piece at the Labor Day picnic."

"Moosey and Christopher," Rich said to me. "They asked me last week if they could look for some. I told them to go ahead and find all they wanted. Luger was even out there with them."

"That devil-dog," hissed Larlene. "We want it shot."

"Shot," agreed Harmony.

"No dog's getting shot," I said. "What's with you people? Everyone wants dogs shot lately." Just then Savannah Jean came hobbling out of the doorway separating us from the examining rooms. A young ER doctor was right behind her writing on a chart.

"What's the damage, Jim?" I said.

"Ah," he replied, looking up and seeing me. "Evening, Hayden." He looked down at his watch. "Or rather, morning." He checked his chart. "Nothing too bad. Seven stitches. Has the dog been quarantined?"

"No need," said Rich. "I have his papers right here." He produced a sheaf of documents and handed them over.

"You still need to watch him," said Jim, looking over the papers. "Keep him on a leash for two weeks." He looked over at Savannah Jean and gave her a thin smile. "You won't need the rabies treatment."

"That dog needs to be shot," insisted Larlene. "Shot, then buried, then dug up and shot again!"

"You can't just go sicking your dog on everyone that comes around," said Savannah Jean to Rich.

"I didn't sick Luger on anyone. He's a war hero."

"Listen, Savannah Jean," I said. "You too, Larlene. You had no business in Rich's yard. It is illegal to go into anyone's backyard and steal their property. Four-leaf clovers are property. As far as the law is concerned, he was protecting what was his."

"God told me to take them clovers," said Savannah Jean. "In a dream. He said Satan put them there. Are you saying that the laws of men outrank the laws of God?"

"Thou shalt not steal," I said.

"Thou shalt not have any gods before me," countered Savannah Jean. "That includes four-leaf clovers."

"And God said, 'Let the earth sprout vegetation, plants, and fruit trees on the earth.' And God saw that it was good," I said. "*That* includes four-leaf clovers."

"Do not turn to mediums or witches; nor superstitions, and so make yourselves unclean by them: I am the Lord your God."

"Have nothing to do with irreverent, silly myths. Rather, train yourself for godliness," I said.

"Where is that found?" asked Savannah Jean warily.

"First Timothy," I said. Maybe the verse was in First Timothy, maybe it wasn't, but until they looked it up I was safe. "You ladies stay out of Rich's yard. I'm not joking. Next time you'll find yourselves, like the Apostle Paul, in the hoosegow."

"Huh," grunted Savannah Jean, but turned on her good heel and led the Hickey twins, glaring all the way, out of the emergency room and into the parking lot.

ρ

It was late afternoon and I was relaxing on a bench in Sterling Park, the one nearest the Holy Grounds coffee shop, waiting for Meg. I had two coffees with me, and a couple of noshes as well. The leaves still hadn't begun their metamorphosis, but it was one of those afternoons where you could feel the change coming. The meteorologist might characterize it as a slight drop in temperature with very low humidity and prevailing breezes. We'd say, "Fall is in the air."

Sterling Park made up the center of the town square. It featured uncommonly large trees: giant maples, oaks, and poplars, some dogwoods, a few hemlocks. Considering the leafy canopy over the park, it was amazing to me that any grass would grow, but grow it did, thanks in no small part to Billy Hixon and his lawn crew. They fertilized, mowed, raked, clipped, and pampered the turf till it looked like something on a golf course, and woe unto that pet owner who didn't clean up after a walk. There was a gazebo at one end of the park, opposite from where I was sitting, right across from the Ginger Cat, and I saw some folks with the same idea I'd had, relaxing and enjoying the afternoon. A few kids ran across the expanse chasing a dog that was barking happily and trailing a leash behind it. Two college students, a boy and a girl, were lying on a blanket, pretending to study. I noticed some other people walking around the square on the sidewalk, peering in shop windows. For a late Saturday afternoon, the park was not crowded. Birds were singing, a few butterflies were taking advantage of the late blooms.

"This is beautiful," said Meg, walking up behind me and kissing me on the neck. "It's like something right out of a movie."

"Bucolic," I said.

"Ah," said Meg. "Not so much bucolic, I think, as halcyon. I think of bucolic as more of a pastoral setting. Cows and sheep, some fainting goats, maybe a truffle pig."

"Now you're just showing off."

"Yep. Is that my coffee?" Meg had decided that, even pregnant, she wasn't giving up coffee. Not for nine months. Wine, okay. Beer, sure. Not coffee. There were plenty of medical studies, she said, that showed coffee was actually healthy for an expectant mother and her unborn baby. Or, if not healthy, at least, not unhealthy. She'd switched to decaf though, and limited herself to two cups, and after the first couple of weeks, when she was miserable anyway, made the transition.

"Here you go. Decaf, two sugars. This is your lemon square, but if you're feeling queasy, I'll be happy to eat it for you."

"No, I'm feeling fine this afternoon, thanks." She sat down beside me.

"Been shopping?"

"A bit. Did you know that Gucci makes a diaper bag? Only $1,279."

"I did not know that, and I didn't want to know that."

"I have a list," said Meg, and produced a piece of paper from her non-Gucci purse. "A baby list."

- Dolce Bella Baby Bottle: one bottle and one crocodile skin bottle holder —$580

"For one bottle?" I said. "I'll bet we could get an illegal wet nurse for less than that."

Meg smirked at me and continued.

- Oval high chair by PoshTots in a black and ivory leopard print — $1,200
- Aston Martin Silver Cross Stroller — $3,115
- Onda Luxy Bubbles: an Italian made infant bath set — $3,038
- Deluxe Infant Stimucenter — $3,069
- Italian Cherubini Crib: Silver and gold gilding with appliquéd cherub moulding — $4,400

"It's a good thing we're rich," I said. "How about those diapers made out of pages from the Gutenberg Bible?"

"Sorry. Not on the list."

"Sheesh," I said. "This is getting expensive, and we haven't even started thinking about college."

"Don't worry, sweetie. We're not getting any of that junk. The baby stuff at Target is just fine. You might like to know that, according to the latest figures, it costs almost two hundred fifty-thousand dollars to raise a child to age eighteen."

"That include college?"

"No, but I already started the college fund."

"You did? Great! Anything I need to worry about?" Meg was an investment counselor by trade and a fine one. She had brokered my small fortune into a large one. Now I just stayed out of the way.

"Nothing in particular. It's a standard, self-directed ESA. We should probably open another trust account as well."

"Excellent work," I said, having no idea what she was talking about.

"Have you thought any more about the baby's name?"

I shook my head. "Nope. It's your choice."

"That's sweet, but I want your input. Not your silly names. Your considered choices."

"Why don't you pick some and I'll tell you if I like them?"

"Hmm." Meg took a sip of her coffee and nodded my attention toward the front doors of the church. They had just opened and Dr. Mallary Clochette had emerged followed by three other people, two women and a man.

"Who are those three?" asked Meg.

"I have no idea. Grad students maybe? I think Mallary must be on her sabbatical by now."

She spotted us sitting on the bench watching her, turned and headed our way, clipping along at a no-nonsense pace.

The Maestro was a terror: a choral genius with an AA, a BME, an MME, a PhD, and a DMA in conducting from Florida State which is not a diploma mill, I don't care what they say. The letters trailed after her name like her doctoral students, educated baby ducks, waddling advertisements of her brilliance. When she sneezed (as she did often, being allergic to Eric Whitacre) all the letters flew out her nose and the students gleefully wiped up the pure vowels and exaggerated consonants with bath towels and sold them on eBay.

But I'm getting ahead of my story.

"What?" said Meg. "Did you say something?"

"I hope not," I replied, as Mallary and her troupe came up the sidewalk toward us. "Just muttering to myself."

"You're doing that a lot lately. Are you sure you're okay?"

"I'm fine. Really."

Mallary Clochette strode up to us. Really strode, taking striding to an art form. I didn't get up as politeness would dictate. I was already slumped on the bench, my legs crossed, my arm around my beloved, a perfectly good coffee in my hand. And, as Pete had pointed out, I was getting old. It just seemed like too much trouble.

"Good afternoon, Hayden," Mallary said. She smiled thinly at Meg, but obviously couldn't remember her name.

"Meg," Meg said.

"Meg, of course. I'm sorry. I've met so many people lately."

"No need to apologize."

"A lovely afternoon," I said. "I hope you're having a good day, Dr. Clochette."

"I'm having a very productive day," she said, then gestured for her minions to come forward and present themselves.

"These are my graduate assistants. As you know, I'm on sabbatical this fall, and since they're all in the final year of our doctoral program, I've gotten permission for them to join me."

"Fabulous," I said.

"Of course, this quaint little town isn't New York," said the man, his disdain showing. "We all would have preferred New York, or at least Boston." He looked at the two other students. "At least, *I* would have." He said this pointedly and the comment was obviously directed at Mallary. "The Maestro prefers to be in Podunk, North Carolina."

"Maestro?" Meg said. "Wouldn't that be *Maestra*?"

"I prefer to be addressed by my students as maestro," said Mallary, "just as many women actors chose to be called that and not actresses. We do not call women astronauts astronettes, women pilots aviatrix, nor do we call Emily Dickinson a poetess."

"Fair enough," Meg said. "Distinction noted."

"This is Jeremy Gevrik," Mallary said. "He has the manners of a boor, but he has the makings of quite a good choral conductor. This is Julia Tullum and Jenny Kunick. Jeremy assumed we were heading to New York." She gave Jeremy a withering look. "Or at least to Boston."

"You as much as told us we were going to New York ..." he said, but was stopped by her upraised hand.

"Plans change," said Mallary. "Circumstances change."

Jeremy appeared to be in his early thirties. He had dark hair, cut and styled by someone who knew what they were doing, and was wearing khakis and an expensive designer polo shirt, tucked in. Slip-on leather shoes, no socks. He was thin and in good shape, the kind of shape you get in by going to the gym regularly. He sported small, rectangular, Euro-style glasses, and a three day growth of beard that had been carefully cultivated to look like he'd forgotten to shave that morning because he'd received an emergency phone call from Helmuth Rilling asking his advice on the interpretation of a newly discovered C.P.E. Bach cantata.

Julia was his female counterpart, right down to the glasses, the short stylish hair, and the attitude. She was wearing gray slacks, a black silk blouse, and short heels. Understated makeup. She had on a small strand of pearls with earrings to match. Nothing ostentatious, just noticeable. She was shorter than Mallary by a few inches, but taller than Jeremy.

"Jeremy, Julia, and Jenny," I said. "Three Js. That's cute." It wasn't cute, but I'd already had enough of Jeremy.

"Strictly coincidence, I assure you," sniffed Julia. "Jeremy's from Dayton, Ohio. His undergrad is from Oberlin and he's got a Master's from Florida State. I guess he just wanted to get to a real city for a change."

Jeremy seethed.

"I'm from Philadelphia," Julia said sweetly. "Curtis Institute. I've *been* to New York."

There was an awkward silence, then Meg said, "Where are you from, Jenny?"

"Knoxville, originally, but I've been up this way a lot growing up, especially during the summers. I have my Masters from UT."

"So you know the area," I said.

"Sure. I worked at the Farmhouse Restaurant one summer. You know, doing the singing waitress thing."

"I remember it," I said. "It was still going when I moved up here, but it's gone now. Sold for the value of the property. The new owners tore it down and built a mansion."

"That's what I heard," said Jenny, "but I haven't gone back up. It's too sad."

Jenny was older than the other two by fifteen years or so. She was wearing slacks as well, and a cream colored blouse that even I could tell was far cheaper than Julia's silk one. She was attractive, but had the look of someone who had worked for quite a few years, a look that neither Jeremy nor Julia could manage. There were worry lines around her eyes and mouth, and a few gray hairs.

"We're putting together my book," said Mallary. "*LadySong: The Art of Conducting Women's Voices.* All the research and writing has been done, all the examples decided on. We just have to pull it all together and get it off to the publisher."

"We could have pulled it all together in New York," growled Jeremy under his breath, but loud enough for us all to hear him.

Mallary gave him a look, then said. "I just spoke with Thomas. He indicated that there's a large room next door to your office that we might use as an editorial suite. He said that it's currently not being used for anything but storage."

"And not much of that," I said. "He's right. What's in there can easily be moved."

"Thomas indicated that I should ask you, to see if our being there would be satisfactory. Why you," she shrugged, "I don't know."

"I don't know either, but it's certainly fine with me."

"Excellent. We'll set up a couple of tables, some chairs, and bring in our laptops and printers. I have an electric piano I'll be moving in as well. We may need to play through some things, but I don't think we'll bother you."

"I don't see how you could," I said. "I'm hardly ever there."

"If you'd like to sing with the St. Barnabas choir while you're in town, we'd love to have you," said Meg, always the welcoming optimist, but Mallary was already striding away and the contemptuous look that Jeremy and Julia gave her was dismissive at best.

"I'd like to," Jenny whispered, then hurried to catch up with the trio.

Chapter 11

So it was true. I had heard the rumors, but I didn't believe them. Adeline and the priests. Sure, it was common knowledge that all priestly ordinations included kissing a goat. In fact, it was true of all canonical installations and had been that way since the Council of Squirrel Springs in 1739. But goats were one thing. This was Adeline Angora, five-time winner of the Miss Mohair Contest. Looks and talent, she had it all. How these fledgling priests got hold of her was anyone's guess. She'd been missing for weeks and every ecclesiastical goat-roper in the country had his ears pricked. The new Archbishop was due to be crowned in three days and he wanted this particular goat. As everyone knew, what the Archbishop wanted, the Archbishop got. Lips that touched his would be Adeline's or heads would roll.

Jenny Kunick didn't show up on Sunday to sing with the choir, but she may have been busy with Maestro Clochette. I passed her new office as I walked up to the choir loft and, although the door was closed, I could hear quite a bit of activity going on inside. The service went well, but the choir loft felt much different. The broken stained glass image of our beloved saint had been removed and plywood nailed up where he had once been. The scaffolding had gone up outside and covered the entire back wall of the building. The damage from the falling tree had been more extensive than previously thought, taking part of the roof, all the copper gutters, the downspouts, the window, and punching a hole in the back wall of the organ pipe chamber.

We sang a fine arrangement of *Simple Gifts* at the offertory, and the only other surprise was the announcement that the first of the candidates interviewing for the position of Rector of St. Barnabas Church would be participating in our service the following Sunday.

"Are you going to sign up for cuddling?" Pete asked. "I heard all about it this morning."

Pete was wiping the counter down following the Monday morning breakfast rush, such as it was. I'd just arrived and was pouring myself a cup of coffee, since Cynthia seemed to be busy filling salt and pepper shakers. Other than the three of us, the Slab was empty.

"I am not signing up," I said. "I do not want to cuddle or be cuddled, especially by someone I'm not currently having cuddling relations with."

"That narrows it down for you, my friend," said Pete, "but I see your point. Cuddling, as far as I'm concerned, is a means to an end. It may be what is required afterwards, but that's a different discussion altogether."

"Thus says the foremost expert on cuddling," said Cynthia sarcastically.

"Well," said Pete, "I hate to toot my own horn, but I have been told that I give great cuddle."

"By whom? One of your three ex-wives?"

"Yep. Two of them didn't like to cuddle that much, but the second one did. She was a big girl, warm in the winter and shady in the summer."

"The important thing here," I said, "is that I not be involved in any fashion. There are three ways this cuddling ministry thing can go: badly, horribly wrong, and, with disastrous effects."

"Monica Jones has a friend who's a professional cuddler," Cynthia said. "She says she makes a pretty good living at it. Charges a hundred dollars an hour."

"Don't even think about it," Pete said to Cynthia. "You are *not* signing up! Anyway, a professional belly dancer cannot also be a cuddler. It's in the bylaws, or the U.S. Constitution, or something. Besides, these are volunteer cuddlers."

"Don't worry, I'm not signing up," said Cynthia, "but it makes a certain amount of sense. Kimberly Walnut came by this morning and gave me a flyer. She's going all out on this one."

"She's finishing up her book," I said. "Dr. Walnut, published author and resident expert on Christian Formation Ministries."

"Look on the bright side," said Pete. "She'll be looking to upgrade her position soon, and head for a bigger and more appreciative congregation."

"Amen," I said. "What's the flyer say?"

Cynthia read, "Are you a compassionate and empathetic individual? Do you have light and love to give to individuals who are in need? For one reason or another, many of us do not get the level of human contact that we want or need to be our optimal selves. Jesus said, 'Love one another.' Touch has the power to comfort us when we are sad, heal us when we are sick, encourage us when we feel lost, and above all else, allow us to accept that we are not alone. Sarah's Snuggery is a St. Barnabas ministry that will provide nonjudgmental, platonic touch to improve people's lives."

"Sarah's Snuggery?" I gave an involuntary shudder.

Cynthia nodded. "It was going to be called Sarah's Snuggles, but the rector decided that all snuggling should be done at the church. Hence, Snuggery."

"Did Kimberly Walnut say where in the church these cuddlers were going to ply their trade?" I asked.

"Yep. The Snuggery will be in the library. I guess there's a pullout sofa in there. Plus, the door can be locked and the curtains pulled. Privacy is very important to cuddlers."

"No overnight cuddles, I'm guessing," I said. "Plenty of supervision?"

"One hour maximum," said Cynthia. "Kimberly Walnut will do all the scheduling. Cuddlers must take the class and be certified."

"Certified by whom?" I asked.

"Hmm," said Cynthia, looking at the flyer. "Good question. It doesn't say, but I'm sure there is some kind of ecumenical compliance agency."

"For *cuddlers*?" I said.

"Listen to this," said Cynthia. She'd flipped the page over. "Scientific studies show that we thrive on contact. A lack of human interaction can contribute to depression, stress, high blood pressure, and aggression. Even minimal personal contact, on the other hand, releases a chemical called oxytocin into the brain, effectively lowering high levels of stress and blood pressure. Human touch reduces anxiety, physically accelerates the healing of injured body tissue, boosts the immune system, and creates feelings of calm and happiness."

"I'm not arguing the science," I said. "I'm not even arguing the incredible silliness of having it at St. Barnabas. In fact, I affirm Kimberly Walnut and wish her all the best in her next job."

Cynthia laughed. "She doesn't have one. Not yet."

"The amazing thing is that the priest is on board with this."

"Yeah," said Cynthia. "I'll bet there are a few of the ladies that will want to be cuddled by him. He's a good-looking middle-aged man. Keeps himself in shape."

"Are they going to do same-sex cuddling?" Pete asked. He'd finished wiping the counter and had moved to the task of cutting up onions for the lunch crowd. "Hasn't the Episcopal Church affirmed same-sex cuddling?"

"It doesn't say," said Cynthia. "I presume so, if that's what the cuddlee wants."

"Ah, progress. It brings a tear to my eye," said Pete. "Well, the onions do anyway. Any more news on our deceased girl?"

"Nope," I said. "Jeff Pigeon didn't know her. That was a long shot anyway. Ron won't be home till Friday. The camp director in 1977 was a guy named Hank Townsend. He died in 2002, so that's no help. He was a high school principal during the school year, from Tifton, Georgia. That's all we've found out. There's no camp roster, and we've put out the word for anyone around town who was at camp that summer to come talk to us."

"Any takers?" asked Pete.

"Two," I said. "Keith Kendrick and Alan Lawrence. Neither one of them remembers her. Not surprising. They don't remember Ron being there either. Jeff said maybe Ron was a CIT that year, but he was in college and working that summer in Washington, DC, and doesn't remember for sure."

"CIT?" said Pete.

"Counselor in Training."

"Oh. Well, Ron will know who the girl is," Pete said. "Of course, he's the main suspect, him with his arm around the murder victim."

"True enough," I said, "but I know Ron. He doesn't seem the type to kill someone."

Moosey McCollough was twelve years old, and as a twelve year old boy with mischievous tendencies, finding out that there is something in the world called Tennessee Fainting Goats is one of the best discoveries you can make. Helen, of course, called the police station immediately.

"Nine-one-one!" yelled Helen into the phone, loud enough for both Dave and me to hear, even though Nancy was the one lucky enough to answer. "Nine-one-one!"

"Helen," said Nancy, "you don't have to yell 'nine-one-one.' You've gotten us. This is the police department."

"This is an emergency! Nine-one-one! Moosey McCollough is riding his bike beside my fence."

Nancy gave a huge sigh. "And?"

"And he has a bike horn. You know, the kind with the huge bulb on the end. He honks it every time he rides by."

"And?"

"And the goats fall over." Helen heard Nancy snort into the phone. "It's not funny! These are very rare and expensive goats!"

Nancy handed me the phone, shaking her head and biting her lower lip against laughing.

"Helen, it's Hayden."

"Hayden! Moosey McCollough is scaring my goats. On purpose."

"Yes, I heard," I said. "Honking his bike horn."

"Exactly. I want him arrested. That should fix his wagon. He's a little juvenile delinquent!"

"Helen, it's not against the law to honk your bike horn."

"It's cruelty to animals," she said.

"Huh," I said, then, "I thought the goats didn't get hurt when they fainted."

"It's cruel to scare them. That's just common sense. It's cruel to scare any creature."

"You do have a point, but they may just be startled, not actually scared."

"It's the *same thing*," huffed Helen, exasperation in her voice. "I want Moosey locked up, Hayden. Send him to juvie!"

"I'm not sure I can lock him up, Helen, but I'll speak with him."

"Here he comes again!" Helen squealed and I could hear the phone drop, then Helen's voice from some distance away. "You little hooligan! You're going to the big house!" Then the horn honking, then Helen again, this time a sorrowful wail. I hung up the phone.

"Figures that Moosey was the first one to figure that out," Dave said.

"It's only a matter of time now," said Nancy. "Every kid in town is gonna know about this by supper."

I walked out in front of the station and waited, knowing that Moosey would be riding by momentarily. The Pigeons' house was on his route home from school, followed by downtown St. Germaine, the Wine Press, Piggly Wiggly, and Dr. Ken's Gun Emporium. He didn't usually make every stop, but the chances were good he'd appear shortly, riding the old BMX bike that he'd bought for ten dollars at the thrift store. He'd fixed the bike, painted it bright green, then added the horn which announced his presence regularly around town.

It wasn't ten minutes before I saw the mop of hair, the striped T-shirt, and the torn dungarees covering red, high-top Keds. I gave a loud whistle and waved him over. He tore across the park, standing on the pedals and pumping his legs for all he was worth, then, when he hit the asphalt, slammed on the brakes and slid the back end of the bike around in a perfect half-circle.

"Hiya, Chief!" he said, grinning broadly. "What's up?"

Moosey was still waiting for one permanent tooth to come all the way in, but he now had most of them. His wire-rimmed glasses were sitting crooked on his nose, mainly from being bent and re-bent so many times that they had lost all semblance of symmetry.

"Do me a favor, would you?" I said.

"Sure."

"Please ... really, *please* stop making Helen Pigeon's goats faint."

Moosey looked concerned. "I only did it a couple of times. Am I in trouble?"

"Nope. But Mrs. Pigeon is making our lives miserable. If you promise not to scare them more than once a week, I'll give you two bucks."

"Hmm," said Moosey, thinking, then countered, "Three times a week. Four bucks."

"Twice a week, two bucks, and an ice cream on Fridays."

"Deal!" said Moosey, then shrugged. "I probably woulda done it for nothin'. I felt kinda bad seeing all those goats lying upside down."

"Well, there you go," I said. "You drive a hard bargain. Have a good afternoon." Then I added, "Don't forget to do all your homework."

"I will," said Moosey.

"Hey," I said. "Are you taking trumpet lessons?"

He shook his head. "Just playing in the band."

"Would you like to?"

"Sure!"

"Let me see what I can do. You'll have to practice, though. Every day."

"I can do that. I like playing the trumpet."

"I'll let you know," I said.

"Can I have the two dollars now? Bernadette has a couple of old Barbies she wants to sell me."

"You're buying Barbies?"

"I'm gonna blow them up. I got some firecrackers left over from the summer."

"You be careful with firecrackers," I said. "I knew this one kid ..."

"I know, I know. Two bucks?" He stuck his hand out and gave me his most winning smile. I smiled back, reached into my pocket, and paid him the two dollars in quarters.

Dave came out and stood beside me as I watched him go.

"You paid him off?"

"Yep."

"We going to pay off all the kids?"

"Two dollars a head ... might cost the town a couple hundred bucks."

"Well worth it," said Dave.

Chapter 12

"Adeline Angora's not the only Tennessee Kissing Goat in the milking chute," I said. "Anyway, what do you care?"

"I don't really," she said, "but I'm on a job."

She dropped two C-notes on the desk, then drizzled a look on me like I was a frosted cupcake and she was Paula Deen on a diet.

"I'm undercover, working for the new Archbishop. My real name is ..."

Suddenly a shot rang out, an arrow whizzed by, a stick of dynamite fell through the mail slot, and a noose dropped from the ceiling. Maybe someone was trying to tell me something, but I wasn't one to take a hint. Not until it smacked me right in the mush.

Stormy smacked me right in the mush. "Pay attention! My real name is ..." She suddenly grabbed her throat with both hands and began to turn blue. "Urgle wobllech hrrrgk," she sputtered, trying to catch her breath.

"Mind if I call you Urgle?" I asked. "The rest of that is rather unpronounceable."

"It's Brungarian," said Urgle, smoothing out the skin that had bunched up on her throat like one of those Shar-Pei dogs, but not as cute. "A highly guttural language."

"Very interesting," I said, not interested in that at all. What was more interesting to me was the red stain slowly spreading across Urgle's abundant frontage like a spilled glass of wine if the wine was spilled inside Urgle and then leaked out a hole the size of a bullet, which coincidently was the same size as the one Urgle was currently leaking from. Her eyes rolled back, then front, then back again, and she slumped to the floor like a hundred and fifty pound gunny sack full of Easter pudding, the kind without bones in it.

"Urgle," she croaked again, red bubbles blossoming on her lips like bubble-blossoms if there is such a thing, and if there's not, there should be.

"I know," I said. "I heard you the first time."

"Urrrrrgle ..."

"Got it," I said. "Your name is Urgle. Now about that goat ..."

"This is codswallop!" said Marjorie, usually the first to comment on my prose, "Total godwottery!"

"Are those even words?" asked Tiff St. James.

"If they are in Hayden's story, probably not," said Meg.

"Codswollop?" said Tiff. "Godwottery?"

"Perfectly good words," answered Marjorie. "If education were anything like it was when I was a girl, you'd have a decent vocabulary. You've been mollycoddled."

"I've been what?"

"Mollycoddled, dear," said Marjorie. "You've been mollycoddled by a bunch of snollygosters." She turned to Meg. "Speaking of mollycoddling, we've mollycoddled you two long enough. What are you going to name that baby? We don't even know if it's a boy or a girl."

Meg gave her a smile and said, "We haven't decided yet."

"You haven't decided if it's a boy or a girl?" said Phil Camp.

"It's one of those," Meg said. "Definitely."

As rehearsals went, this one was par for the course. Mostly singing, some snide comments about my prowess as an author, some prayer requests, announcements, and Meg being grilled about baby particulars.

"You're not going to tell us, are you?" said Randy Hatteberg. "How will we know what color booties to crochet?"

Meg smiled nicely.

"You should name that baby 'Urgle,'" said Steve. "That works for either a boy or a girl."

"Don't be ridiculous," said Sheila. "You wouldn't know if someone were calling the baby or drowning. Anyway, if Meg and Hayden want to keep it all a secret, they certainly may. It's their prerogative."

"Absolutely," agreed Elaine.

"I couldn't agree more," said Bev.

"It's their God-given right," said Rebecca Watts.

"If they want to be mean about it," said Sheila.

"Keep us in the dark," said Elaine, "for their own selfish reasons."

"Even though we're supposed to be their friends," said Bev.

"Not that they would want to brighten our dreary lives," said Rebecca. "Why should they?"

"I guess we could have a baby shower for the Unknown Baby," said Marty. "We could all bring generic diapers or something."

"Meg's *very* busy," said Rhiza. "Instead of a shower, maybe we should just get her some discount coupons for baby powder."

"All right, all right!" said Meg, laughing. "It's a girl, okay? It's a girl."

"Hurrah," said Fred May, less enthused by the news than the ladies. "Now maybe we can get some singing done."

"Absolutely not," said Marty. "Not with news like this. What's her name?"

"We're not telling," said Meg. "Because we don't know yet."

"I'm leaning toward Abishag," I said. "Or Cornelia."

"He is not!"

"How about Tawni?" said Lena. "Or Dixie? I love thinking up baby names! What about Destini, with an 'i?'"

"Those sound more like stripper names," said Mark Wells.

I'd heard enough. "Sopranos," I called loudly, putting an abrupt end to the discussion. "Back to the anthem. *Thou Art the King of Glory*. Let's begin at measure forty, two before you come in."

"Could we hurry it up?" said Goldi Fawn. "I gotta get to cuddling practice."

"Sure. We have just twenty minutes before Susan and Zeb show up."

"Who are they?" asked Hollie.

"Susan Sievert's the new trumpet teacher at Appalachian State. Zeb Martin is on the voice faculty. He's sung with us before."

"I remember," said Elaine. "He was one of the bears in *Elisha and the Two Bears*."

"Indeed he was," I said. Zeb had a huge, dark voice and had sung in an opera house in Germany before coming back to teach at Appalachian State.

"I wish we could have done something with an alto solo," said Lena. "Even a soprano solo. I would have tried out."

"He never has try outs," said Goldi Fawn. "He just picks people, his favorites." She glared across the choir, spotted the object of her annoyance, and said, "Usually Ian."

True enough, but I ignored her and started the organ introduction. Twenty minutes later we were fairly well prepared. Susan and Zeb appeared at the door of the loft.

"C'mon in," I said. "Let me introduce you."

"You all sound fabulous," said Susan. "This will be fun."

The St. Barnabas staff meeting had been moved to Friday morning so we could all meet the first of the candidates who would be interviewing for the rector's position. I arrived late and found that the staff meeting wasn't so much a meeting as a reception taking place in the Parish Hall, everyone standing around, coffee cup in hand, chatting with our visitor. The staff, such as it was, was there: Marilyn, me, Father Walmsley, and Kimberly Walnut. We hadn't had a sexton for years, the janitorial duties now handled by a cleaning company, and the church locked and unlocked by whomever happened to be available with a key.

The worship committee had been invited: Mattie Lou Entriken, head of the kitchen committee; a few Sunday School teachers; Georgia Wester, the senior warden; Mark Wells, the junior warden. A few vestry members were also in attendance, Meg being one of them.

Father Walmsley was in the big huddle that included our interviewee. He waved and motioned me over when he saw me. I found myself a cup of coffee, dolefully ignored the beautiful cupcakes Diana Evarts had provided, in deference to my waistline, and joined the group.

"Hayden," said Father Walmsley, "this is Carter Ousley from Atlanta. He's currently at St. Timothy's."

"Pleased to meet you," I said, and extended my hand. He didn't take it, but instead clapped me on one shoulder. "Likewise," he said.

"I read your vita," I said. "It looks very impressive."

Carter was in his mid-forties. Thinning blond hair, blue eyes. He was wearing a dog collar, but where Father Walmsley wore his over a traditional black shirt, Carter's shirt was orange. His suit was natural linen, stylishly rumpled. He had a silver cross on a chain around his neck. His vita included a brief stint in England at a small vicarage outside Winchester, as well as St. Timothy's. He was a second-career priest, but that was nothing unusual in our denomination. His college degree was in history with a minor in music and he'd been a junior college administrator before joining the priesthood four years ago.

"I've told him all about you," said Father Walmsley, "the church, and our wonderful tradition of topnotch music."

I doubted that. If Father Walmsley knew all about me, and even partially what had gone on at St. B's for the last six years, he would have run screaming into the hills like a little girl.

"We snuck in last night and heard the beginning of your rehearsal," said Carter. "When you were rehearsing the hymns. Say, do you ever do any kind of descants? With sopranos and maybe a trumpet?"

"Well, as a matter of fact ..." I was cut off by Kimberly Walnut who had been busy until that moment at the cupcake table. Now she came up to the group and forced a maple-iced confection into Carter's hand.

"You'll love these, Carter," she gushed. "We sometimes have them at staff meetings."

"Um, yes ... thank you."

"Go ahead, try it. Has Father Walmsley told you about my book? Archangel Publishing will be putting it out next year. I just have a few more chapters to finish up. We've decided, Father Walmsley and I, that St. Barnabas will be the perfect ministry laboratory."

"It's a very exciting prospect," Carter said.

"I've just finished my doctorate," said Kimberly Walnut. "My project was on ministries for growing your congregation and I guess that this book was just a natural outgrowth of that. My major professor, Dr. Alfred Pignus, says that when it's published, this book may be one of the foremost tools available for Christian Development and Ministry as well as ... "

"Excuse me," I interrupted. "It's good to meet you, Carter, but I have to go. You have plenty of people to meet. I'll see you on Sunday."

He nodded at me and looked as though he was about to answer.

"As I was saying," rattled Kimberly Walnut, glaring at me, "before we were so rudely interrupted, this book is going to be the definitive word on growing your church through ministry formation for the next ten years. The title is *Fifty Nifty Thrifty Ways ...*"

I left the conversation, waved to Meg, who was engulfed in a discussion with Bev and Carol Sterling, no doubt about babies, then took a cupcake off the table for Nancy and an extra, because you never know when you might need a cupcake, and walked out the door and into the morning.

Ron Pigeon was waiting for us when we arrived at his home. We'd called ahead, but I'm sure he had already been filled in by Helen. Helen was not known for keeping any kind of confidence. Ron was sitting on his front porch at a small table, working on his laptop. The porch was a beauty, an old-style, wraparound, covered porch that afforded a view of the wide street. Nancy and I had walked over since it was a beautiful day and Ron's house was on Oak Street, only four blocks from the station. It was an old neighborhood featuring large trees shading the sidewalks and houses dating from the '20s up through the '50s. Ron had been involved in an ugly divorce last year. Becky had taken the kids, both in high school, and moved down to Florida to be near her parents. The children hadn't been happy to leave, but Becky wasn't going to stick around, not after she was the only one in town who didn't know about Ron's affair with his real estate partner's wife, including the partner. She wasn't about to leave the kids. Becky pretty much took everything Ron had, save this house, which had been a rental property that the firm owned. Ron bought the house from the company after the divorce was final. The partner packed up and moved, with his wife, to Wilmington, as far away from St. Germaine as he could get and still be in North Carolina.

"C'mon up," said Ron, looking up when he heard us. "I'm just catching up on some work. A real estate agent's work is never done. You know, those cruises are fun, but you have to pay out the nose for internet service and even then it's so slow, it's not even worth the trouble. The best I could do was answer a few emails."

"Where did you go?" I asked as we walked up the stone steps.

"It was a singles cruise. Left out of San Diego and headed down the Mexican Coast and back."

"Helen didn't tell us."

"That's because Helen didn't know. If she had, she would have told you. Helen's not one to keep a secret."

"Then you know why we're here," I said.

"Oh, sure. Helen called me as soon as the ship hit port. She said you were looking for a missing girl that had been murdered and that I would know who it was." He stood and offered us chairs. "Here, sit down. Show me what you've found."

Nancy had the long photo in a cardboard tube. She opened it, then unrolled the picture and stretched it across the table. We sat down across from Ron and showed it to him.

"Summer, 1977," she said. "This is you, right?" She put a finger on the figure that Helen had identified as Ron.

"That's me, sure enough. I was fifteen and working as a CIT that year. Camp Possumtickle. Wow. That brings back some memories."

"Specifically, we're interested in the girl that you have your arm around," I said.

"Huh," grunted Ron, and looked more closely, as if he hadn't noticed his arm around the girl's shoulder, or hers around his waist.

"See," I said, "you're not with your cabin in this picture. In the other pictures that summer, you were with your cabin. Here, you're standing with this girl."

"I remember. This is the last session that summer. Is that the girl you found in the woods?"

"You tell us," said Nancy, and produced the artist's sketch.

"Wow. It sure looks like her," said Ron. "Not exactly, but it could be." He tapped the photo. "This girl's name is Barbara McCuwen. She was working in the kitchen that summer. If I remember right, she didn't come up till July. The rest of us were already working. She was in college in Florida. Music major, a sophomore I think."

"And you, a precocious fifteen-year-old," said Nancy.

"Well, I was mature for my age."

"That's what we all thought when we were fifteen," I said. "More likely, we were all hormone-crazed adolescents hitting on any girl that would give us the time of day."

Ron laughed. "Or that."

"So this was a summer fling?" said Nancy.

"More like three days," said Ron. "We took the pictures around the middle of each session as I recall. The kid's parents would buy them when they came to pick them up at the end."

"So around the 3rd or 4th of August," Nancy said, making a note in her pad.

"Something like that. Not to speak ill of the deceased, but, as I recall, Barbara wasn't shy about making friends." He gave me a long look. "You know what I mean."

94

"Tell me."

"She was, you know, an easy date. She went through the counselors like a beaver through a birch basket, as we used to say, pardon my French. I'd even heard rumors that she'd done the camp director."

"Hank Townsend," said Nancy.

"Nah, not him. He was a straight arrow. Maybe I'm thinking of the assistant director. He was a coach."

"You remember his name?" I asked.

"No. Sorry, I don't."

"She was sleeping with several of the counselors?"

"Several. More than several, if memory serves."

"And you being fifteen ..."

"Exactly. She was my first." Ron looked at Nancy and gave an apologetic shrug.

"So you were in love," said Nancy, not unsarcastically. Nancy had been friends with Becky and didn't have much use for Ron.

"Of course I was. Who wasn't when they were fifteen? Hey, it was the seventies. It was over in a couple of days. She moved on."

"You remember any of the other counselor's names? Or even campers?" I asked.

"Jay Gore was a counselor that year." Ron thought for a long moment. "He's the only one I remember and that's because he was the head counselor in my cabin and he got me the job in the first place. You know Jay? He used to live here, but he moved a long time ago. Maybe just after college."

"I've met him. Lives in Tryon, right? He had a giant Bullwinkle the Moose balloon he brought up for the Christmas parade a few years ago."

"That's him. He bought it in New York. It was a Macy's reject."

Nancy made a note.

"Anyone else?" I asked.

"Not really. Not that I can remember. It was a summer job when I was fifteen."

"Okay," I said. "We'll check with Jay. You've been very helpful. Thanks."

"I was hoping it wasn't her," said Ron. "I really was. I was thinking about seeing if I could find her after all these years. Maybe reconnect."

"You should try oldfartsmatch.com," said Nancy. "That's your best bet."

"I got a look at his computer screen," I said, as we walked back to the office. "He was on a dating site."

"Yep," said Nancy.

"Call the newspapers, will you? Give them Barbara's name. Maybe that will jog someone else's memory."

"Will do. You know, Ron sure remembers a lot for it being thirty-three years ago. A lot of certain things, not so much of other things."

"It was his first roll in the hay. You don't forget that, much less the girl."

"I guess," said Nancy. She gave me a sideways look.

"Don't even ask," I said.

♫

"This is Jay," said the voice coming from my cell. I'd gotten his phone number from Cynthia. She kept a Christmas Parade rolodex.

"Hi, Jay. This is Hayden Konig, Police Chief in St. Germaine."

"I remember, Chief. How're you doing?"

"Fine, thanks. Listen, we're investigating a missing person and maybe some foul play. Do you happen to remember working at Camp Possumtickle in 1977."

He thought for a moment, then said, "Sure. '77. That was my last year."

"You were a counselor?"

"Right. In the Sioux cabin. I also taught archery and canoeing."

"Ron Pigeon was your CIT?"

"Ron Pigeon," Jay said. "We called him Ronald. Yeah. I knew him from youth group. I got him the job I think."

"That's what he remembers, too."

"Is Ron okay? Something happen to him?"

"Ron's fine. We're looking for a girl who worked in the kitchen. Barbara McCuwen."

"Oh, man ..." Jay paused, then, "Yeah, I remember Barbara."

"Can you tell me anything about her?"

"She came in late, that I remember. Maybe in July sometime. Most of us were there at the beginning of June. She might have been from Florida. She was ... umm ... friendly."

"Ron indicated that she had been friendly with a number of the counselors. Maybe even the staff."

96

"So you know that part then. Yeah, I think she was."

"You?"

"Nope. Not me. I was already going with Betsy."

"Anything ugly happen?" I asked. "Amongst the guys working there? Jealousy, maybe?"

"There might have been some words at first. Not much. Then, after the first couple of weeks, everyone knew the score. I do remember that she was one of the ones to leave early. A couple of the guys were sad about that."

"There were others who left early?"

"Sure. Always, but they didn't get asked back."

"I'm sorry to tell you that we think we found Barbara's remains in the woods by the camp."

"Oh, man ..." said Jay again.

"You wouldn't have any thoughts on this, would you?"

"I really don't. I didn't know her that well, but she was a nice enough girl. Kinda messed up, but nice. I had the feeling that she might have been into drugs, you know, a little pot, maybe some pills, but I don't know that for sure."

"Might you remember the names of any of the kids working there with you that summer?"

"Sure. I still keep in touch with three or four of them. Give me your email and I'll send their contact information, although I can't imagine they'll tell you any more than I have. A couple of them may have had a one night stand with her. They might even admit it, although I doubt it."

"What about the staff?"

"I can't imagine. I think I heard that Hank Townsend — he was the director — died a few years ago."

"The assistant director?"

"Moose Kilchert. Sorry, I don't know his real first name. He was a football coach at Mr. Townsend's high school. He was about ten years older than Townsend, I think. If he's still alive, he'd be ancient. The rest of the staff were women, the nurse, the head cook, maybe a couple of secretaries. I don't remember their names."

"Thanks, Jay. I'll look for that email."

"Sure thing, Chief."

I gave him my email address and phone number, and hung up.

Chapter 13

Dave managed some police work on Friday afternoon. He'd finished his book, and gotten on the internet, working a hunch. After an hour, he had some information for us.

"Barbara Jean McCuwen was born in November of 1957. She was reported missing by her foster parents in September, 1977. She was nineteen at the time, almost twenty, and not living with them anymore. She was fostered by them from age eleven to thirteen, but then went back to the Methodist Children's Home in Enterprise, Florida. Apparently, they tried to keep in touch with her, even after she went back."

"Where's Enterprise? I've never heard of it."

"Volusia County. Somewhere between DeBary and Deltona."

"Which is where?" I asked again.

"In between Daytona Beach and Orlando."

"Did the foster parents say why she went back to the Methodist Home?"

"Well, they're both dead, so no."

"How about the home?"

"They say they don't know. They did look it up for me once I explained, but there's no record of why she went back. Just that she did."

"You found all this on the internet?" I asked.

"Sure," said Dave. "Well, most of it. Volusia County Beacon ran an article in September, 1977. It was in their archives. Just had to log on and do a search."

"How did you know where to look?"

"The article popped up on Google. Anyway," said Dave, "according to the article, Barbara was a student at Stetson University in Deland, studying music. Oboe, to be exact, with a minor in piano. Her foster parents reported that they'd talked to her in June and she'd decided to study with her teacher during the summer term at the university. Of course, there was a missing persons report filed. I called down to the Sheriff's Department for the reports. They said they'd look, but weren't hopeful. All their stuff was paper thirty-three years ago and not filed very well."

"Well, we have the article," said Nancy. "Good work, Officer Dave. Those girly vampire mysteries are paying off."

"Any other pertinent information?" I asked.

"Sure. The ex-foster parents thought she was in Deland the whole time and so didn't file the report until mid-September when they hadn't heard from her for a couple of months."

Nancy began taking notes.

Dave continued. "According to her college friend, a girl named Peggy Wist, Peggy called her up from the camp where she was working and told Barbara about a job. They were both in the music department at Stetson, same year, but Peggy was a horn major. Anyway, the kitchen at the camp was short handed and they'd asked the counselors if they knew anyone who might be able to come work on short notice. So Peggy called Barbara and Barbara, who was finished with her summer term, decided to come up. She took a Greyhound. It was early July."

"So we have her in North Carolina," I said.

"At Camp Possumtickle," Nancy said.

"Right," said Dave, "but here's the thing. According to Peggy, she gave Barbara a ride back to Deland after the camp was over. She said they drove to Deland, then she went home for the Labor Day weekend. She headed back to school, but never saw Barbara after that."

"So now we have Barbara back in Florida," said Nancy.

"Maybe," I said, "maybe not. Both Jay and Ron said that Barbara McCuwen left early from the camp, before the other staff. How could she have done that and gotten a ride with Peggy?"

"Gotta talk to Peggy Wist," said Dave.

"Yep. Let's find her."

Since we were on a roll, detecting-wise, I decided to dial up the names Jay had given me. Four calls later, I had no further information. Two of the four said they didn't remember Barbara McCuwen, and I was pretty sure that at least one of those was lying. One admitted to knowing her very well, in the Biblical sense, both Old and New Testament. One didn't answer the phone. The story was the same in each case. She showed up in the middle of the summer, was a girl happy to have a good time, and left Camp Possumtickle early, before her contract was up.

I also googled Moose Kilchert, the assistant director of the camp. His given name was Mitch and he was a high school football coach. He was a loving husband and father, and a deacon in the local Baptist Church, fond of his hunting dog, Bo, and an inspiration to all who knew him. So said his obituary.

"What'd I miss?" said Dave, coming backwards through the police department door. His hands were full: in one a box of donuts from the bakery, and in the other, three coffees from Holy Grounds in a cardboard cupholder.

"What did you miss?" said Nancy. "Everything. We've solved the case."

"C'mon," said Dave. "I was only gone ten minutes. Fill me in."

"I dunno, Dave," said Nancy. "What kind of donuts did you get?"

"Bear claws."

"Oh. Okay, then."

We each had a bear claw, and sipped our coffee while filling Dave in on what we'd discovered since we sent him for snacks ten minutes ago, which was basically nothing. Then we all had another bear claw and were thinking seriously about dividing the last one into thirds when Dave said, "I forgot! I found Peggy Wist while I was waiting in the coffee line."

"The friend from college," said Nancy with a nod.

"The very same. I called the college. No luck, so then I got in touch with the alumni association. Still no luck. They had no information."

"So, how did you do it?"

"I just did a people search on my phone. Peggy Wist, born 1957. That was the year that Barbara was born, and since they were both in the same year at Stetson, I figured that was a good place to start."

"And?" I asked.

"There are nine Peggy or Margaret Wists listed in the US, only one born in 1957. She's listed as Peggy Wist Young — a musician. Maybe it's not her, but I'll bet it is. I'm texting you her address and her phone number. The area code is Philadelphia."

"Nice work, Dave," I said, picking up my phone and checking. Sure enough, there was Dave's info. I pushed the dial button. Three rings, then, "Hello?"

"Good morning, Peggy. This is Chief Hayden Konig of the St. Germaine Police Department."

"Is this a joke? Is this you, Bill?"

"This is not Bill. This is the Police Department in St. Germaine, North Carolina. Where Camp Possumtickle was located. I'd like to ask you a few questions about Barbara McCuwen."

Silence, then, a quavering, "Who?"

"You know who, Ms. Young. I can come over with the Philadelphia police if you'd rather and we can talk with them present, or I can ask you a few questions over the phone and we'll be finished."

"Umm ... okay."

"Thanks," I said. "We'd really appreciate your help on this."

"Go ahead," she said. "Ask."

"When Barbara was discovered missing, you told the police that you gave her a ride back to Deland after camp was over."

"Yes."

"Everyone else remembers that Barbara left camp early, about a week before everyone else."

Nothing.

"So, I guess the question is, why did you lie to the police about this?"

A heavy sigh, then, "I haven't thought about her in so many years. Is she okay?"

"Why did you lie to the police, Ms. Young?"

"Barbara just up and left. I told her to wait a week and I'd drive her home, but she was determined to hitchhike. I told her it was dangerous."

"Why didn't you tell the police that?"

A pause, then, "Umm. I'd already told my parents that I stayed with Barbara at her apartment in Deland for a few days."

"But you didn't."

"No, I was staying with my boyfriend in Daytona Beach. He got us a motel room. My folks would've killed me. They never would have let me go back to school. They only let me go to Stetson because it was a Baptist university. They really wanted me to go to Bob Jones University up in Greenville."

"I get it," I said. "So, just to be clear, the last time you saw Barbara was at Camp Possumtickle, before you left in August."

"Yes."

"Did you know a CIT named Ronald Pigeon?"

"Maybe I knew him back then. I don't remember him, though. We didn't hang out with the CITs. They were all ninth and tenth graders. Plus, I was in the girl's camp. We got together sometimes with the boy counselors, in between sessions, but not a lot."

"Barbara didn't mention him? Ronald?"

"I didn't hang around with Barbara that summer at all. I got her the job, but she was like, acting out or something. She brought a stash of pot with her and was all over the guys. By the end of camp she had quite a reputation, but it was like she didn't care."

"Okay. That's what I need to know."

"Is she okay? Barbara, I mean."

"No. She's dead," I said. "She was killed that summer in the woods, but no one thought to look for her there because everyone thought she was in Florida."

"What?" then, as the realization set in, "Oh, no!"

I hung up. Granted, it wasn't the most courteous way to end our conversation, but I wasn't feeling particularly courteous.

Nancy said, "What do you think?"

"She's lying, but she's good at it. There's something else, too. Something I can't put my finger on."

Chapter 14

Buxtehooters was a pipe organ bar with real class: beer-fräuleins in tight dirndls, enough suds to float a U-boat, and Baroque organ music from a three-manual Flentrop with a heckelphone stop that sounded like two fifty-pound ducks in the throes of passion. I walked up to the entrance just as the first show was letting out. It was couples only night. The queue to get in looped around the block as usual, but I knew the bouncer, so I gave him the nod, grabbed a chippy from off the line, and waltzed in like I was somebody.

"Gee, thanks, mister," the chippy squealed delightedly. "My name's Mystique." I knew her type, a dame with a body that would make a guy write bad checks, although with overdraft protection he probably wouldn't have to pay the exorbitant bank fee, still, it would go on your permanent record like your high school guidance counselor warned you about, either that or give you an STD, that kind of dame.

"Too bad you couldn't get my boyfriend in, too," she said.

"Yeah," I said. "Too bad, Toots. Now beat it."

She gave me a puzzled look, shrugged and danced her way up to the bar. I spotted Pedro a minute later, back in a booth reserved for the uncouth. Pedro LaFleur was my right hand man: a man who ate danger for breakfast, then switched to lemon tarts, had a couple of burritos, then back to danger again. I sat down across from him and gave him the stinkeye.

"Why do your characters always give each other the stinkeye?" asked Meg, looking up. "I don't even really know what the stinkeye is."

"It's like this," I said, screwing up my face and giving her the stinkeye. "A look that conveys distrust, disdain, or disapproval. Possibly all at the same time."

"Oh," said Meg.

"It's also known in finer literary circles as the skunk eye or the ol' hairy eyeball."

"Good to know," said Meg, and continued reading. "Don't do it again."

ρ

"Why are you givin' me the ol' hairy eyeball?" Pedro asked.

"You know why. It's Stormy. Stormy Knight. She's dead as a Lutheran sermon on dispensationalism."

"It flies in the face of orthodoxy," muttered Pedro, taking a bite of his lemon tart. "She's dead, you say?"

"Caught a bullet in my office."

Pedro nodded. "You know, more people get killed in that office than on crocodile day at the petting zoo."

It was true, but I had no stomach for it, having been working out diligently using the Richard Simmons workout DVD that I got for a dollar at the "Only a Dollar" Store where everything was a dollar.

He said, "You tell Dirk yet?"

"Nope. You know about the goat?"

He gave me a long stare, lemon-yellow crumbs dusting his three-day old stubble like the first frost on a pile of newly mown hay after a dog had discovered it.

"Yeah, I know. That's why I sent Stormy to you."

"I'm taking the case," I said.

"I knew you would," foreboded Pedro.

ρ

I offered to go through the service music with Father Carter Ousley, our first tryout priest, prior to the service, but he declined. He'd be speaking the parts of the mass that the congregation wasn't singing. That was fine with me. Thomas Walmsley would be assisting, and our order of service was reasonably straightforward so there were no worries that I could foresee.

Then again, I couldn't foresee everything.

We heard the opening sentences, and began the procession with *O Praise Ye the Lord*, the great hymn with music by Hubert H. Parry. Benny Dawkins was in attendance, as well as his young protégé Addie Buss. Benny was one of the foremost thurifers alive, and although St. Barnabas was his home church, he could generally be found, on any given Sunday or major feast day, at one of the great cathedrals of the world. As a premiere smoke jockey, he would wield his incense pot and make the clouds of incense come alive. Addie was getting to be almost as proficient, although Benny kept taking his art to new heights. His latest passion seemed to be creating Biblical scenes and this morning the congregation was treated to a breathtaking vaporous recreation of a seated Jesus surrounded by the little children. Addie supplied the smoke rosettes on the way down the aisle, each one perfection, as the puffing pot spun on the chains in her little hand. Then, when they reached the front of the nave, Benny began his magic. First the stone appeared, hanging in mists above the altar, then a seated Savior, and finally, children playing at his feet. We didn't gasp anymore, we'd become used to Benny's artistry, but most of the congregation stopped singing the third verse, their mouths agape in wonder.

Benny finished, made his turn, then censed the altar, and ended up in front of his chair, Addie beside him in front of hers. The choir made their turn and headed back down the side aisles for the choir loft. The acolytes, crucifer, deacon, and two priests walked up the steps to their respective places.

We sang the *Gloria* and the psalm, a version with a congregational refrain. Then, lo, Kimberly Walnut, true to her form, got up and announced that it was time for the Children's Moment. She did this on occasion and never told us when it was going to happen. Father Walmsley didn't seem to mind since Kimberly Walnut had been the one to do them. I should have suspected that she'd be showing off for the new fellow.

"Children, I'd like for you to come to the front for our Special Time Together," she said.

Children's groans went up across the congregation.

"Just the children between the ages of three and six. C'mon now." She gave a smile that might have been meant to be nurturing. No one moved and so she started calling out names. "Jared? Hiram? Gabby?" I see you out there. Come on down. Toby? Brittany?"

Little rear ends were shoved into the aisles by parents who didn't want any more notoriety than was absolutely necessary, and the children walked tentatively up to the front, still unsure what would be expected of them. Oh, they'd been prepped before the service, but during the last Children's Moment, Kimberly Walnut offered them all a marshmallow peep, then took them all away to teach them about the hardship Job went through. They (and we) never did get it and one three-year-old little girl cried all the way back down the aisle. Now the parents, if not the kids, were understandably gun shy.

But still they came.

Kimberly Walnut waited at the front, her deacon's stole hanging a bit crooked, her hands working knots in front of her. She didn't have any props. That might be a good sign, we couldn't tell yet. When the eight children were gathered in front her, she sat down on the steps and bade the little tykes do the same. They did, and for a moment, it was a picture for the front of Kimberly Walnut's book.

"Now, children," began Kimberly Walnut, "I have a question for you. If I sold my house and gave all my money to the church, would I get into heaven?"

"NO!" hollered the children, confident of the answer since Kimberly Walnut had told them what to say.

Jared felt Hiram's elbow nudge him. Probably not on purpose, and not much, just a little bit, but Jared was five and Hiram only four. Hiram needed to understand the pecking order so Jared gave him a bit of elbow back. Not too much, just enough to say, "I'm five and you're four so get out of my space." Hiram was almost five and slightly bigger than Jared, and so the next nudge said, "I don't give a rat's rear end if you're five, nudge me again and you're gonna meet Jesus." Jared was apparently okay with meeting Jesus, so he turned and walloped Hiram, this time with an elbow into his ear.

"Waaaaaa!" wailed Hiram, who was, after all, still just four.

"What?" said Kimberly Walnut. "What's wrong?"

"Jared hit me in the ear!"

"What?" Kimberly Walnut said again, not comprehending the situation. "Who did what?"

Jared's father, Axel Trimble, was already coming down the center aisle toward the front, a look on his face that would freeze molten lava. Axel was a high school principal and an ex-Navy SEAL. Jared saw him coming, his eyes widened, and his mouth started moving, no sound coming out. When Axel was about six feet away, Jared made a break for it, trying to dart around the end and make it back to his pew and maybe, just maybe, the safety of his mother and grandmother. Axel was having none of that. He snatched him off his feet, stuck him under one huge arm, feet facing front, and began the long march to the front doors. Little Jared's head was sticking out the back of his father's rough embrace, his arms pinned to his sides. He knew what was coming.

There was deadly silence, save for Axel's heavy footsteps on the flagstone floor and Jared's whimpers, and as they reached the narthex we all heard his tiny quavering voice fill the church.

"Pray for me ... pray for me ..."

The door opened and they were gone.

Kimberly Walnut gave a horrified glance toward Father Ousley, but the priest had a look of perfect placidity. In accordance with the Kimberly Walnut School of Liturgy, she decided to plow ahead, obeying her untenable doctrine that says once something starts to go wrong, it can only get better.

"So children ..." she continued.

"Is Mr. Trimble going to come back and get me?" asked Hiram, and started crying again.

"No, Hiram," said Kimberly Walnut. "He's just going to deal with Jared. Let's get back to the lesson, okay?"

Hiram's mother was already on her feet and coming to take the boy back to the bathroom to wash his face and make sure there was no permanent damage to his ear drums.

"Jared's gonna get a beating," said Brittany. "I've seen that look before."

"Yeah," agreed Gabby glumly.

"He'll probably just get a time out," said Kimberly Walnut, but that idea was discarded as the first wails came from outside the front doors.

"A beating," said Brittany with a solemn nod of her head. The other children nodded as well.

"So," said Kimberly Walnut, trying desperately to change the subject, "if I came and cleaned the church every day, and mowed the yard, and cooked dinner for everyone, would I get into heaven?"

"No," muttered the group, knowing the answer, but their little souls no longer into it. One of their number had gone down. One had been taken off to the bathroom. What was left for them?

"Well then, how do I get into heaven?" asked Kimberly Walnut.

No comment. Kimberly Walnut seemed confused. She'd already given the kids the answer, but they weren't responding. She tried again.

"If I give all my money to the church, and clean everything nice and tidy, and mow the lawn, and fix meals for everyone, and I can't get into heaven ..."

She looked back at Father Ousley and smiled a knowing smile.

"Then how *do* I get into heaven?"

Toby, a six-year-old whose mother had sent him to the front with a Tonka truck, now stood up, threw down the truck with enough force to break it and yelled, *"You gotta be dead!"*

He stomped off down the aisle without bothering to pick up his truck. The rest of the children got silently to their feet and followed him, single file, dropping into their respective pews along the way.

"Umm," said Kimberly Walnut. "Right. Exactly. You have to give your life to Jesus." She turned and gave the priest another halfhearted smile, but his eyes were closed as if he was praying, which he might have been. I know I was.

ρ

It was during the Sequence Hymn, our second hymn of the morning, that we got our second surprise. We were singing *Lord of All Hopefulness*, a beautiful hymn to the tune *Slane*. When we reached the last stanza, Father Ousley pulled out a trumpet, *his* trumpet, that he'd stashed on an instrument stand beside his chair, out of sight. He had a small, marching-band-sized sheet of music in his left hand and he'd decided to favor us with an original descant. I shot a panicked look at Susan Sievert, sitting in the back of the choir loft waiting her turn. We'd practiced a descant on the last hymn, *God of Grace and God of Glory* and she was going to play it. I hadn't planned on a trumpet descant for this one.

And that was why I was playing the hymn in E Major. A brighter key, I thought, and the top E's in the melody weren't that high. The hymnal, however, had the hymn in E-Flat and that was the key that Father Ousley was playing in.

I recognized the problem right away, but after playing three verses in E, could hardly justify dropping down a half step. So I just kept going, thinking that a musician, *any* musician, would stop as soon as they could end a phrase, or, even better, make the adjustment and play it up a half-step.

But alas.

Lord of all gentleness, Lord of all calm, took on a new meaning that morning. *Whose voice is contentment, whose presence is balm.*

We finished the hymn, a fitting tribute to Charles Ives, who neither wrote it, nor to my knowledge, ever sang it, but who certainly would have appreciated the bitonality.

Our offertory, however, was over the top. Zeb Martin and Susan were both pros and the piece was Handel at his best, a movement from the *Dettingen Te Deum* written in 1743, just a year after *Messiah* was premiered.

Thou art the King of Glory, O Christ.
Thou art the everlasting Son of the Father.

The bass and the trumpet dueled brilliantly for two pages, and then the chorus came in echoing the text and finished triumphantly. The congregation of St. Barnabas was not prone to applause, but they just couldn't help themselves, and we launched into the doxology and finished that with a trumpet flourish as well.

ρ

Our third surprise came during communion. The choir was getting ready to go down the stairs to the table after we'd sung the *Sanctus*.

"What's he doing?" Georgia asked in a hushed voice. She gestured up to the altar.

Elaine squinted down at the front of the church. "He's putting on gloves. Latex gloves."

"What?" said Georgia. "*What?*"

"Hey, what's he got on his hands," said Marjorie, a little louder than most of us thought prudent. I started playing something. Something soft and sweet.

"Latex gloves," whispered Elaine. "He's wearing latex gloves to give us communion."

"Oh, crap," said Georgia, shaking her head. "That's it then."

"Maybe he's a germaphobe," offered Meg. "That doesn't mean he's a bad priest."

"Maybe he's got leprosy," said Marjorie, "or the Spanish Pox. I remember back in the war ..."

"Hush," said Meg. "Let's go take communion. And no comments."

Zeb stayed in the choir loft with me and sang a solo that would make the seraphim weep. It was written by an American composer, Carlisle Floyd, known chiefly for his operas. This was from a song cycle for bass-baritone and orchestra, "Pilgrimage," transcribed for piano, then again for organ: *For I Am Persuaded*. The choir came back up to the loft in awe and perfect silence as Zeb finished singing the benediction, smiles creeping across all their faces. I didn't hear any more about the latex gloves for the rest of the service.

Susan let rip on the final hymn, *God of Grace and God of Glory*, high Ds echoing from the rafters, and we were finished. Father Ousley's trumpet, blessedly, did not join us for that hymn, as he was processing out at the time.

I thought about going to the coffee hour after church but decided I'd had enough for one morning and I really didn't want to relive the service through the recap. Not today, anyway. Meg went though, and gave me a full report.

Chapter 15

The St. Germaine Labor Day picnic was put on by the Rotary Club and held each Labor Day in Sterling Park. The town Memorial Day get-together was covered by the Kiwanis Club, and they both vied for premiere spots to set up their Christmas Crèche during December. Being "in charge" meant that the Rotary Club had first dibs on selling barbecue sandwiches and soft drinks, and was entitled to gather a nominal fee from any other vendors. They also had to arrange and pay for a couple of musical entertainments, which generally consisted of a bluegrass band or two from somewhere close. They made a few hundred bucks on the enterprise and everyone was happy.

The Bear and Brew had paid their vendor fee and set up a tent at the end of the park just a few feet from their pizza ovens. They always did a brisk business since everyone enjoyed pizza, and they were the only tent that offered beer. There were others: the Girl Scouts were busy selling cookies; Bun in the Oven had cupcakes and donuts, cookies and other delectables; the Holy Grounds Coffee Shop had brewed a number of gourmet varieties available for sample and purchase; and the obligatory arts and crafts vendors always showed up. Bud was in his element at the Wine Press tent, offering an extensive variety of colors and vintages.

Codfish Downs had parked his old Pontiac in front of the library and was doing a brisk business selling mountain trout out of his trunk. We'd never caught Codfish stealing these trout from one of the local fish farms, but there had been accusations thrown around over the years. The trunk of the Pontiac was loaded with ice chips and beautiful, two-pound fish, being offered for six dollars each. Codfish had a line waiting.

"Hi, Bud," said Meg as we walked up to the Wine Press tent.

"Hello, Mrs. Konig," said Bud.

"We were thinking of trout for supper," I said. "Maybe grilling it out."

"Excellent," said Bud. "I would recommend spreading a little mayonnaise on it before you grill it."

"Really?" said Meg,

"The mayo keeps it moist and it adds a great flavor. You might also consider grilling some fennel wedges and scallions as well. Then roasted artichokes and fresh tomato slices, since we're nearing the end of the season."

"Where are you getting this stuff?" I said. "I know you're a wine guy, but now, recipes?"

"Gotta keep up," said Bud, grinning. "Stay ahead of the game." He looked around his tent for a moment, then chose a bottle and handed it to me.

"Richly smoked or grilled fishes are a little drier and need wine pairings that quench them. Try this Tapeña garnacha rosé. The palate is beautifully balanced with a crisp refreshing acidity, a soft round finish of red fruits and a hint of minerality. It's like an autumn day in the Spanish Pyrenees."

"Of course it is," I said, taking the bottle. "Better give me two, we may be having company. Put this on our account, will you?"

Bud laughed. "On account of you own the store?"

"Exactly."

The neighborhood churches were out in full force, offering games for the kids — sack races, fishing pools, ring tosses, and the like, most of the prizes being a new Gideon Bible or maybe a glow-in-the-dark dashboard Jesus if the winners were lucky and there were any left.

Moosey found Meg and me almost immediately.

"Hiya, Chief," he said, then, with a little bow, "Good afternoon, Mrs. Konig. How are you today?"

I gave Meg a look.

"We've been working on our manners," she said.

"You wanna buy a four-leaf clover? I've got 'em here in baggies. Only a dollar a piece."

"Are these the ones from Mr. Newport's yard?" I asked.

"Well, sure," said Moosey, looking a little concerned, "but we asked permission and he said we could keep whatever we found."

"Excellent. I'll take three," I said. "One for me, one for Meg, and one for little Abishag here."

Meg gave me the stinkeye.

"Hooray!" said Moosey. "That's ten sold already. We may have to go pick some more."

"Make sure you offer one to Brother Hog," I said.

"I already did," said Moosey, giving me the stinkeye, too. I was getting the stinkeye from everyone, it seemed. "He preached at me for ten minutes," said Moosey. "I finally escaped when somebody came around with pizza."

"How was your trumpet lesson?" I asked. I had arranged for Moosey to begin his musical study with Susan Sievert, taking private lessons from her. Bud had been conscripted to drive him over to the university on Tuesday afternoons.

"Great! I love it. Miss Sievert says I'm a natural. I can blow a high G!"

Meg giggled. Moosey gave her another small bow and said, "Mrs. Konig, it's been a pleasure to share your company." Then he raced off to find his cohorts.

"You're doing good work with that whippersnapper," I said. "I almost believed that he was being polite."

"Oh, he was," said Meg. "Bev and I have the rest of the gang, too. We're teaching an etiquette class on Wednesdays at the church."

"The kids agreed to that?"

"They were bribed. We're taking them to *Carowinds* at the end of the month. All expenses paid."

"Wow," I said. "That's gonna be expensive. Who's picking up the tab for all this?"

As soon as the words exited my mouth, I knew the answer. Meg just gave me her second best smile, the one that made me agree to almost anything. Her *best* smile was nothing to be trifled with.

"It'll be well worth it," said Meg. "The little delinquents are doing wonderfully well."

"Little delinquents, eh?"

"And if you repeat that, you shan't see my *best* smile for a long time."

Brother Hogmanay McTavish was married to Noylene Fabergé-Dupont, of the Wormy Fabergé-Duponts, and he'd been the pastor of New Fellowship Baptist Church for a time. Now he made an excellent living as a traveling tent revivalist. If he could manage it, Rahab, his and Noylene's son, would be in attendance for the revival's finale, but only if Noylene could get away. She wouldn't let Hog take Rahab without her. Since his business was mainly in the hills and hollers of North Carolina, Virginia, West Virginia, and Tennessee, it was usually a day trip for Noylene and Rahab. Hog would go early, pay some folks to set up his tent, do a few warm-up services, then bring Rahab in for the big finish on Sunday evening. The toddler evangelist was always a hit. Rahab, now three and one-half years old, couldn't really be considered a toddler. He was a "preschooler," but Brother Hog had decided that he could bill Rahab as "The South's Only Toddler Evangelist" for one more season and get away with it, Rahab being small for his age.

Rahab was skilled at his craft, and his craft was speaking in unknown tongues. His glossolalia was always interpreted by a member of the congregation, as required by New Testament doctrine. This wasn't set up by Brother Hog in any way, but there was no shortage of interpreters.

"Shiba shullaba, shundra bacar becara beshundra," little Rahab would sing into the microphone.

"Thus saith the Lord," hollered a man, halfway back, standing up from his folding chair. "Thus saith the Lord, you will hear of many things. Blessed is the one who hears aloud the words of this prophecy. These things must take place, but no one knows the day and hour, not even the angels of heaven, nor the Son, but the Father only."

"Amen!" agreed the congregation, sure they knew exactly what Rahab, through his interpreter, was talking about.

The little sprat would go on for a while, and then Hog would take over, inviting his flock forward to receive the blessing of the Spirit. They'd sing some hymns and spiritual songs, take up the collection, several of the folks would receive healing, and everyone would go home refreshed in the faith.

On this day, Labor Day, Hog and Rahab were handing out flyers inviting everyone to the fall revival at Mount Jefferson State Park put on by New Life Deliverance Temple up in West Jefferson. It wasn't a long drive, about thirty minutes, and Brother Hog still had a following at the Baptist church and around town. He could expect a crowd from St. Germaine. Both he and Rahab were decked out in matching white suits and white patent-leather shoes and belts, a yellow tie providing color to their ensembles.

I took a flyer from Rahab, thanked him, and watched him run off in another direction, hunting for converts.

"Hog," I said, shaking the big man's hand, "how are you doing?"

"If I was any better, I'd drop my harp plumb through the cloud. How about you? You looking forward to the blessed event?" He gave Meg a huge smile, reached over to pat her belly, then, seeing her eyes narrow, thought better of it and let his hand drift up and across his comb-over, smoothing his hair.

"We can't wait," Meg said.

"Boy or girl?" asked Hog.

"It's a girl," I said. "Abishag. Abishag Louise."

"Abishag," said Brother Hog with a nod. "A woman of Shunem distinguished by her beauty. She has quite a checkered story, though. There are those that say that Abishag is the female protagonist in the *Song of Songs*."

I was always astonished at Hog's knowledge. He gave off every vibe of being a country preacher, and I often forgot that he had a Harvard PhD in religion, something he didn't advertise, and something I found out quite by accident.

"Really?" said Meg. "We just sang something from the *Song of Songs* with a turtle in it. I never heard of Abishag until Hayden brought the name up."

"Loveliest woman in the kingdom, as I recall," said Hog. "Quite a looker, and known for her charms. They brought her in to see if Old King David still had what it took to be king, if you get my meaning. Tossed her right in the bed, naked as the day she was born. Old King David didn't perform up to snuff. You know what they say, just because a chicken has wings don't mean it can fly."

"Well, that tears it," said Meg. "We're not naming her Abishag Louise."

"I'm sure she'll be a beautiful child," said Hog, "whatever her name is. I hope you'll invite me to the christening, or the dedication, or the infant baptism, or whatever you infidels call that thing where you squirt the baby with some water." Hog was a zealot when it came to "believer's baptism," the doctrine that holds that a person is only baptized on the basis of his or her profession of faith.

"We call it an ecumenical spritzing," I said. "Of course you'll be invited."

ρ

Meg and I stopped to watch three men on the St. Barnabas scaffolding working on the damaged back wall. Apparently Labor Day holds no vacation time for construction crews being paid by the job. They weren't moving fast, but they were moving.

"How long till they're finished do you think?" asked Meg.

"Maybe a week. The window won't be shipped back until late this month. I bet they'll finish the rest pretty quick."

115

Nancy walked up and watched the progress with us for a few moments, then said, "I was talking to Ron Pigeon about a half hour ago. What a horndog! He asked me out three times in ten minutes. I was just trying to see if he'd thought of anything else since we'd talked last. I guess he doesn't remember that I was one of Becky's friends."

"I guess not," said Meg. "There he is chatting up Lena Carver." She pointed over toward the gazebo and there was Ron, leaning against a big maple tree, talking with Lena. Lena looked interested, leaning in and putting a hand on his arm, then laughing. We heard the laugh but couldn't hear the conversation.

"I saw him making the move on one of those doctoral students before Lena," said Nancy, "and Father Walmsley's wife before that. Those grad assistants are single I suppose."

"I dunno," I said. "The two women are Jenny and Julia. The man is Jeremy. Three Js. I can't remember their last names. Getting old, I guess."

"Which is the older one?" asked Nancy.

"That'd be Jenny," said Meg. "She's from Knoxville. Used to work at the Farmhouse Restaurant years ago."

"That's the one he was talking to. I guess Lena's on his radar now, though. Look at that! She's hanging on him like a cheap suit."

"Are you jealous?" I asked.

"Of course not," said Nancy, "but it's only good manners to pretend to be aggrieved by my rebuke. At least for an hour or two."

"Maybe he's pretending right now," Meg said, watching the drama unfold. "Lena will want to make him feel better, so now she's pretending to go with him to his car."

They strolled the short distance to Ron's Toyota minivan.

"Now she's pretending to get in," said Meg, "and now Ron is pretending to start the car, and now they're both pretending to drive to Ron's house on an impromptu date."

"Horndog," said Nancy.

Chapter 16

"You'd better come," said Nancy. I'd answered the phone, just out of the shower. I hadn't even dressed yet, much less had breakfast or my morning coffee.

"What's up?"

"Ron Pigeon," she said. "He's shot himself."

♪

It had been two days since I'd seen Ron at the Labor Day picnic. Helen and Jeff were on the front porch of Ron's house when I drove up. The ambulance was parked in front of the house, a Watauga County Sheriff's car right behind it, probably Bert Coley's car. I noticed Nancy's motorcycle parked on the lawn.

Jeff had a terrible look on his face, grief mixed with anger I supposed. Helen just looked sad, but I saw no sign of tears from either one of them.

"I'm so sorry," I said, coming up the front steps. I held out my hand to Jeff when I reached the porch, and he shook it, but there was no strength in his grip. I let go and turned to Helen. She grabbed me and hugged me and there was no getting away from her for several moments.

"Who found him?" I asked, extricating myself from Helen's grasp.

"Jeff did," said Helen.

"We were supposed to have breakfast this morning," said Jeff. "At the Slab. He didn't show, so I came by the house to wake him up. I figured he just overslept."

"You have a key?" I asked.

"The door was open. Ron never locked his place up. He had nothing to steal." Jeff thought a moment. "Maybe his laptop, but even that wasn't worth much. Becky got everything in the divorce."

"He was really depressed lately," said Helen. "Really. Last month he went in for angina. The month before that it was fibromyalgia. Before that, he called it paralyzing migraines. I'm sure it was all stress. We were encouraging him to get out, meet some people, maybe go out on a few dates. He went on this singles cruise, you know ..."

"He was taking medication for the depression," said Jeff, "but I didn't think it was this bad."

117

"Was he taking medication for angina, too?" I asked.

"Yeah, probably. I guess."

Nancy came to the front door. She had her camera in her hand. "Better come in," she said. "Bert's here. Mike and Joe, too, but they'll wait. I asked, they have nothing pressing unless another EMT call comes in. You want me to call Dave?"

"Yeah. Give him a call and let him know what's going on, but he doesn't have to come over. We have it covered." I turned to Helen and Jeff. "Will you two wait out here?"

"Yes," said Jeff, sadness thickening his voice. "We'll wait."

The house was void of everything that makes a house a home: no pictures, no books, no rugs, nothing on the walls. The front room featured an old recliner and a new, large, flat-screen TV on a stand. The dining room was empty. The kitchen, basically the same, save for a Formica table, circa 1965, and two chairs.

Ron was seated at the table. He was slumped over, his lifeless gaze looking directly down at the surface, his nose mashed into the Formica. His left hand was flat on the table, his right hanging by his side. There was a dark wound just above his right ear. There wasn't a huge amount of blood, and what there was had trickled down in front of his ear and had gathered in a black pool. He was wearing jeans and a cheap polo shirt. The gun, a Taurus revolver, was on the floor beside his chair, just beneath his dangling hand.

"It's a .22 magnum," said Nancy. "There's no exit wound. Not the sort of gun I would have shot myself with, but I guess it's what he had handy."

"Why?" said Mike. "What would you have used?"

"Something bigger for sure. You don't want these things to go wrong. Once you've made the decision, better to go big. I wouldn't want to be a vegetable living in a nursing home because I was too cheap to buy a .38."

"Well, it worked for him," said Bert.

"Yeah, it did," agreed Nancy.

"Did you check it?" I asked.

"It's an eight round cylinder," said Bert. "There's one spent shell, seven live shells."

"Anything else?"

"Sure," said Nancy. "A suicide note explaining everything."

"Right."

"No, really," said Nancy. "I'm not kidding." She produced a sheet of lined notebook paper. "This was on the floor under his chair." She handed it to me.

This isn't the way I wanted it to end.
Barbara, you were my first love and I am terribly sorry.

"Barbara, huh?" I said.
"Barbara McCuwen," said Nancy. "That's my bet."
"I can see it," I said.
"He's depressed anyway, then we start poking around about a thirty-year-old killing that he probably did when he was a kid. Might have been accidental, but maybe not. Anyway, he knew that we were going to find out the truth eventually."
"Makes sense," I said. "Find anything else?"
"Nothing. The whole place is Spartan, but dirty. Glasses in the sink. Nothing in the pantry. He's got one dish and one bowl in the cupboard. A couple of forks, knives, and spoons in the silverware drawer. Half a pizza from the Bear and Brew in the fridge, artichoke and spinach, the receipt on the box dated last night. That, and a couple of PBR beers. His computer is on the counter over there. We might check it, see what he was doing on the internet."
"Let's do that," I said, "but I don't really want to know."
"I don't either."
"Did you get all the pictures you needed?" I asked.
"Yeah," said Nancy.
"Man, Becky must have really cleaned him out," said Bert.
"Not that he didn't deserve it," said Nancy. "Anyway, I haven't looked through the rest of the house."
"You and Bert do that, will you," I said, then to Joe and Mike, "Pack him up and take him to Dr. Murphee."
"Will do," said Mike.

"Looks like a suicide," I said to Jeff and Helen.
"Oh, man," said Jeff. "I didn't even know he had a gun."
"There was a note. Did you see it?"
Jeff shook his head. "No. I just saw Ron lying with his head on the table, then the blood, and then I called 911."

"It was under the table by his chair. Must have fallen down there. Do you know what Ron's handwriting looks like?"

"Maybe," said Jeff with some hesitation. "It seems to me as though he always printed. We all took penmanship back then, learned cursive and such, but Ron never used it. He generally printed everything, even back when he was a kid."

"Like this?" I handed the note over to Jeff. Helen sidled up beside him and peered over his shoulder.

"Yes. Just like that."

"So it's Ron's printing?"

"I can't say for sure because I'm no expert, but it sure looks like it to me."

Helen said, "Oh my God! Barbara. I'll bet that's Barbara McCuwen!"

It hadn't taken long for Barbara McCuwen's name to make it around town via the St. Germaine grapevine.

"So Ron's the murderer?" said Helen. "He killed himself out of remorse? How terrible!"

"It's not true," said Jeff. "He would never murder anyone."

"Barbara McCuwen's death thirty years ago might well have been an accident," I said. "She may have fallen while they were hiking and hit her head, and he, being a kid, panicked and covered it up. Or they might have had a fight and something awful happened. Or, he might have killed her with malice and intent. We just don't know."

"And now we never will," said Helen.

Chapter 17

The pipe organ kicked it up a notch for the nightly sing-along. Dirk Knight was leading the patrons in a rendition of "Achy Breaky Heart" set to the tune of "Cantique de Jean Racine" and the crowd had started their line-dance.

"Hi there," purred a voice I recognized. I looked up and squinted into the darkness.

"My name's Trillium."

"Huh," I grunted. "I thought you said your name was Mystique."

She giggled. "Potato, potahto. This here's my boyfriend, Turg. The one you left on the sidewalk."

I knew it then. We'd been set up, set up like the third Hobbit movie which wasn't as bad as the second, but almost.

"Youse wanna come outside?" said Turg. His sloping forehead receded into a nose that had been pushed all over his puss. Beady eyes, teeth like yellow Chiclets, and small pig-shaped ears decorated a mug that looked like a bucket of smashed crabs. He'd been hit more times than a YouTube kitten video. "Outside or in here," he mucked, "it don't make no matter to me."

"You don't need me, do you?" asked Pedro. "I'm still eating."

"Nah," said Turg. "Just the shamus."

I looked at Pedro in disgust. "Outside, I guess. We don't want to disturb the customers."

"C'mon then," said Trillium, née Mystique, with a big smile. She grabbed hold of my necktie and led me toward the back door, Turg following closely behind, either cracking his knuckles or breaking walnuts in his fists and I didn't see any walnuts.

She ushered me into the alley, then pushed me against the back wall.

"Hang on," I said. "Before you do what you gotta do, I gotta know one thing. Who ordered the hit?"

"What do you think this is, a detective novel?" trilled Trillium. "We don't gotta tell you nothing." She gave the nod to Turg and he moved in like an unwanted relative, not that uncle in Chapter 2, but a worse one, like Dick Cheney or Marie Osmond. He reached into his pocket and pulled out a sap. This was gonna hurt.

"Blam!" went Pedro's gat, "blam! blam!"

Turg looked as puzzled as Jigsaw the Syrian Donkey when he stepped on that land mine. He peered down quizzically at the various fluids now sprouting from his striped zootsuit, tiny geysers of red and green, like a punch bowl at an Italian wedding.

"Green?" I said, making a face. "What's he got that's green?"

"I think that's his liver," said Pedro, "or maybe his gall bladder."

Turg spurted gaily for a few moments more, then fell over on his face with a thump, and lay there like a dead man, a timely analogy if ever there was one. Trillium shrieked and made a run for it, but Pedro's gat barked again and she tumbled, trollop over teacakes, into the alley.

"You might have left one of them for us to chat with," I said to Pedro.

Pedro shrugged and stuck his roscoe back in his flogger. "She's not croaked. I only winged her."

I smiled.

"If God dwells inside us, like people say," he muttered, heading back into Buxtehooters, "I sure hope He likes burritos, because that's what He's getting."

"What's the skinny on the Ron Pigeon case?" asked Pete. He was relaxing after the Slab's breakfast rush, sitting at the back table, nursing his coffee.

"The skinny?" I said, and pulled up a chair to join him. I turned over an empty cup sitting on the red and white checked vinyl tablecloth and waved it at Noylene. She dutifully ignored me.

122

"You know, the skinny, the dope, the four-one-one, the poop, the lowdown."

"Ah, yes, the skinny." I waved the cup at Noylene repeatedly, but was ignored. "You should really get some better help," I said. "The wait staff here is awful."

"That's because you don't tip," said Pete. He nodded toward the Bunn coffee maker behind the counter. "Get your own coffee. Your leg's not broke."

"It's nice to know that good restaurant service is not dead," I said, getting to my feet.

"Not as dead as Ron," said Pete. "So what's the verdict?"

I poured myself a cup of coffee and returned to the table. "Looks like a suicide. Kent's got the body. He'll go over it and give us a call."

Nancy came through the front door, saw us, and headed over, Dave right behind her. They pulled out a couple of chairs and sat down.

"Better get your own coffee," I said, gesturing with my head toward the coffee pot. "Noylene's in a snit."

"About what?" asked Dave.

"No idea," I said.

"She and Hog had a big brouhaha," said Pete. "I don't know why she takes it out on all the male customers."

Noylene appeared at the table and filled Nancy's coffee cup, sneered at Dave, then headed for the kitchen.

"Probably because you're all sexist pigs," said Nancy.

"Exactly," said Noylene over her shoulder, then disappeared through the swinging door.

The clanking sound of the old bell against the glass announced that Georgia and Bev had arrived. Seeing the four of us sitting around the table, they came right over.

Georgia said, "Well, I hope you're happy. The priest is a no-go."

"Why would that make me happy?" I asked.

"Of course, you didn't like him."

"Make no mistake," I said. "I'm staying out of this."

"Meg said you didn't like him," said Bev, pointing an accusing finger at me.

"I never told Meg that."

"Well," admitted Bev, "Meg didn't actually say that. I was just trying some of that police trickery on you. I saw it on PBS, one of those mystery shows."

"We should get Bev to interrogate our suspects," said Nancy. "She's sooo good at it."

"No need to be snarky, missy," said Bev.

"Anyway," said Georgia. "It was all too much, with the trumpet playing, and the latex gloves."

"And his sermon was awful," I said, "not that I'm putting in my two cents worth or anything."

"Yes, his sermon was awful," Georgia said. "Plus, Kimberly Walnut didn't do him any favors either with her stupid Children's Moment."

"True," said Bev. "Anyway, he's off the list. We'll have another candidate in a couple of weeks. As soon as we recover."

"Listen," I said, "don't rush, take your time, pray about it. The right person will show up. God has a plan for St. Barnabas."

"I agree," said Pete. "You should do God's will, whatever the hell it may be. There's a big difference between the ox and the whiffletree."

"What?" said Georgia, incredulously. "What does that even mean?"

"How about some coffee?" asked Noylene, appearing from the kitchen door. "I can seat you two over here next to the window."

"Thanks, Noylene," said Georgia. She and Bev glared at Pete, then followed Noylene and her carafe of freshly brewed coffee to the empty table.

I watched them sit and have their coffee nicely served, then said to Nancy, "Anything to report?"

Nancy pulled out her pad and flipped some pages, consulting her notes.

"The gun had a serial number that we traced to Atlanta. It was originally registered to a guy named Lawrence Stillwater, but he sold it at a gun show. That's what he says and there's no reason not to believe him."

"Did Ron Pigeon buy it?" asked Pete.

"No way to know," I said. "Since the guy wasn't a dealer, he didn't even have to register the sale."

"I told Kent to check for gunshot residue on Ron's hand," said Nancy. "I asked him to check what meds he was on, you know, just in case there might have been some foul play."

"Did you talk to Lena Carver yet?" I asked. "She was with him on Monday."

"Not yet. I thought you might want to be there."

"Yep," I said. "We'll do it this afternoon. According to Jeff, he spoke with Ron on the phone Tuesday afternoon and confirmed their breakfast meeting, then found him on Wednesday morning. So, according to our timeline, he shot himself on Tuesday night."

"That seems to be right," said Nancy. She tapped her pen against her pad. "We should also try to find out who he was seeing. Romantically, that is. Lena for sure. That other doctoral student."

"Jenny," I said.

"Yeah, her. I have his computer at the station. I can maybe log in to his dating site and see who he's been in contact with. That is, if he hasn't shut down the browser. Even if he has, he may have his password automatically saved. A lot of people do that."

"I do that," I said.

"It's not safe," said Nancy.

"Do we need a warrant?" asked Dave.

"Nah," said Nancy. "Just a death certificate."

Lena Carver came into the police station after lunch.

"What?" she said.

"What, what?" said Dave, looking up from his paperwork.

"What am I doing here? I got a message from Hayden telling me to come in for the third degree."

I came out of the office and gave Lena my second friendliest smile, the one that sometimes makes criminals confess just out of gratitude.

"Don't give me that smarmy grin," growled Lena. "What do you want?"

"I just have a couple of questions about Ron Pigeon," I said, and saw Lena pale.

"Oh ... well ... umm ..."

"So, I saw you get into his minivan and drive off on Monday afternoon. You were both in the park for the picnic. I guess you went to his place?"

"Well ... yeah ... I guess so."

"You guess so?"

Lena huffed through pursed lips, then said, "Okay, I did. He asked me over to his place for dinner and ... and I went."

"You don't seem very broken up about his suicide."

"No, I'm not really very broken up."

"You weren't ... umm ... really good friends?"

"Listen," said Lena, pointing a finger at me. "I'll tell you what. He was like an octopus. Eight arms and a beak. We ate some Chinese we got from Mr. Won's, and we were watching a movie on Netflix and, all of a sudden, he was all over me like stink on cabbage. I'm no shrinking violet, and I've been around the block a few times, but that was nothing I wanted. He told me he had some Viagra if I was worried. I said, 'No, thank you,' and got out of there."

"You didn't go back on Tuesday?"

"No way. Why would I?"

"I don't know. Maybe you felt empowered. Wanted to have a few words with him? Maybe get even?"

Lena gave me a smirk. "Don't be ridiculous. You think I can't handle some potbellied, middle-aged guy with Viagra in his pocket?"

"Just asking," I said.

Chapter 18

I sat behind my desk and slugged down a shot of rye.

Trillium was tied up in the chair across from me. Pedro was right, he'd just winged her. Not too serious. A flesh wound they called it: a clip, a through-and-through, a little lead poisoning. I chewed up a piece of Bazooka Joe, stuffed it in the hole and called it good. "You want a drink, Trill?" I asked.

"The name's Gina," she said.

"I can't keep track. How about I call you Monika?"

She went as white as a Presbyterian congregation. "B-b-but …" she sputtered frothingly and uncomprehendingly, "but, how did you know?"

"Oh, I've caught your act a couple of times. I sat in the back by the squeeze box. Now, who was the ankle you sent to drag me into this?"

"I didn't send her. It was Dirk. He thought we looked a lot alike."

"Like two dissimilar peas in a pod," I said.

"You still don't get it, do you?"

"Give me the skinny," I said, wanting more fat than skinny.

"The Maestro," she hissed snakily, her tongue forking out, as if she were using her vomeronasal system to taste the presence of small mammals, a category into which, thanks to my inherited genes and the fact that I snorked down sausages like popcorn, I did not fall. "It's the Maestro."

"Let's begin with the psalm," I said. "Last week didn't go so well."

"That's because we were still laughing at the Children's Moment," said Steve. He raised his eyes to the ceiling and intoned, "How can I get into heaven?"

"You gotta be dead!" chanted the rest of the basses in unison.

"Be that as it may," I said, "we should have done better."

"I find this fascinating," said Jenny Kunick, holding up my story. "Fascinating and hilarious. I'm sure that Dr. Mallary Clochette will be doubly amused." Jenny had made it to choir rehearsal and managed a seat in the Back Row Altos. Lena was miffed.

"Let's not show her," said Meg. "She may not find the humor in it. Lord knows, I can't."

"May I take this back to the university with me and pass it around?"

"Sure," I said. "It will do those students good to see some real writing for a change. Not all that academic blather."

"Twaddle," corrected Marjorie. "Academic twaddle. Blather is more often the spoken word."

"I've never heard either one of those words," said Tiff. "Twaddle? Blather?"

"Then this is an education for you, isn't it dear?" said Marjorie.

The Maestro: always resplendent in her garnet and gold mohair doctoral hood. My blood ran cold, as if I had hot and cold running blood and the hot wasn't working, like when you spend too long in the shower and that's all I'm saying about that.

She was a terror: a choral genius with an AA, a BME, an MME, a PhD, and a DMA in conducting from Florida State which is not a diploma mill, I don't care what they say. The letters trailed after her name like her doctoral students, educated baby ducks, waddling advertisements of her brilliance. When she sneezed (as she did often, being allergic to Eric Whitacre) all the letters flew out her nose and the students gleefully wiped up the pure vowels and exaggerated consonants with bath towels and sold them on eBay.

The Maestro. The case was coming together like two things that come together and make one thing, and there you have it, one final thing.

"She wants you out of the picture," Monika said.

"It's the Castrato Brothers?"

She nodded her head negatively, side to side.

"It's the codpieces?" I questioned, surmizedly.

"No."

"It's the mohair?"

"No," she said. "Sheesh! Do I have to spell it out for you?"

Spell it out? I felt like that stupid kid in the Spelling Bee that got the word "chiaroscurist" and left out the "a." What a bonehead!

Then it hit me like a goat tossed off an interstate overpass. "It's the goats."

"Of course it's the goats," she said, then slumped forward in her chair, dead as an old goat: one that died, maybe from being thrown off an overpass, maybe of liver flukes, maybe of hoof-and-mouth disease, you never know with a goat.

"I think I'm allergic to Eric Whitacre, too," whispered Jenny to Marty, sitting next to her, "but if you ever say I said so, I'll deny it."

"Culpable deniability," said Marty. "It's what makes the world go round."

"Jeremy and Julia both love him. Same for Maestro Clochette."

"No doubt," said Marty, then, "Hayden! Why haven't we sung any music by Eric Whitacre?"

"Too many notes," I said. "Plus, you're not good enough."

"Who says?" said Elaine.

"I says."

Chapter 19

"Hayden?" said the voice on the other end of the phone. "This is Jerry Jarman. You remember, over at the Renaissance Park? The old camp?"

"Sure, Jerry. What can I do for you?"

"You should come over and look at this. We found something when we were demolishing the last cabin."

"What is it?"

"A cigar box full of letters. They were under the floor, stuck in between a couple of joists. There was a piece of wood nailed up like a shelf, and this box of letters on top of it."

"Did you look at them?" I asked.

"Sure," said Jerry. "A box of letters. We didn't know."

"Know what?"

"They're all written to that girl. The one in the newspaper. Barbara McCuwen."

Nancy and I were at the old camp inside half an hour, pretty good considering it was still before eight o'clock. We walked up to the office, still being used by Jerry, and he met us at the door.

"You guys start early," said Nancy, looking around. There was nothing left of the camp except the pavilion and two cabins, one of which had been moved.

"The crew found it last night just before they knocked off. They left it on the steps for me. I came in at about six and found it. Then, as I was flipping through some of the notes, I recognized the name, so I called. I figured the police force would be up by seven."

"Hmm," I said. "Of course we would."

He handed me the old cigar box. There was no doubt about its age. The price was still on it. There was no way you were going to buy a box of Don Pepin Garcias these days for $17.59. Inside the box was a stack of letters. No envelopes, just the letters. Some might be considered notes, short and sweet, but others were multiple-page missives."

"There are sixteen of them," said Jerry.

"May we take these?" I asked.

"Sure," said Jerry. "I figured you'd want 'em, them being addressed to the dead girl, and all. Probably a clue."

"Probably," I said.

"I'm almost done here," he said. "I've got everything laid out, and the infrastructure guys are coming tomorrow. You know, underground electric, gas, septic tanks, sewer lines, that sort of thing."

"When will you start construction?" Nancy asked.

"Next month, but I'm not in charge of that part. I'm heading back to Texas. We'll have a general contractor up here. We'll do what we can before the weather stops us, then start again in the early spring. The park should be up and running by next year at this time."

"Sounds great," I said. "Thanks for calling us."

We spread the letters out on the counter of the police department and Nancy and I each read through them. There were sixteen, Jerry was accurate in his count.

"He read all of these," Nancy said.

"Of course he did," I said. "Nothing we can do about that though."

"Probably messed up the DNA," said Nancy, miffed.

"Probably. You know how hard it is to get a sample from paper anyway."

The letters, missives, and notes were all to Barbara and all from Ron Pigeon. He may have underreported his infatuation with Barbara Jean McCuwen, seeing as the sixteen letters were written over just nine days. They were dated and time-stamped by the love-sick adolescent.

"This must have driven Barbara crazy," said Nancy. "She plays what she thinks is a quick game of slap and tickle with a fifteen-year-old and he goes all gaga on her."

"You ever have that happen to you?" I asked.

"Not exactly," said Nancy, with a smile. "Look here, the first couple of letters are all 'I love you, we'll always be together,' the next few, some adolescent love poems, not that bad, either. Then, 'How could you do this to me? I know we mean more to each other,' then, 'I can't live without you, if this is love I'd rather die,' then finally, 'If I can't have you, no one can.' All addressed to Dearest Barbara, all signed Ronald."

"The classic devolving of the lovestruck," I said.

Chapter 20

"Look," said Pete, "do you even know for sure if these bones are Barbara McCuwen's?"

The four of us were sitting around the kitchen table, smelling Meg's lasagna cooling on the counter. We'd contemplated having the trout we'd gotten from Codfish on Monday, but by Thursday, Meg and I had already eaten it, so now, lasagna. The pasta had to rest, Meg said. Twenty minutes, that was the family recipe. I couldn't argue: it was the best lasagna I'd ever had. The salad was ready, the wine was poured, a wonderful Chianti that Bud recommended, although Meg was not partaking, and the garlic bread was ready to go into the oven.

"Actually, no," I said, "and there's no way to find out. We can get the DNA, sure, but we have nothing to compare it to. We might make a familial match if there were a sibling or a parent left, but we can't find one."

"Cousins?" asked Cynthia. "Second cousins once removed?"

"Maybe. She was brought up in a Methodist Children's Home. There weren't any relatives that they know about. Anyway, right now it's an assumption. We're assuming that the skeleton is that of Barbara McCuwen, and that she met with foul play."

"Are we assuming that Ron did it, then shot himself in some sort of remorseful, depressive state?" Cynthia asked.

"We could assume that, I suppose."

"Let's assume," said Meg, "for the sake of assuming, that he didn't do it, but you, in your cleverness, do manage to find a killer with motive and opportunity to kill Barbara, and you can prove that this person did it."

"Okay," I said.

"Wouldn't a defense attorney have a field day, since you couldn't even prove that the dead person was Barbara?"

"Absolutely. If it wasn't Ron, and I'm not saying it wasn't, eventually we'll have to do both, prove beyond a shadow of a doubt who the killer is, moreover, who the victim is."

"You have your work cut out for you," said Meg. "I don't think it was Ron."

"Sometimes a cigar is just a cigar," I said, "to quote Sigmund Freud. We have a suicide note explaining why he killed himself and apologizing to Barbara, love letters to her when he was fifteen, sometimes two a day, in which he says, 'If I can't have you, no one can.' He's a recently divorced man, taken to the cleaners by his wife, now obsessed with dating, and obviously suffering from depression and a host of made up diseases. Then we find the bones of his old girlfriend and start questioning him about it. There's a lot of guilt, stuff he hasn't thought about for years, and that pushes him over the edge."

"Exactly," said Meg. "There's no pencil."

"Huh?"

"There's no pencil. Why is there no pencil? Look, here in Nancy's picture."

I had brought Nancy's crime photos home with me. Not exactly dinner viewing, but a darn sight better than Pete and Cynthia's vacation pictures from South Dakota.

"Okay," I said, looking at the picture. "What are you talking about?"

The photo was of the scene we'd come upon. Ron Pigeon was sitting at the table, face down, his nose pressed into the tabletop. Blood was leaking from a hole on the right side of his head and trickling down behind his ear. His left hand was flat on the table, his right hanging loosely beside his chair. The gun was on the floor just under his hand. In this photo, Nancy had managed to get the note into the picture. It was under the table just in front of his shoes. It might have fluttered off the table when Ron's head banged down, or a breeze might have caught it anytime in the next twelve hours or so. The windows in the kitchen were open, so that was an easy explanation.

"Where's the pencil?" said Meg.

My mouth dropped open. "That he used to write the note ..." I said, slowly.

"If you write a suicide note, planning to then shoot yourself, you don't then get up and put the pencil away."

"No," I said. "You don't."

"Don't you think that the box of love letters being found in the last cabin being torn down is just a little too coincidental?"

"Well, sure, but ..."

"Wow," said Cynthia, "is this how you solve all your crimes? You just let Meg do it?"

"Usually," I admitted.

"Well, it's not solved yet," said Meg. "The murderer is still un-apprehended, and the lasagna's ready."

Halfway through our meal, the phone rang.

Meg answered since she was the closest, then handed it to me. "Kent," she said.

"Good evening, Doctor. You're working late."

"Nah. I'm wrapping up and heading home. I usually finish up around six. You eating supper?"

"An early supper," I admitted.

"Oh, sorry. You want me to call back?"

"No, go ahead. We were just talking about the case. Here, let me put you on speaker. I have the mayor and her paramour here as well."

"Good evening to all," said Kent.

"Good evening," the group answered.

"You have some results?" I asked.

"I do. You want them over the phone or in a report?"

"Can you give them to me over the phone and then get me a report?"

"That will cost you double," said Kent. "Two bottles of Kentucky's finest."

"Done."

"Your boy died of a gunshot wound, sure enough, probably by his own hand. He had GSR on his right hand. The bullet wound was above his right ear, so that all shakes out right."

"How about the tox report?"

"He was taking nitroglycerine, probably for a heart condition, although I couldn't tell you what that was. He hadn't had a heart attack lately. I can tell you that."

"We found the nitroglycerine pills in his bathroom, but no prescription on the bottle and we don't know who his doctor was. Jeff, his brother, says he might have been taking the pills for angina."

"Probably," said Kent. "I've seen those unmarked bottles before. He might have gotten them on the internet. You can buy that kind of stuff now, especially if you don't have insurance or much cash. Mexico, or Canada, or even South America."

"Helen thinks all his troubles were stress related. He was complaining about fibromyalgia last month and migraines before that."

"Could be. It also could be that he was on WebMD way too much. Self-diagnosis is a real problem for some personality types, then they order their own meds. It can put them in such a downward spiral they might never come out of it."

"So, your professional opinion is 'death by suicide?'" I looked over at Meg and she was shaking her head.

"Oh, I didn't say that." I could almost see Kent Murphee smiling.

"What are you saying then, Doc?"

"There's always something interesting whenever I get a body from St. Germaine."

"And?"

"And ... it seems as though Mr. Pigeon was fond of taking Viagra. Maybe even a double dose."

"We'd heard that," I said. "Well, not about the double dose. And this pertains to our case how?"

"If you take Viagra while you're taking nitroglycerine for your heart condition, the chances are extremely good that you won't be functioning for quite some time. Nitrates and Viagra don't mix. They both relax the smooth muscle of the vascular system. You mix the two and your blood pressure drops like a stone. You'll pass out in no time."

"Will that kill you?"

"Well, theoretically it is possible, but it's not likely. You'll wake up with a hell of a headache in a few hours."

"He was mixing them?"

"Boy, howdy," said Kent. "He probably didn't know because he never saw a doctor, just bought his pills on the internet. But, like I said, he died of a gunshot wound."

"Yeah," I said. "Gunshot. Anything else?"

"I'll let you know if I find something else, but that should be it."

I said, "Thanks, Kent," and hung up the phone.

"Well, there it is," said Meg.

Chapter 21

The New Anglican Nourish and Nurture Interspecies Ensemble (NANNIE) had been garnering rave reviews. As a women's chorus, they couldn't be bleat, although many had tried. The Maestro had them singing at all the choral competitions, and people wept openly to hear them. The Maestro might have been splendiferous in her mohair gown and hood, but, when performing, the singers wore angora. Same goat, sure, but "vive la différence!"

The NANNIEs started out as your usual interspecies choir — oh, they had fun, singing Advent shanties, frolicking in the meadows, playing kick the can, and catching fireflies in the twilight — but as the stakes rose, it became less about the fun and more about the choral sound. The Maestro was hired and she went through the choir like the grim reaper, or at least the grim gardener, weeding out the chaff like dandelions from a patch of posies, plucking them one by one and blowing on their heads till their hair flew off. Altos were fired, then hired, then fired again, until they couldn't take it any more and went to work at Home Depot. Sopranos were made to sing higher and higher until their throat pouches burst.

Then came the Tennessee Kissing Goats.

The regular goats — Nubians, Alpines, Toggenburgs, and the rest — never stood a chance, most preferring to end it all than to suffer the ignominy of being sent down to the Kid's Chorus. It was a bloodbath, and one that will never be forgotten at the Tryon Meat Market where mutton was going for two dollars a pound. Fortunes were made that fateful day, but so was sadness if sadness can be made, but fortunes for sure.

The Kissing Goats sang like angels and the most beautiful of them all was Adeline Angora. Higher and higher she warbled, her celestial song calling across the ages. Then she was gone, gone like the "Amens" in the new hymnal that the committee decided were liturgically redundant, leaving us unfulfilled both Plagally and spiritually. I mean, really. How do we know the hymn is over? Because the organist stops? Not always the best plan.

ρ

By the time the coroner had released Ron Pigeon's body for burial, the service had been planned. Sunday afternoon funerals were always well attended. People didn't have to leave work, they were already in their church clothes, and, except for a football game on television that no one cared about (Arizona versus Oakland), there wasn't much going on.

Ron Pigeon hadn't been a member of St. Barnabas, and neither were Jeff and Helen, but they'd been attending as of late and Kimberly Walnut was ever hopeful, going so far as to keep Helen on the prayer list as an "unspoken request." Ron hadn't been attending anywhere, and so it was decided that his service might as well be Anglican as anything else. Plus, New Fellowship Baptist had already scheduled their church-wide business meeting for two o'clock. Helen had been in charge of the arrangements, as far as she had been willing, which wasn't too far. She'd asked me to find a bagpiper, if possible, to pipe the casket out of the church, and then play *Amazing Grace* at the graveside. She'd seen this in a movie.

Visitation took place in the parish hall from one until two, then the mourners and well-wishers moved into the sanctuary. I stopped by for a moment, said my words of comfort to Jeff and Helen and then went to the choir loft to get my music in order. The casket was in front of the fireplace at one end of the hall, on its bier, this one a collapsible aluminum version on wheels, making it easy to push around the church. Mercifully, the lid was closed. The pall bearers, who included Jeff, Pete, Mark Wells, Lynn Cooper, and two men I didn't know, would have their work cut out for them carrying the casket up the front steps of the church and then again, from the hearse to the gravesite in Wormy Acres, but the rolling bier would be a great relief on the flat sections.

It was a beautiful day, seventy degrees and sunny. Many of the folks who knew Ron and Becky when they were a happy couple were planning on attending, although I'd heard that Becky and her children were not. The parents with children of an independent age — anywhere from five on up — decided to let the children play in the park during the service. This was small town living (and dying) at its finest.

At two o'clock I began to play. Helen had chosen several hymns for the prelude, and I was happy to oblige, but I interspersed the Albinoni *Adagio*, and even had time for some Buxtehude. By 2:20, the casket was rolling down the aisle covered with a white pall as the congregation sang *A Mighty Fortress*.

"I am the resurrection and the life, saith the Lord," said Father Walmsley having ascended the steps. "He that believeth in me, though he were dead, yet shall he live; and whosoever liveth and believeth in me shall never die."

There were a number of choir members who had come up to the loft for the service, as they did for most services, even though they weren't singing. It was easier, they said, and they had a good seat. Besides, they were used to sitting there. So now, Georgia, Meg, Bev, Rhiza, most of the altos, Randy Hatteberg, Bob Solomon, and Fred May, were all upstairs looking down at the service.

"O God, whose mercies cannot be numbered," continued Father Walmsley, "accept our prayers on behalf of your servant, Jeffrey Alan Pigeon, and grant him an entrance into the land of light and joy, in the fellowship of thy saints; through Jesus Christ thy Son our Lord, who liveth and reigneth with thee and the Holy Spirit, one God, now and for ever."

"Amen," said the congregation in unison.

"Hang on," hissed Meg. "Did he say Jeffrey Alan Pigeon? Jeff?"

"Holy crap!" whispered Georgia. "Helen's gonna blow."

Helen did not blow, thankfully. She might not even have noticed, such was her honking in the first pew. I hadn't noticed her fondness for Ron before, but now, apparently, grief was overwhelming her.

We heard the *23rd Psalm*, then a reading from Paul's letter to the Romans. The Gospel lesson was John 10:11-16, "I am the good shepherd." We sang a hymn, *The God of Love My Shepherd Is,* and Father Walmsley stepped to the pulpit for his homily.

"We have come here today to remember Jeffrey Pigeon," he said, "loving father, beloved husband, faithful servant of God."

We all looked down at Helen. She had her head on Jeff's shoulder, her face in her hankie, and he couldn't have moved if he wanted to.

138

Father Walmsley continued. "I never had the pleasure of knowing Jeff, but I have spent some time on his Facebook page, and I have been left with a very clear impression of the kind of person that he was. Jeff wasn't one for too much fuss or ceremony so I won't go on for too long, and I will be keeping to his more recent past because that is something you will all be more familiar with."

Mark Wells, sitting in the second row with the pallbearers, pulled out his handkerchief and was barking softly into it. It was not a bark of grief.

"Jeff and Helen met in Boone twenty-five years ago; he was then, and always was, a solid, reliable all-round good guy, someone you felt at ease with, someone that you instinctively knew you could trust and rely on."

The choir started snickering, albeit quietly, and into their sleeves. Jeff still hadn't moved, and Helen was still slumped over on his arm.

"Jeff Pigeon was a well-liked and respected man, he had many friends and although he didn't see them as often as he used to, they still kept in touch with each other, safe in the unspoken knowledge that they were there for each other if needed. He was a chiropractor by profession and, although it was a job he enjoyed doing, his life was his family, especially his wife, Helen. She meant more to him than anything."

Now we saw Helen sit up ramrod straight and glare at the priest. He saw her and seemed startled, pausing in his eulogy for a few moments. In that silence we heard some clanking sounds coming from the roof. Most of the congregation looked up, but there was nothing to be seen. The clanking stopped.

Father Walmsley went on for ten more minutes, extolling Jeff's virtues as gleaned from the internet: Jeff loved hiking, Jeff loved all kinds of music, Jeff enjoyed camping with his friends.

"Jeff enjoys going to funerals," whispered Bob. "Especially his."

"Jeff enjoys the afterlife," added Rhiza. "Walks in the clouds, rainbows, and streets of gold."

Now the laughter was obvious, and Helen was livid. There was nothing she could do. By the time she'd decided to pay attention, Father Walmsley had already been nattering for five minutes.

"We will shortly spend a few moments in silence," concluded the priest, "and you can each remember Jeff in your own special way, and afterwards Dr. Walnut is going to lead us in the Lord's

Prayer. Perhaps also during this quiet time we can spare a special thought and offer our sympathy, our love and support, to Jeff's family, his wife Helen, and the two children who ... for some reason ... couldn't be here today."

He stepped down from the pulpit and returned to his seat behind the altar. Kimberly Walnut jumped up to lead the prayer, but Father Walmsley put a hand on her arm and she sat back down. A few moments of silence was the directive.

Quiet again, and we all heard the low bark of a big dog coming from outside, probably from Sterling Park, across the street. Then, strange clanking, again from the roof. Then, nothing.

We recited the Lord's Prayer and the Apostle's Creed, and, there being no communion, went forward to the conclusion of the service.

"Give rest, O Christ, to your servant Jeff, with your saints," said Father Walmsley.

"Where sorrow and pain are no more," answered the congregation, reading from their bulletins, trying not to giggle. "Neither sighing, but life everlasting."

"Ron's name is on this bulletin," muttered Meg, "clear as the nose on that priest's face. Service of Resurrection for Ronald G. Pigeon."

The door to the choir loft opened and Kevin Brode came in, dressed in his Scottish regalia, complete from bonnet to spats. His tartan was of the Clan Brodie, and he had all the necessary accoutrements: kilt, brooch, sporran, doublet, tartan stockings, and pins. His bagpipe was stuck under one arm. He waved to me with the other, then made his way through the choir and over to the bell tower. The tower had a large slatted window which opened, and Kevin was intending to play his pipes from the tower.

Father Walmsley: "You only are immortal, the creator and maker of mankind; and we are mortal, formed of the earth, and to earth shall we return. For so did you ordain when you created us, saying, 'You are dust, and to dust you shall return.'"

"Amen," said the congregation, laughing again to see Jeff, now standing in the front row.

I heard a small commotion coming from under the choir loft, in the narthex, just by the front doors.

"Excuse me," said a child's voice. I didn't recognize it.

"Into your hands, O merciful Savior, we commend your servant Jeff," intoned the priest.

140

Jeff could take it no more. "You idiot," he hissed, unfortunately loud enough for everyone to hear. "*I'm* Jeff!"

"What?" the priest whispered back.

"I'm Jeff." He pointed at the casket. "That's my brother, Ron!" More laughter.

"Excuse me," said the small voice again from the back of the sanctuary.

"What do you mean, that's Ron?" said Father Walmsley, now obviously horrified. He turned to Kimberly Walnut, standing beside him. "Why didn't you say something?"

"I ... uh ... umm ... you ..." said Kimberly Walnut.

The priest gave her a look that could kill, then turned back to his prayer book. "Acknowledge, we humbly beseech you, a sheep of your own fold, a lamb of your own flock, a sinner of your own redeeming."

"Excuse me!" said the little voice, now much louder and further down the aisle.

"Receive him — receive *Ron* into the arms of your mercy," chanted Father Walmsley, "into the blessed rest of everlasting peace ..."

"Excuse me!" hollered the boy who I now recognized as Jared Trimble, the little five-year-old from Kimberly Walnut's Children's Moment. I saw Jared's mother, Baylee, leap to her feet as she realized it was *her* child interrupting the solemn proceedings, but she was at the front of the church, seated on the outside of the pew, and Jared was a long way away.

"Jared!" she said in a loud stage whisper. "Come here this instant! Just wait until your father hears about this! He's gonna tan your hide!"

"... and into the glorious company of the saints in light."

Just then a goat came trotting down the aisle. It was a mostly white, long-haired goat with horns and a beard. It grabbed Jared's shirttail in his mouth and started chewing. This was too much for the congregation, and they started hooting.

"Where did you get that goat?" Baylee Trimble hissed.

"That's what I been trying to tell everybody."

Father Walmsley was just hoping to get finished. "Let us go forth in the name of Christ," he bellowed, trying to be heard over the laughter.

Helen turned to look and hollered, "That's my goat! What are you doing with that goat?"

The goat, now noticing the commotion, promptly fell over in a dead faint, Jared's shirt clamped between his teeth. Jared, being only five and not weighing as much as the goat, tumbled down on top of it.

"Let us go forth in the name of Christ," Father Walmsley tried again, hoping for a congregational response. He got one, but not the one he'd hoped for. Gales of laughter met his commendation.

"Why did you bring that goat in here?" demanded Jared's mother, finally getting to her son and trying to pry the goat's mouth open.

"I didn't," cried little Jared. "The goats ..."

"What about the goats?" said Helen, now into the fray.

"The goats are on the roof."

Helen was up to the pulpit in seven bounds. "*Everybody, FREEZE!*" she whispered into the microphone. "Not one word."

We all did as we were bidden, not knowing what was going on, but sure it was out of the ordinary.

"Not a sound! Not ... one ... sound!"

"What?" whispered Bev.

"Goats on the roof," whispered Meg in reply. "Fainting goats."

Helen ran back to Jared. "Tell me," she said in a hushed voice.

"We saw them climbing up the ladders in the back," said Jared, now obviously scared.

"The scaffolding?"

He gave a terrified nod.

In the quiet we heard the sound again, a clanking sound, the sound of goat hooves on a slate roof.

"Oh, my God," said Helen. She pointed at Jeff. "Get out there and see what's going on."

Jeff took off down the aisle at a dead run. Helen stood up and addressed the congregation. "Please, no noise. No noise at all."

We heard the front doors open, then close, and we all imagined Jeff racing into the park to see the Pigeon Retirement Plan dancing delicately upon the pinnacle of St. Barnabas. Unfortunately, the only person who saw Jeff exit the church was Kevin Brode, standing in the bell tower, waiting for the signal to play *Highland Cathedral*. The huge, wooden-slatted window was open and, although Kevin couldn't see the goats since he was facing the opposite direction, he told us later he could hear them.

"It was surreal," he said. "I heard bells tinkling, and some goats bleating. Then I saw Jeff come out and wave, so I started to play."

From the inside of the church, it was terrible. Not as terrible as outside, but terrible nevertheless. With the first sound of the bagpipe's drones, Helen's face registered her panic.

"No!" she whispered. "Nooooo!"

Then the chanter kicked in. We heard the first goat fall over, a thump, then listened in horror as the large animal scraped and flopped its way down the steep roof, following its progress by sound until it reached the edge and dropped, its shadow appearing briefly behind the stained-glass window before crashing into the landscaping.

"Ahhhhh!" wailed Helen, her cry now a full-throated squall.

"Har-ronk!" went the bagpipe with a sound designed to strike terror into the hearts of the Scots' enemies. There is nothing quite as loud, or as alarming, as a piper playing in close proximity.

The startled goats fell over like dominos, then, one by one, slid down the slate and dropped off the edge. We watched them fall, their stiff bodies briefly silhouetted behind the sunlit stained-glass images of the saints. They hit with sickening thuds, the sound leaving little doubt the Tennessee Fainting Goats wouldn't be getting up again.

Helen was sitting in the middle of the center aisle, sobbing. Little Jared's shirttail was still clamped in the goat's teeth. The goat was upside down, its four legs in the air, unconscious, but very much alive. Jared's mother was standing beside Helen, not sure what to do next. The congregation was stunned into silence.

"Let us go forth in the name of Christ," said Father Walmsley, this time sadly. He turned and walked out through the sacristy door.

The six pallbearers shrugged, walked to the front, and began to push the casket out.

"Ron would have liked this," said Pete Moss. "I know I would have."

"I'm having goats at my funeral," agreed Mark.

Chapter 22

"What was the total?" Pete asked.

"Ten goats deceased," I said. "One goat recovering from 'shirttail stomach.' Helen's not doing well, although Jeff told me he'd insured the herd for a good bit of cash. More than he bought them for, anyway."

"Maybe we should insure our pig."

"Already did," I said. "If Portia falls off the roof, we'll be rich."

"That was a first for me," said Pete. "I've never seen anything like that. It was Goatpocalypse."

"It was. On the bright side, Jeff and Helen are having a barbecue on Friday."

"We're all invited?"

"Sure. We have a lot of goat to eat."

"I can't wait," said Pat Strother, sitting at the next table over with Pam McNeil, but happy to join the conversation. "I love a good barbecue."

"I don't believe I've ever eaten goat," said Pam.

"I've eaten goat," said Stacey Lindsay. She was sitting at the counter with Terry Shager, the town electrician. Stacey worked at the bank. "I hated it," she said. "It was all stringy and gamey and such."

"*Barbacoa de Cordero*," said Pat. "That's the way to eat goat. *Barbacoa de Cordero*." Pat worked part-time as chef at the Ginger Cat, but her main business was catering. "Chilis, cumin, cloves, oregano, onions, thyme, and two pounds of dried avocado leaves. Cook for seven hours. Oh, my. It's delicious!"

"*Si!*" said Manuel, who had come out of the kitchen and overheard her. "*Muy maravilloso*. Maybe Señor Pete will get us one of those goats. I will make a *birria*. Goat and chili stew."

"I thought avocado leaves were poisonous," Stacey said.

"That's the Guatemalan avocado," said Pat. "Mexican avocado leaves are no problem."

"It was horrible what happened to those goats," said Pam, "although, that may have been the best funeral I've been to for a long while."

Nancy came into the Slab, saw us, and walked over. Noylene and her coffee pot made it to the table just behind her.

"Breakfast?" Noylene asked. "We have shrimp and grits. Manuel got a recipe from somebody he knows in Charleston, then Rosa tweaked it. It's good."

"*Si*," said Manuel. "Very good."

"Sounds great," Nancy said. "Sure."

"Me, too," I said, and Noylene and Manuel left for the kitchen.

"Any thoughts on the goat wranglers?" said Nancy.

"Goat wranglers?"

"The ones who opened the Pigeon's fence and let them out."

"I have some thoughts."

"What thoughts would those be?"

"Helen and Jeff's property is right next door to Rich Newport's house."

"Yeah?" said Nancy.

"So, if you were on a holy quest to destroy all Satanic four-leaf clovers, and one of the places that you were sure they were growing was next door to a herd of goats, what might be your next move?"

"Ah," said Nancy. "It was those two nitwits, Larlene and Harmony Hickey."

"And Savannah Jean Butts," I said.

Pete said, "So they let the Pigeon's goats out to eat the clover at Rich's house?"

"Then Luger the German shepherd herded them over to the park. I saw him when I came out of the church."

"Why didn't the goats faint when the dog chased them?" asked Pete.

"Luger doesn't bark, not unless he's supposed to. That's his training. Probably he just prodded them gently downtown. I did hear him bark once, maybe when the goats started climbing."

"You want me to go and give Savannah Jean and the twins the third degree?"

"I don't know for sure they did it, but they'll tell you if they did. They won't lie about it."

"And if they *did* let the goats out?"

"I've been thinking about that. There's really nothing we can do except scare them a little, not unless we can make a case that they could reasonably foresee the end result: that Rich Newport's dog would herd the goats into town, that the goats would climb up the scaffolding onto the roof of St. Barnabas during a funeral, that Kevin Brode would ascend the bell tower and start playing his bagpipes, and that the goats would then faint and fall off the roof to their death."

"It's a stretch," said Nancy, smiling in spite of herself. "Maybe Helen and Jeff could sue them."

145

"They could, but they wouldn't win. Same problem. I doubt they'll pursue it."

"Meanwhile, back at the ranch," said Pete, lowering his voice to a conspiratorial whisper, "another murder."

"There is that," I said, my voice now low as well. "We haven't made that public, of course, so keep it under your hat."

Our breakfast arrived at the same time as Dave.

"Did you order me any of that?" he said, pulling out a chair and sitting down.

"Sure we did," said Nancy. "It should be here any minute."

Noylene rolled her eyes, set the bowls down in front of us, and went to rustle up one more order of shrimp and grits.

Back at the office, we put our heads together and reviewed the facts.

"So Ron Pigeon was murdered," said Dave.

I nodded. "We're going on that assumption. He had the GSR on his hand and the bullet came from that gun, but he had probably passed out by that point. The Viagra would have reacted with the nitroglycerine he had in his system."

Nancy had fingerprinted the house, and there were plenty of prints. Too many. They'd be no help unless we had a suspect and the suspect denied being there. The only prints on the gun were Ron's.

"We agree it's a woman?" asked Nancy.

"Yep." I looked over at Dave. He shrugged and said, "Okay, but why?"

"He wouldn't have taken Viagra if it was one of the guys coming over for pizza."

"Good point," said Dave.

"The letters found in the demolished cabin?" I said.

"A red herring," said Nancy. "Another road sign pointing toward Ron killing Barbara McCuwen in 1977. Then, in his remorse, committing suicide."

"We don't think he killed Barbara McCuwen, do we?" I said.

"No, we don't," said Nancy.

"We think," said Dave, "that whoever killed Ron was also probably the person who killed Barbara McCuwen, then killed Ron to cover it up."

"Correct," I said, "but that would only make sense if Ron knew something. Maybe he saw the killer murder Barbara. Maybe they were in it together. At the very least, the killer must have thought that Ron might rat her out."

"There's another possibility," said Nancy. "What if Ron's killer was a friend of Barbara's and this was a revenge killing?"

"Maybe," I said, "but we couldn't find any friends of hers around here. No one except Ron even recognized her."

"True," agreed Nancy.

"I'll bet," I said, "that whoever did this is in that Camp Possumtickle picture."

Chapter 23

"My concert choir has their fall tour coming up," said Maestro Mallary Clochette. "We've had a cancellation in our itinerary, and I wonder if we might sing a concert at St. Barnabas?"

The other members of the worship committee looked at me from across the table.

"Sure," I said. "What's the date?"

"A week from Sunday. We'd like to do a late afternoon concert if that's possible, then we'll take our bus down to Asheville. The choir has hotel rooms already reserved and paid for."

"Will you be conducting?" I asked. "I know you're on sabbatical, but we'd all love to hear the choir under your direction."

"I already anticipated your request," said Mallary, with a small smile.

I usually brought my calendar to the worship meeting, that is, when I showed up. Now I flipped it open. "We don't have anything going on. Kimberly Walnut has a Blessing of the Animals service scheduled for the next week, October 4th, it being the feast day of St. Francis."

"Oh, right," said Kimberly Walnut.

"Maybe we could have the concert at four," I suggested, "and follow it with a reception."

"I think that would be fine," said Mallary, standing up now that her business was finished. "Why don't we put it on the calendar?"

She handed me a sheet of paper, then passed more copies around the table. "You'll handle the printing of the programs, of course," she said.

"Sure," I said, perusing the list quickly. Monteverdi, Bach, Mendelssohn, Poulenc, and some others. "Looks great. Something for everyone."

"You'll note there are no women composers included," said Mallary with a sniff. "This is what happens when you take a sabbatical and your replacement is a male-centric jackass. I'll certainly remedy that for the Christmas concert."

"I like how you spell your name," said Lena. "That's different. I'm always looking for different spellings. My niece had a baby and wanted to name her 'Cindy,' and I talked her into spelling it 'Syndee.' I think it's much more interesting, don't you?"

Maestro Clochette gave her a hard, unsmiling look, but didn't answer, then turned back to me. "You'll notice that I have my grad students each conducting one short piece. They need the practice." She stood up to leave.

"Excellent!" said Father Walmsley, rubbing his hands together. "Just excellent!"

"How's your project going?" I asked. "Your book on conducting?"

"It's going very well. We should be finished right on schedule." Mallary walked out the door and disappeared down the hall.

"What else do we have?" asked the priest. He looked over at me. "Anything special for Sunday?"

"Boilerplate," I said. "Proper 20, the seventeenth Sunday after Pentecost. We're singing Wesley's *The Lord Hath Been Mindful of His Own* for the anthem. The service music will stay the same. Marilyn has the list of hymns."

"That anthem is great," said Marty. "I love it."

"In other news," said Bev, "I got a report from Billy. The repairs to the roof are finished. The old oak tree has been removed, sadly, and the other damage has been fixed. We're waiting on the big window. We're expecting delivery in a week or so."

"That is good news," said Father Walmsley. "What about that scaffolding?"

"We're leaving it, but they've taken the boards off the first two levels. There shouldn't be any more climbing, not by goats anyway."

No one said anything as we all silently contemplated the tragedy for a long minute.

"Amen," I said.

"Amen," everyone answered.

"Anything else?" asked Father Walmsley.

"Cuddling," said Kimberly Walnut.

Marilyn shot me a look and I saw her jaw muscles clench.

"Cuddling?" said Bev. *"Cuddling?"*

Kimberly Walnut ignored her. "This Sunday, we have the commissioning of the Sarah's Snuggery," she said. "We should do it at the end of communion. Maybe right after we send the lay eucharistic ministers out."

I glanced over at Marilyn and she, very unobtrusively, drew a finger slowly across her throat. I gave her an almost imperceptible nod. We were in this together.

Our lay eucharistic ministers were charged with taking communion to members of the congregation who were unable to be present at the celebration of the eucharist because of illness or infirmity. It was a job they took very seriously.

"No," I said, "if you must do such a thing, you should do it at another time. Maybe during the announcements before the service starts. I don't believe we want to trivialize the Lay Eucharistic ministry by throwing some cuddly claptrap on top."

"We're not trivializing anything," huffed Kimberly Walnut, "and we are not throwing some cuddly claptrap on top. You forget that I, myself, was a LEM before I was a deacon."

"Oh, I'm not forgetting anything," I said.

"I've already written that part of the service. The cuddlers will come forward and get into a huggle. Then Father Walmsley and I will offer a prayer of thanksgiving and commission them into the family and ministry of St. Barnabas with a Litany of Cuddling."

"A Litany of Cuddling?" said Marty. "A huggle?"

"Hayden is right," said Bev. "If we have to do it, such silliness should be done during the announcements rather than as part of the service."

"I agree," said Marty Hatteberg.

"It is *not* silly!" fumed Kimberly Walnut. "Here, look at this!" She passed out photocopied sheets to everyone at the table.

Commissioning the Cuddling Ministry

The cuddlers to be commissioned are called forward to the front of the church. Then the following prayer is offered.

O God, whose nature it is to enfold us in your mothering arms, grant that these, your servants, may encircle those with a hunger for human touch, cradle those yearning for understanding, coddle those who covet an embrace, and all for your Son's sake.
Amen.

Then, as the candidates form a *HUGGLE**, the Litany is said:

*HUGGLE — a hug from a person who stands behind another person and wraps his/her arms around the person in front. May be done with several people in a line.

150

Leader:	What would it look like ... if our church followed the example of Sarah to care for the lonely and depressed?
Congregation:	**Come and be cuddled. I will gather the lambs in my arms.**
Leader:	... if our church made a commitment to the awesomeness of a hug?
Congregation:	**Come and be cuddled. I will gather the lambs in my arms.**
Leader:	... if our church celebrated the healing power of an embrace?
Congregation:	**Come and be cuddled. I will gather the lambs in my arms.**
Leader:	For one reason or another, we do not get the level of human contact that we want or need in order to be our optimal selves.
Congregation:	**Come and be cuddled. I will gather the lambs in my arms.**
Leader:	Touch has the power to comfort us when we are sad, heal us when we are sick, encourage us when we feel lost, and above all else, allows us to accept that we are not alone.
Congregation:	**Come and be cuddled. I will gather the lambs in my arms.**
Leader:	Jesus said, "I will gather the lambs in my arms."
Congregation:	**O God, may we praise you with snuggling and cuddling, with our hearts and minds, arms and legs. Come and be cuddled!**

Congregational Song: *Come and Be Cuddled*

*Come and be cuddled, God has a place
Where we can feel happy within an embrace.
As we rest in each other's arms, now we can say
That the kingdom of heaven is a snuggle away.*

© Dr. Kimberly H. Walnut, D.Min.

"Oh, my sweet Lord," muttered Bev.

"I wrote the song myself," said Kimberly Walnut, handing me another sheet. "Just the melody and the chords, but I'm sure you can make it work."

I looked at it for a second, then set it aside. "I might just point out here," I said, "that, even if we ignored the part about Sarah the Snuggler being our model for comforting the disenfranchised — a dubious premise at best — Jesus never said 'I gather the lambs in my arms.' That was Isaiah. Isaiah said, '*He* shall gather the lambs in *his* arms.'"

"Same thing," said Kimberly Walnut.

"It might be nice," said Lena Carver, "to do it during the service. Just for a change of pace rather than having the same boring thing every Sunday. Over at Sugar Grove Methodist, we changed things up all the time."

Marilyn gave me the look.

"I believe the prayer book is rather clear on the subject," I said.

"The prayer book is just a guideline," said Kimberly Walnut with a snort. "This commissioning service will be included in *my* book."

"Here's the thing, Kimberly Walnut," I said. "Unlike most other denominations, we in the Episcopal Church do not consider our prayer book to be a collection of optional resources. It outlines procedures approved by General Convention, and all Episcopalians, by definition, make a commitment to follow it."

"What?" said Kimberly Walnut.

"Clergy make this commitment at their ordination. You, Kimberly Walnut, made this commitment at *your* ordination, even though you are just a deacon."

"I did?"

"The Book of Common Prayer is a covenant we make with one another," I said. "We promise to use it faithfully so we will be shaped by a shared vision, and we promise not to force upon one another liturgical practices that fall outside of the boundaries that we have agreed upon."

"Huh?"

"I'm afraid Hayden's right this time," said Father Walmsley. "We should do this during the announcements."

"Well ... just ... fine." Kimberly Walnut closed her eyes tightly, took several deep breaths, and seemed to try to find her happy place. Then her eyes opened, and she feigned composure. "Fine. We'll do it during the announcements." She got to her feet. "Excuse me for a moment." She walked stiffly out of the room and closed the door behind her.

"See what you've done," said Lena, eyeing me coldly. I gave her a shrug and poured myself a cup of coffee.

Marilyn gave me her sweetest smile and half a wink.

"Nicely done," Bev whispered to me. "Where did you come up with that?"

"Marilyn and I looked it up last week," I whispered back. "We kind of suspected we'd be up against it eventually."

"We'll be having the second of our candidates here a week from Sunday," Georgia announced. "As you all no doubt know, we've decided not to invite Father Carter Ousley from Atlanta to be our priest."

"I thought his trumpet playing was a bit off," said Joyce Cooper.

"That's putting it mildly," muttered Pam. "Then there were the latex gloves."

"The next candidate will not be doing a Children's Moment either," said Georgia. "The vestry has decided that until we find a full-time rector and he or she makes the final decision, the Children's Moment, if there is one, will take place in the chapel after the second hymn."

Kimberly Walnut had come back into the room during this announcement and immediately barked, "The vestry can't just make a pronouncement like that. We're in charge of worship! Me and Thomas. Umm, Father Walmsley." She paused. "Well ... and Hayden."

"And us," said Georgia. "That's why we're agreeing with the vestry on this."

"But ..."

"That's it then," said Georgia.

On my way out, I stopped by Dr. Clochette's makeshift office, knocked on the closed door, and was invited in.

"Morning," I said.

"Good morning, Hayden," said Jenny. Jeremy made a grunting sound. Julia ignored me altogether. They were, all three, sitting at Mac laptops, working on what appeared to be page layouts. Mallary wasn't there. The two tables in the room were covered with stacks of papers. On the wall was a whiteboard filled with notes. On another table was a copy machine, two printers and a scanner.

"How're things in the world of publishing?" I asked.

"Coming along," said Jenny, distractedly, not taking her eyes away from her screen. Jeremy and Julia said nothing, but squinted harder at their computers as if trying to will me out of the room.

"Jenny, may I speak with you for a moment? Outside."

She glanced up at that and gave me a quizzical look. "Sure," she said, then closed her laptop and got up to follow me. I led her next door into my office, then shut the door behind us.

"What's up?" she said.

"You know Ron Pigeon? He was the fellow who committed suicide."

"I heard about the funeral, of course. It's all over town. We were all down in Asheville yesterday, Dr. Clochette, Jeremy, Julia, and me. There's a retired choral director from California that Dr. Clochette thought we should meet and talk to. Willam Björkman. You know him?"

"I know *of* him, sure. He directed one of those Swedish Radio choirs for years, then ended up in Los Angeles. Quite a composer as well as a first-rate choral guy. I didn't know he was in Asheville, though."

"He retired to Asheville last year. Dr. Clochette knows him very well." She paused, then said, "*Very* well."

"Huh. Anyway, I wonder if you ever saw Ron Pigeon. Socially, I mean."

"You mean like a date?"

"Yes, like a date."

"No." She gave a light laugh. "I'm married, Hayden. I've been married for fifteen years."

"Ah."

"I did meet him though, during the Labor Day picnic. Julia and I were wandering around. She'd gone into the jewelry shop and I was talking to Rebecca, from the choir. She's the librarian, right?"

I nodded.

"So Ron came up and Rebecca introduced him to me, then followed Julia into the store. We chatted for a few minutes. That was it. I left shortly after that and made a trip back home to see my husband."

"Ron didn't ask you out?"

"Sure he did. I told him I was married."

"Okay," I said. "Thanks."

I sat at my desk, my cigar clamped firmly between my teeth, a bottle of Old Foghorn Ale in my hand. The typewriter sat in front of me, beckoning like a neglected woman, the kind with glass alphabet keys where her heart should have been. I reread my story from the beginning. It was starting to make sense, something I've always found to be a problem.

She slumped forward in her chair, dead as an old goat: one that died, maybe from being thrown off an overpass, maybe of liver flukes, maybe of hoof-and-mouth disease, you never know with a goat.

"Liver flukes, eh?" said Meg, reading over my shoulder. Not that I minded. Her face was next to mine. I could smell her hair, and she was definitely doing something to my ear.

"Mmm. Liver flukes drive me wild. When you're quite finished, how about coming to bed?"

"You are becoming quite brazen in your gravidity," I said. "One might go so far as to say 'lascivious.' It's not even seven o'clock."

"I know," she said with a huge sigh, then flopped down on the sofa. "I just don't know what's come over me. I expect it's the hormones."

"I'm not complaining," I said. "Not at all. I see this as my husbandly duty."

She jumped to her feet. "Good! I'll give you ten minutes," she said, and left the room.

Ten minutes, with that kind of incentive? It was all I needed.

Another body and it wasn't even noon. Pedro opened the door to the office, walked in, and plopped down on the davenport. "Dead, eh?" he said, looking at Mystique-Trillium-Gina-Stormy-Monika slumped in the chair. "Who iced her?"

"She's dead in my office, tied up to my chair, and you wanna know who did it?"

"Well, not you certainly," said Pedro, lighting up a smoke. "This is about the goats."

"How do you know that?"

Pedro shrugged. "It's what you pay me for. Gimme a shot of rye, some of that Old Overcoat you've got in the bottom drawer."

My best stuff, but Pedro was my best friend. I counterpoised the choice, then slid open the drawer.

"Counterpoised, eh?" said Pedro. "Big word for a gumshoe."

"So, spill it," I said, spilling some of his drink, and hoping he appreciated the symbolism.

Pedro slurped his hooch and gave a rye smile, no doubt hoping I appreciated the homonism.

ρ

"Ten minutes is up!" came the call from the bedroom. I looked at my watch. Three minutes had gone by.

"On the way."

ρ

At eight o'clock we had a light supper. I fed Baxter, let him outside, and started to do the dishes when the electric window above the kitchen sink opened and in stepped Archimedes. We hadn't seen the owl for about a month now. This wasn't unusual while the weather was good. In fact, in the past few years, Archimedes spent most of the summer on his own. We might catch sight of him now and then sitting on the roof of the shed, or the house, but mostly, he was his own owl. When the weather turned, he came back, preferring the warmth of the house to whatever warmth his nest might offer. It wasn't particularly cold out, although, halfway through September, the nights were dropping into the high forties.

Archimedes sat on the sill of the open window and preened his feathers. Meg and I watched him in silence. It was always an amazing realization for us, that this wild creature might grant us his friendship, or, if not friendship, at least his impassivity to our presence. Meg preferred to think of it as friendship, and who's to say she's not right?

The owl stepped lightly beyond the window and down onto the granite behind the farm sink.

"Oh my!" whispered Meg in astonishment.

Right behind Archimedes, now standing on the sill and looking around the kitchen, were three little owlets, carbon copies of their father, but in miniature.

"Do you think they'd like a mouse?" asked Meg, her voice still hushed.

I moved slowly to the fridge. We kept a coffee can in the back of the crisper with a few deceased mice in it. I got them from Kent Murphee who had a friend in the medical service industry. I had a case of mice and a couple cases of baby squirrels in the freezer out back, saved against the cold, hard months of winter when owl food was scarce. Every few days, we tossed the mice out into the yard and let whatever animals ate such things have them, then replenished our supply from the freezer. Dead mice don't keep very long, even in a refrigerator. I took out two smallish mice, holding them by their tails.

I handed one to Archimedes which he took with a talon, then leapt back through the open window, over the owlets, and took off in a silent fluff of feathers. Two of the owlets, startled, went with him, but one stayed put, looking at Meg and me through large yellow eyes. I offered him the second mouse and he took it in his beak, then cocked his head to one side, blinked, and disappeared the way his siblings had gone.

"Baby owls," said Meg, wonder in her voice. "Baby owls!"

"Now I don't think I can sleep," said Meg. She was on the couch in her robe, her legs tucked up under her, watching a recorded episode of Downton Abbey. "This is your fault."

"I'm happy to take the blame."

I gave a big yawn. I was back at the typewriter, hoping to finish up before the local news came on at eleven. By eleven-fifteen, I'd be out like a light.

"Okay," Pedro said, "I got the dope from this lady priest I'm dating. They're on the warpath. No more codpieces, no more kissing a nanny goat at ordinations."

"That's un-American," I said. "It's uncivilized and unholy. These are liturgical traditions that go back for centuries."

"Sure," said Pedro, "but there weren't any lady priests back then. Now that there are, they want equal treatment."

"Billy goats?"

Pedro nodded. "For a start. And not ugly ones. Cute ones."

"And the codpiece?" I said.

"They'll settle for mohair Spanx."

"You know," said Meg, clicking off the TV, "since neither one of us can sleep ..."

Chapter 24

"What the hell is this?" said Marjorie, waving her newly discovered music.

"This is the cuddle song," I said. *Come and be Cuddled.*"

"Are you serious?"

"Well, I thought we should go over it at least. We have to sing it for Kimberly Walnut's Commissioning of the Cuddlers."

"I'm not singing it!" said Marjorie. "I have my standards."

"Marjorie," said Randy, "you have no standards. You once sang *Baby, Don't Judge* for communion."

"That was years ago. Anyway, it was a request."

"Where was I?" I asked. "I think I would have remembered that."

"Oh," said Marjorie, "it was one of those times when you got miffed and quit." She cleared her throat and sang in her warbling tenor, "Baby, don't judge, only God can be our judge ..."

"Thanks for that," I said, interrupting her. "We do have some work to do, though. The anthem for Sunday, then the other music in your folders. Let's go through this cuddle song first, as bad as it is."

"Baby, don't judge," chirped Marjorie happily. "Only God can be our judge ..."

♪

We went through the 1977 Camp Possumtickle pictures again, but didn't recognize anyone else. We were at a standstill.

♪

Friday was Barbecue Day. Jeff Pigeon had decided that Barbecue Day was the perfect time to announce his candidacy for the 5th Congressional District. The election was coming up in a little over a year and Jeff thought that he'd better go ahead and declare his intentions. Added to this was the fact that he had ten goats that needed to be eaten. He'd already collected the insurance, so the barbecue was lagniappe, good will to be garnered at little to no cost. It was another beautiful day in Paradise. Jeff had called the Watauga County jail and arranged for some deputies to come to Sterling Park with their two huge wood-fired barbecue pits. They started cooking around four in the morning, and planned on serving the masses from noon to 1:30. At Pete's suggestion, Jeff had donated a goat to the Slab, and Pete had arranged for Pat Strother and Manuel Zumaya to add their culinary expertise to the mix, Pat with her *Barbacoa de Cordero* and Manuel with his *birria,* a Mexican goat stew. They had a table set up outside the Slab on the sidewalk. The food smelled delicious.

Jeff had a bluegrass band lined up to play in the gazebo and by lunchtime there were tables set up to dispense the meat, buns, coleslaw, potato salad, and brownies to whomever might want to enjoy the event. There was iced tea and lemonade, and beer available at the Bear and Brew if you liked your barbecue with suds. Helen had told us that Jeff would be giving his speech at 12:30, before everyone went back to work.

Billy and his crew, two brothers named Randy and Lester Kleinpeter, had mown the grass the day before. They'd have to mow one or two more times before they were done for the season. As it was, the grass wasn't growing much, but Jeff had wanted it perfect, and had made the necessary arrangement with Billy.

"Baptists and crabgrass are takin' over," said Billy. "Mostly the crabgrass. We're going to have to do some maintenance next spring, that's for sure."

Meg was in Greensboro for the day, doing something with the nonprofit financial counseling business for low income families that she had started with Bev Green. They'd set it up a few years ago, didn't charge anything and, were busier than one-armed paper hangers. She and Bev were hunting up grant money and they had scheduled a corporate meeting long before the goats had decided that the roof of St. Barnabas was a fine place for seeing the town. I got a cup of coffee from Kylie Moffit, then wandered for a few minutes, shaking hands and chatting with our neighbors. I saw Nancy and Dave doing the same on the other side of the park. We weren't really patrolling, just out and about, being visible.

The Mallarites, as the three grad students had become known around town, had come out of their dungeon-like existence to see the sunshine and get a free lunch. Jeremy, Jenny, and Julia were sitting side-by-side on a bench, Jeremy and Julia looking particularly cranky. All three had paper plates in their laps, each holding a sandwich, potato salad, and a pickle. Jenny, at least, was eating her sandwich: the other two sat staring down at their

160

vittles, and none of them looked happy. I walked up and said hello just as Noylene came over with some brownies.

"This isn't how I envisioned the last year of my doctoral program," said Julia. "Sitting in a North Carolina town eating a goat."

"I thought you three were thrilled to help with Maestro Clochette's book," I said.

"Not really," said Jeremy. "Sure, we get a mention in the acknowledgements, but we're little more than slave labor. Oh, she's a great choral conductor and we need to do our time and get our credentials, but I'm ready to get out of this dump and make some money."

"You want one of these brownies?" asked Noylene. "I ain't got all day."

"Yes, please," said Jenny, taking one from Noylene's platter.

"I sure don't want to end up like you," said Jeremy, shaking his head sadly. "We were talking about it this morning. Living hand to mouth, working two jobs, one of them a part-time church gig, always kowtowing to some committee, never getting to perform quality choral music."

"Well, it's not that bad," I said.

"Right," said Julia. "What does a church job pay in a town like this? Twelve thousand? Fifteen?"

I shrugged.

"Are you kidding?" said Noylene with a hooting laugh. "Hayden's worth probably twelve million or so. You kids are out of your league."

"What?" said Julia.

"The trick," I said, "is to get the church to pay you what you're worth."

"How're you doing, Chief," said a voice behind me. I turned and saw Jay Gore, a plate full of food in his hand.

"Jay, right?" I said, moving away from the forlorn trio of doctoral students.

"Yep. Jay Gore. I'd shake your hand, but it's got goat all over it."

"Good to see you again. What are you doing in town?"

"I came over for Jeff's announcement. Tell you the truth, I think he'll make a fine congressman, but this barbecue's terrible."

"I don't know why. The meat was tenderized from quite a great height."

Jay laughed. "So I heard. Anyway, it's probably time for a change. I still have a house over here, so I'll be voting for him."

"Tell you what," I said. "Dump that plate and come with me."

We walked across to the Slab and found there was quite a line in front of the table where Pat and Manuel had set up. I led Jay around to the back, tapped Rosa on the shoulder and whispered, "Police emergency."

She laughed. "How many, Chief?"

"Two."

"You want any of the *barbacoa?*"

"Yes, please."

"Coming right up."

We took our plates into the Slab and had no trouble finding seats.

"Wow," said Jay taking a bite of the stew, "this is delicious!"

"I agree," I said.

"How's the investigation coming? Did any of those guys whose names I gave you help?"

"Nope. A couple of them said they remembered her, but no help really."

"Ah, too bad. I was sorry to hear about Barbara. She was a nice enough girl. Just had some problems."

"Hey, when we're finished, would you mind coming over to the station? Maybe you can put some names to a few more faces in the camp photo."

"Sure. Happy to do it. Then I won't have to listen to all of Jeff's speech."

Twenty minutes later, we were in the police station and I was digging out the Camp Possumtickle photos. Nancy and Dave came in, followed by Cynthia.

"What's up?" said Cynthia. "I saw everyone coming in."

"You sure are nosey," I said.

"I'm the mayor," sniffed Cynthia. "Besides, I don't really want to listen to Jeff. Why can't these politicians just say, 'I'm running for congress, enjoy the afternoon?'"

"Welcome to the club," said Jay. "I'm just here to look through a couple of camp pictures."

"You're Jay Gore, right?" said Cynthia. "The Bullwinkle balloon?"

"That's me."

"We met when you came up for the Christmas parade. I'm Cynthia Johnsson, mayor and professional belly dancer."

"Not in that order, I hope," he said with a laugh.

"Jay was a counselor in 1977," I said. "He's going to name names."

I found the photo I was looking for and spread the panoramic shot out on the counter.

"There I am," said Jay, pointing to a scrawny kid with curly blonde hair, and a big smile. "I was running track back then. Cross country. I was quite a bit thinner."

"Weren't we all?" I said.

"There's Ron Pigeon," said Nancy, pointing at the figure on the back row, "and there's Barbara McCuwen." She tapped the picture of the girl draped by Ron's arm, her hand sneaking out from encircling his waist.

"No," said Jay. "That's Peggy Wist. He looked for a long moment, then pointed to a girl that looked very much the same, but with blonde hair, seated, Indian style, on the ground, her hands on her knees. A girl at the opposite end of the photo. "Barbara's right here," he said.

"That's not Barbara?" said Nancy, her attention back to the first girl.

"That's Peggy Wist."

"Son of a gun," I said. "Ron lied to us. Do you know anything about Peggy?"

"I remember Peggy. She was at the camp two summers, '77 and the year before. She liked it up here. I remember that she was from Florida, but grew up in one of those children's homes. You know the kind I'm talking about? An orphanage, but we didn't call them that."

"I know exactly what you're talking about."

"Holy cow," said Cynthia.

<p>

Jay had gone out to hear the remainder of Jeff's campaign speech, leaving the four of us.

"Okay," said Dave, "just to be clear. The girl who we thought was Barbara McCuwen, isn't Barbara. It's Peggy Wist."

"Right, so far," I said.

"So the skeleton would be who?"

"That's a good question," I said. "The drawing we got from the forensic artist ..."

"Max Dunlap," said Nancy.

163

I nodded. "The drawing sure looks like Peggy. Really, it also could be Barbara. Imagine her with blonde hair, standing up maybe. From this picture they look an awful lot alike."

Nancy said, "I suspect they were both at the Methodist Children's Home in Enterprise, Florida at the same time."

"*What?*" said Cynthia. "Really?"

"Probably," I said. "It would be a heck of a coincidence if they weren't. I don't know how many Children's Homes are in Florida. Quite a few I suppose, but my bet would be that they were both there, became friends, went to college together. We'll check on that."

"So why would Ron lie?"

"That's the question," I said. "He obviously knew that the girl he had his arm around wasn't Barbara. Yet he told us it was."

"He knew that we'd found a skeleton and the picture matched the girl he had his arm around," said Cynthia.

"This is getting complicated," said Dave.

"Indeed," I said. "I think I'll drive down to Enterprise. This Sunday would be a good day for me to skip church anyway."

Chapter 25

On Saturday morning I got up early and headed south on a nine hour drive. I didn't mind the driving, and, truth be told, I'd rather drive than fly. I'd called Edna Terra-Pocks, my go-to substitute organist, and she was happy to play for Sunday's service on short notice, even going so far as to offer to noodle around on Kimberly Walnut's cuddle song during communion. My words to her were, "Knock yourself out."

Once I hit the interstate in Charlotte, it was smooth sailing before finally leaving I-95 in Daytona Beach and picking up I-4 twenty miles north of Enterprise. The landscape and the weather had changed dramatically and, when I opened the door of my truck, having arrived at the Children's Home, I was greeted with an eighty-eight degree blast of warm air even though it was now four in the afternoon.

I'd called ahead and talked to the director of administration at the central campus. She'd agreed to meet with me after talking to her boss, and was waiting for me at Hardin Hall, the largest building on campus, and now the Welcome Center. It was a large 1920s neoclassical, red brick building, with a pediment, pillars, moldings, and a gabled front entrance that sat under roof. It was surrounded by some huge trees dripping Spanish moss. Karen Dixon was waiting for me as I walked in.

"Chief Konig?" she said. "Right on time."

I shook her hand as she introduced herself. "GPS is a wonderful thing," I said. "I'm here within two minutes of its prediction."

"I have a meeting at five," she said. "So we can't chat too long, but I do have some information for you and a surprise as well. Come on in and sit down."

We took two facing chairs in the lobby and were the only ones in the room. Apparently, four o'clock on a Saturday afternoon wasn't a busy time.

"We were established as an orphanage in 1908 by Florida Methodists," said Karen. "By the 1950s we'd changed our emphasis to caring for abused, abandoned, neglected, or dependent children. Boys and girls are accepted without regard to race, creed, or national origin."

I listened politely, although I'd already read most of Karen's spiel on the website.

"We have one hundred acres here on Lake Monroe. We're very proud of our work."

"You should be," I said.

She pulled out a folder. "I can't give you too many specifics about the girls, but I have their report cards for the last year and a couple of pictures for you. They were taken during our school year in 1975. That's the last year they were here." She passed them to me. "You can keep them, if you like."

"Thanks."

"You can ask questions, and if I'm allowed to answer them, I will. Other than that, we'll need permission from the girls."

"And if one or both of them is dead?"

"A death certificate or a court order."

I looked at the photos, school photos from the 70s, the kind taken by the yearbook publishers and hawked to the parents in various sizes and formats. The girls looked similar, but different. Their hair was long and straight, although Barbara's was blonde and Peggy's was light brown. They had the same coloring, the same high forehead, the same nose. Their mouths were different, but not much. They could have easily been sisters, or at least cousins.

"Okay," I said. "Fair enough. Can you tell me when they resided here at the Children's Home?"

"Peggy Wist was here from 1965 to 1975 when she turned eighteen. Barbara McCuwen came to us in 1966. She was taken into a foster home 1968 to 1970, but then came back to us and stayed until 1975."

"Can you tell me why she came back?"

"I can't, and not because I won't." She shrugged. "I simply can't. There isn't any information."

"How about the foster parents?"

She flipped through some papers and said, "Deceased. Both of them."

"Were these girls related?"

"I can see why you might think that, but no, they weren't. They were both orphans from different parts of the state."

I looked at the report cards. Margaret Hillary Wist — Peggy — and Barbara Jean McCuwen. "Peggy was a good student," I said.

"It seemed so."

"Barbara, not so much. Cs and Ds. But they both got into Stetson at the same time."

"We do have those letters from the University," said Karen. "Barbara was admitted on a probational basis, and just to the Music School. Her SATs were way above average, but, like many kids in these circumstances, her grades were poor."

"Can you tell me anything else that might be pertinent?" I asked.

"Nothing really," said Karen, then shifted her gaze to the doorway and said, "but here's the surprise." Another woman came into the room, late middle age, attractive, with short dark hair and a big smile.

"This is Beth Fountain, our Vice President of Foster Care Services."

"Pleased to meet you." I said, standing. "I'm Hayden Konig, St. Germaine Police Department."

"You found out something about Barbara or Peggy?" asked Beth, concern clouding her face.

"Well ... possibly. Did you know them?"

"I'll leave you two, then," said Karen, standing up as well. She reached out her hand, and I took it. "It's been a pleasure," she said, and disappeared into a hallway.

"Let's sit," said Beth, and we did.

"You speak as if you knew Barbara and Peggy," I said.

"I knew them very well," said Beth. "We were in the same house, along with five other girls. I was raised here. I came here in 1970 at age ten, then left in '78, went to Rollins College, then on to the University of Florida for graduate studies. I came back here to work in 1995 and have been here ever since."

"Can you tell me about the girls?"

"Peggy and Barbara were best friends," said Beth. "They shared a bedroom all through high school. Barbara told me once that she stole from her foster parents just to get sent back, so she could be with Peggy. I told her she was crazy. Most of us would have killed to get into a good foster home, and the Daniels were the best."

"The Daniels?"

"June and Garth. Wonderful people. They fostered kids into the 1990s, then she passed away and he went into assisted living. I think he died about ten years ago. I remember them asking me about Barbara when I first started working here. They kept up with her, but never heard from her after that summer she left college."

I passed the two pictures across to Beth and she looked at them with a sadness in her face. "They sure did look alike," I said.

"They sure did," said Beth. "That's what drew them together I think. They were always joking about how they were two slightly different peas in a pod. Sisters with a different mother. I remember one time, Peggy broke her leg at the swimming pool. It was a bad break, and she was in a wheelchair almost the whole year. Barbara

167

pushed the chair for her everywhere. Wouldn't let any of us take a turn. They really loved each other." She handed the pictures back, took a deep breath, and said, "You found something, didn't you?"

"I'm afraid so," I said. "We think that one of them was killed back in August of 1977. They were both working at a camp in St. Germaine, North Carolina. We found a skeleton in the woods early in the summer. A forensic artist gave us a drawing."

"Oh, dear," said Beth, then gave a huge sigh.

"We can't find the other girl, and we don't know whose skeleton it is."

"Can you do a DNA match?" asked Beth.

"We could, if we had something to match it to. We've already sent it into the lab and we have a DNA profile."

"A relative?"

"We could do a familial search, sure, but we haven't found any relations. How about a dentist?"

"Well, sure. All of us went to Dr. Gerard. He's gone, but the office is still there and we still use it. Lakeside Dental."

"I'll check with them. Thanks."

"You know," said Beth. "Peggy had a trust fund. It wasn't a whole lot of money, maybe fifty-thousand, but it was a lot to kids. Peggy and Barbara used to talk all the time about taking that money and starting new lives in Philadelphia. They'd read about Philly in a magazine, or something. Anyway, Peggy couldn't get the money till she was twenty-one."

"Good to know," I said. "You've been a great help. Thanks again."

I dropped by the dental office, got some records, then spent the night in Daytona Beach. On my way home on Sunday, I gave Nancy the lowdown, chatting with her over my Bluetooth, one of the advancements in technology I enjoyed. But there was something, something I'd heard, something I'd seen. Something I was missing, and it was just ... right ... there ...

I was an hour from home when I had an idea, and called Kent from my truck.

"Are you calling me to ask me to dinner?" said Kent. "Maybe come over and have a drink? If you are, I can't make it. Jennifer and I are packing to go to New Hampshire for a week. It's part of her plan to bankrupt us before I retire."

"What time do you leave?"

"First thing tomorrow morning. It's a long drive."

"I need to know something about that skeleton. Something specific."

"What specifically?" Kent sounded interested.

"I got some dental records, but that'll take a a week or so to confirm. I need to know if she had any evidence of a broken leg? It would have been several years old and healed, but probably a bad break."

"I don't recall that she did, but those bones were pretty beat up."

"Could you go down to the office and check? Before you leave? It's important."

"You mean go right this minute and leave Jennifer to do all the packing?"

"If you wouldn't mind."

"Sure!"

ρ

I was coming into town when Kent called back.

"The answer is affirmative, in my humble opinion," he said. "There was a break to the left tibia, but it had healed nicely. The bone is degraded so badly that my humble opinion probably wouldn't hold up in a court case, but there it is."

"That's all I need," I said. "Thanks."

"Now you just have to answer to Jennifer."

"I'll have Bud put together a case of his finest and send it to the house."

"That'd be perfect."

ρ

"It was Peggy Wist," I told Meg when I got home. "The skeleton belongs to Peggy."

Chapter 26

"Let's wrap this up," I said. "Adeline the Tennessee Kissing Goat is missing and needed for the Archbishop's coronation. She was last spotted at an after-ordination party."

"Yep," said Pedro.

"Everyone else is dead except Dirk and the Maestro."

"It seems so," agreed Pedro.

"And the NANNIEs are singing for the ordination."

"That I did not know," said Pedro. "Probably a bit of the plot that hasn't been revealed till now."

"Where's Marilyn?" I said. "I haven't seen her all day. For a secretary, she's keeping strange hours."

Pedro nodded, gulped the remainder of his drink, sucked down the rest of his smoke, and fondled his gat. He was ready. "Maybe you should listen to your messages," he said, giving a nod toward the blower.

"Later," I said. "Let's get over to the NANNIE's rehearsal. The game is a-hoof."

"How was church?" I asked Georgia on Monday morning, even though Meg had filled me in.

"Awful," said Georgia. "You know, I just want to go to church and not come away mad. Is that so much to ask?"

"No."

"The worst thing was the cuddling ceremony: the litany, the song which no one sang except Kimberly Walnut ... the whole thing. Since we did it before the service, I was mad from the start. Then Edna got lost a couple of times, played the *Sanctus* instead of the *Gloria*. We went ahead and sang the *Sanctus* again during communion. The basses got lost in the anthem and just quit singing. The hymns were too slow. Father Walmsley forgot the creed."

"Wow," I said, although I'd already heard all this.

"This is what happens when you leave. As Senior Warden, I forbid you to ever take a day off."

"Duly noted," I said. "How many cuddlers were commissioned?"

"There was Kimberly Walnut, of course. Father Walmsley is one. Goldi Fawn Birtwhistle, Shea Maxwell, and Kylie Moffit."

"Kylie? Really? She's not a member of St. Barnabas."

"You don't have to be a member. Kimberly Walnut pointed that out. She told us all about her book, *again*, and called attention to the fact that this was a ministry, not only for the *cuddlees* but for the *cuddlers*. Besides, Kylie's still got that Christian massage business going over the Holy Grounds coffee shop. She's into it." Georgia took a deep, cleansing breath. "Any of those you'd like to be cuddled by?"

"Well, Kylie's kinda cute," I said.

"I'll keep that information to myself," said Georgia, smiling. "In other news, we'll have our second tryout priest here on Thursday. Father James Hook. He'll be here until Sunday afternoon. Will you be around?"

"I expect I will. Will you email me his bona fides?"

"I'll be happy to," said Georgia, "but if he's not the one, it's back to the drawing board."

"So what do you think?" said Nancy.

"Why would Ron Pigeon send us in the wrong direction?" I asked. "Why would he tell us that the girl he had his arm around was Barbara McCuwen?"

"He was sending us on a wild goose chase," suggested Dave. "If we thought the skeleton was Barbara, that's it for Barbara. The only reason he'd do that is if he knew that Barbara wasn't dead."

Nancy said, "If he knew the skeleton wasn't Barbara's, then he also knew whose it was — Peggy's. The only way he could know that was if he murdered her."

"That's one explanation," I said, "and it's neat and tidy. The problem is that Ron didn't kill himself out of grief, or remorse, or even depression."

"He didn't kill himself at all," said Dave.

"That's exactly right," I said. "He was murdered."

Nancy said, "So, although Ron knew that the skeleton was Peggy's and not Barbara's, someone else knew as well. That someone had every reason to silence Ron Pigeon."

"He was spiraling downward, by all accounts," I said. "He'd lost everything, his wife, kids, all his money. He was depressed, self-medicating, trying to hook up with anyone he could. My thought is that whoever this person is, she decided not to take any chances."

"And that person," said Nancy, "is Barbara McCuwen."

"That's what I think," I said. "When Dave found Peggy Wist's phone number and I called her, she gave me the story about staying with her boyfriend in Daytona Beach and not wanting her folks to find out."

"She had no folks," said Nancy.

"Barbara McCuwen took Peggy Wist's identity," I said, "and has been using it all these years. They looked alike, Peggy was dead, neither of them had family. She didn't go back to college, and never went back to the Children's Home, so there was no one to know it wasn't her. Probably took her license and Social Security card, colored her hair."

"Why?" said Dave. "Why would she take Peggy's identity?"

"There was a trust fund," I said. "Fifty-thousand dollars or so. She probably knew everything about it. It's not a stretch to think she cashed out on Peggy's twenty-first birthday."

"But they were best friends," Dave said.

"Until Ron Pigeon came along," said Nancy. "Ron himself told us. You read those letters. Barbara was his first, but then she dumped him and moved on. I think he moved on, too, after a few weeks, moved on to Peggy. Then maybe Barbara kept reading those letters over and over. She kept them, that's for sure."

"Treasured them, even," I said. "Saved them for thirty years."

"She might have decided that she wanted Ron back," said Nancy.

"Jealousy?" said Dave.

"I can see it," said Nancy. "Maybe some sort of event."

"So Ron killed Peggy and Barbara knew about it, or Barbara killed Peggy and Ron knew about it, or they did it together."

"I believe that's right," I said.

"So let's go up to Philly and get her," said Dave.

"Evidence, Dave," said Nancy. "We're going to need evidence."

Chapter 27

Sarah's Snuggery had been booked by the cuddlers from ten to three, Monday through Friday. Kimberly Walnut had been right: our parishioners apparently had a want or need for human contact. The sign-up sheet was being monitored by Kimberly Walnut and so we weren't privy to who was being cuddled by whom, but the library was bustling. I suppose, if someone camped out in the hallway, they could find out the particulars.

Thursday morning marked the return of our patron, Good Saint Barnabas. The window had been in St. Louis for several weeks, being expertly repaired, and was now reinstalled in its former position at the back of the church, high in the loft, where the saint might look down kindly upon those who toiled musically in the Lord's temple. There had been some talk of a reinstallation ceremony, but with everything else going on, not much interest could be mustered.

In the afternoon all the good and great were invited to the Parish Hall to meet the second of our candidates. The Rev. Dr. James Hook, according to the vita that Georgia provided, was a priest looking for a nice place from which to retire. He was fifty-nine years old, had already served several large parishes, the last being St. Peter's by the Lake in Florida, and had been considered unsuccessfully for bishop several times. He'd taught at the General Seminary in New York, and had his PhD from Duke University. With his wife and four children, all grown, he seemed almost too normal for us.

"I don't know," said Meg, upon reading his resumé. "I thought we wanted a young, energetic priest to revitalize the congregation."

"That's what everyone always says," I answered, "but revitalize us to do what? We have a great congregation. The pews are full, the fellowship is great, and the programs, despite Kimberly Walnut, are working. We could get eight, maybe ten years out of this guy before he retires. That's as many as we'd get from some young dynamo. Probably more."

"You're right," said Meg.

"When was the last time we had a good priest?"

"Gaylen Weatherall," said Meg. "It wasn't that long ago. It just seems like it."

"So maybe he's the guy. That's all I'm saying."

James Hook made a fine first impression, in his khaki suit, black shirt, and dog collar. A tall fellow, lean, and slightly tanned, he had an outdoorsy look like someone who would be at home hiking the Appalachian Trail. His hair was gray and he was clean shaven. He grasped my outstretched hand with both of his and shook it.

"Call me Jim, Hayden. It's a pleasure to meet you. I've heard great things about the music here at St. Barnabas."

"Thanks, Jim. It's good to meet you, too."

"This must be Meg." He shook her hand as well, then cast a glance toward her ever-burgeoning belly. "And little Abishag."

"I am gonna *kill* Georgia," Meg said through a clenched smile.

Jim laughed. "Abby is a perfectly fine name. My own daughter is called Abby."

"Short for Abigail, I expect," said Meg. "Not Abishag."

"Well, yes," Jim said. "Still, those Old Testament names are very popular." He was joking and we could tell. That was good. If we couldn't tell, that would be bad.

Kimberly Walnut sidled up and inserted herself into the conversation. "I have a sister named Ruth. Like *The Book of Ruth*. I dedicated my book to her. It's called *Fifty Nifty Thrifty Ways to Grow Your Congregation*."

"I heard," said Jim, giving her a smile. "I can't wait to read it." As he spoke, I could see the corners of his eyes narrow just the smallest bit. We'd get along. Yes, we'd get along just fine.

𝄢

Meg and I stayed in town, worked for a bit at the church, copying the current installment of my detective story onto the back of the psalm, then had a lovely dinner at the Ginger Cat, and headed for choir practice. The choir was, mostly, on time.

𝄢

We jumped in the flivver and peeled rubber. "So, who killed Sarah?" Pedro asked.

"Who's Sarah?" I said.

"The skirt in your office. Sarah Bellum. Real smart girl, but can't decide on a name."

174

I frowned and considered the problem. Sarah-Mystique-Trillium-Gina-Stormy-Monika, she had more names than that Abdul guy on the internet. Dead in the chair. Sure, she was tied up, but not that tight. I'd been tied up tighter, we all had. The bullet wound was nothing to speak of, but I'd probably hear about it from Johnny Law once he showed up.

"Any ideas?" asked Pedro.

"Yeah. The big sleep. I'm sure it was meant for you. The ol' poisoned chair trick."

"Huh," grunted Pedro, considering. "How do you figure?"

"That's your chair. Mine's behind the desk."

"Now I'm getting peeved," he said.

♪

"Well, Sarah's dead," Hollie said, reading my latest, "or whatever her name is. We're getting ready for the big finish. I can feel it. Everything's coming to a head."

"That's the problem with these stories," said Randy. "You never really know."

"Hey," said Fred, "our window's back!"

"Thanks be to God," said Steve. "Although we can't really see it in the dark. I guess we'll get a look at it on Sunday morning."

"I expect the new one looks just like the old one," said Marty. "When does the scaffolding come down?"

"It's gone already," said Georgia. "They popped in the window, took down the scaffolding, sent a bill to the insurance company, and disappeared on little cat feet."

"How's the new tryout priest?" asked Bob Solomon. "I couldn't get to the meet-'n'-greet."

"He seems very pleasant," I said. "Cordial, well-spoken, highly educated ..."

"Not crazy?" asked Marjorie.

"I'm not one to speak on crazy," I said, "but he gives every indication of being not crazy."

"He's old," said Sheila.

"He's fifty-nine," said Meg, taking my argument to heart. "Not that old. He might retire in eight years or so, but how long would a young priest stay with us?"

175

"That's a good point," said Sheila.

"Anyway," I said, "he's preaching on Sunday."

"Will he stay for the Blessing of the Animals?" asked Lena.

"That's next week," I said. "This Sunday we have a concert in the afternoon — the Mt. Basil Concert Choir. The Blessing of the Animals is on October 4th. St. Francis Day."

"Oh," said Lena, then, "I'm bringing my ferret."

"Oh, dadgummit," said Marjorie, "I forgot about that Blessing of the Animals thingy. I gotta go find an animal."

"You don't have to go find one," said Goldi Fawn. "You're supposed to bring one that you already have. Your pet."

"So, it's not like the Blessing of the Canned Goods?" Marjorie asked. "I was gonna get a fish or something, then wrap it in white tissue paper and donate it to the soup kitchen."

"Nothing like that," said Goldi Fawn. "You bring your pet and then it gets blessed."

"Hey," said Mark Wells, "what if that animal is an atheist? Or maybe another religion? What right do we have to force it into being blessed?"

"That's a good point," said Bert Coley. "I mean, my dog is a Bible believing Christian, but he's a bluetick coonhound so, of course, he's a Christian dog. He even says grace before he eats. But what about some Muslim dog, like an Afghan hound?"

"Or a chow chow," said Mark. "That dog would be a Buddhist."

"Your pet is what you are," said Goldi Fawn. "It says so in the Bible. My cat is a Baptist."

"Are you a Baptist?" Georgia asked.

"No, but the lady who I got her from was. She even had her baptized. I got the certificate. It's not easy to dunk a cat, but she wanted to make sure Fancy was going straight to cat heaven if she choked on one of her hairballs."

"Right," I said. "So now we should rehearse. How about the music for Sunday?"

We went through the anthem, *The Eyes of All*, a lovely setting by Jean Berger. The psalm was 19, and the communion motet was Attwood's *Teach Me, O Lord, the Way of Thy Statutes*. As we were finishing up, Susan Sievert and Moosey appeared at the top of the stairs, both bearing trumpets.

"What's this?" asked Bev.

"Well, Moosey's been playing with the band at school," I said. "Now he's had a few lessons. We thought it was time he played in church."

"Really?" said Meg. "Wonderful!" If Moosey was capable of looking embarrassed, he did.

"They'll be playing the postlude," I said. "Purcell's famous *Trumpet Tune*, arranged for two trumpets and organ."

"In C," said Susan with a smile.

"In C. Now, if you'll all sit back, may I present Moosey McCollough and his teacher Susan Sievert."

There was wild applause, but nothing like when they were finished. My arrangement was such that Moosey had quarter notes and half notes in the middle of his range, I covered the tune and the harmony, and Susan contributed flourishes, fripperies, fandangles, and enough high notes to give Purcell a nosebleed.

"Sunday," I said when the furor had subsided. "Don't miss it."

Chapter 28

Saturday was not a good day for the clergy. Axel Trimble, the ex-Navy SEAL high school principal, found out that his wife, Baylee, apparently not being appreciated enough at home, came to Father Walmsley for a confidential cuddling session. Unfortunately, on Friday, she was seen coming out of the Snuggery with the priest by Helen Pigeon who just happened to mention it to Marjorie, who was on her way to the Piggly Wiggly, and you know how that Hannah at the checkout register is, always wheedling the latest gossip from whomever is in her line, and, of course, Hannah told her best friend, Amelia, who is the biggest blabbermouth in town. Then, according to Mark Wells, Axel was in Dr. Ken's Gun Emporium on Saturday morning, checking out the latest shipment of assault rifles and Terry Shager, there buying some varmint ammo, kidded him about the cuddling thing.

"Hey, big fella," Terry said, "I hear that Baylee's been getting cuddled."

Axel's eyes narrowed dangerously. "What did you say?" Axel had been at church on the morning the cuddlers had been commissioned and, needless to say, was not at all impressed. He wasn't so much a cuddler as a trained assassin.

Terry, realizing his error, looked down and pretended to study a used Colt .38 in the display case. "Uh ... nothing. Nothing at all."

Axel put a huge hand on his shoulder, turned him around, and backed him into the hunting knife display. "What did you just say?"

"Umm, well ... I, uh, happened to hear, you know, down at the hardware store, that Baylee was, uh, I mean ... oh, crap."

"Spit it out," growled Axel. Axel was a large man and his special services background was evident. He was well over six feet tall, two hundred thirty pounds or so, with arms the size of small tree trunks. His hair was short, self-cut once a week with a pair of dog clippers, and he had a faint scar running from his ear halfway down his cheek, a souvenir from his tour in Iraq.

"Baylee was in the St. Barnabas Snuggery with the priest," Terry blurted out, then shut his eyes and prepared to meet his maker. When he opened his eyes, he saw Axel exiting the front door of the store. "Oh, crap," he said again.

Axel went right down to the church. The doors were open: the altar guild was working on flower arrangements, the janitorial service was getting everything ready for Sunday. Joyce Cooper saw Axel storm in, and called a greeting to him. He ignored her, intent on his mission, and so Joyce, suspecting something must be amiss, followed him. Axel walked down the hall, past the rector's office, turned right, and walked to the library — Sarah's Snuggery. The sign up sheet had been taken down since the vestry had decreed there would be no cuddling on the weekends. He tried the door. Locked. Angry as Axel was, it only took one kick to destroy the door and leave it hanging in splinters from the jamb. He stepped through the wreckage and found Father Thomas Walmsley under a lambskin throw on the pullout sofa, cuddling with Kimberly Walnut — "cuddling" not exactly being the correct term, since neither of them had their cuddle clothes on.

Father Walmsley screamed. Kimberly Walnut screamed. Joyce Cooper screamed.

Axel Trimble tore off a piece of the door jamb, ragged, with a few nails sticking out, and seemed to be focused on teaching Father Walmsley a lesson. Joyce, being a good Christian woman and intent on not seeing murder done, jumped on Axel's back and covered his eyes with her hands. It was the distraction the priest needed. He scooted past Axel and out the door, quick as a lizard, the fleecy pelt hiked around his loins like a hairy diaper, leaving Kimberly Walnut scrambling to pull the top sheet free of the clutter to cover herself. He scurried down the hall and locked himself in his office. Kimberly Walnut was, for once, speechless. Oh, she tried to say something, but all that came out were barnyard animal noises.

Axel reached behind him and lifted Joyce off his back, not gently, but not, at least, in a way that might do her injury. He gave Kimberly Walnut a look of disgust, patted Joyce on the shoulder, and disappeared down the hallway.

"I've never seen anything so horrible," Joyce said later. "There were bosoms and dangly things flopping all over the place. I didn't know where to avert my eyes first."

"I can only imagine," I said.

"I thought I was done for when Axel grabbed that piece of wood. I've never seen anyone so mad, but then it was like, click, something switched off. I went down to see if Axel had smashed in Father Walmsley's office door, but he hadn't. He was just gone."

"You're a good person," I said. "That could have ended very badly. Greater love has no one than this: to lay down one's life for one's friends."

"You mean I laid down my life for Kimberly Walnut?" said Joyce.

"Yes."

"Figures."

After a tearful half-hour in the Snuggery, Joyce finally assured Kimberly Walnut that she wouldn't tell anyone, but, of course, I'd gotten the whole story by lunchtime. After some discussion, Joyce and I thought we might keep it under wraps, just for the time being. Still, I had to tell Meg, that was a given, and it was just too good not to tell Pete and Cynthia. Then Nancy showed up. But we could all keep a secret, at least for the rest of the afternoon. We were sitting at one of the new picnic tables in Sterling Park. Cynthia had brought us sandwiches, chips, and beers from the Slab. Meg had a bottle of water.

"We need more details," said Cynthia.

"Yes," said Meg, "the juicy stuff."

"Alas, I have none."

"You aren't even interested?" said Cynthia. "What about Kimberly Walnut? What did she tell Joyce? Did she spill the whole sordid story?"

Meg joined in. "Yes, and how did Father Walmsley escape from his office? What about the rest of the altar guild? Didn't they hear the commotion?"

"There are other things we need to know as well," added Cynthia. "Certain cuddling particulars. Who was where? What was which?"

I shrugged.

"You are absolutely no help at all," said Cynthia, then turned to Meg. "We're going to have to talk to Joyce."

"Absolutely," said Meg. "Has anyone seen Axel Trimble?"

"Nobody's seen him," I said. "When Joyce told me what happened, I drove over and talked to Baylee."

"That's good," said Cynthia. "She needs to know what's going on."

"How did she seem?" asked Meg.

"Concerned and disquieted," I said. "Uneasy, apprehensive, anxious, yet solicitous. I sensed these and many other feelings. I can do that, you know, sense women's feelings. It's my superpower."

Meg slugged me in the arm.

"Ow. To tell the truth, she didn't seem too worried."

"Probably happened before," said Nancy. "PTSD maybe."

"Maybe," I said, "but if you walk in on two cuddlers cuddling in their birthday suits, and you know that one of those cuddlers has also cuddled your wife, you might jump to a conclusion."

"Hey," said Pete, "what if you name that baby Sierra Rose?"

"What are you talking about?" said Cynthia, incredulously. "Are you even listening to this conversation? Have you got dementia, or something?"

"Probably," said Pete. "I was just thinking. Sierra Rose. It's got a nice ring to it." He looked at the bottle of Sierra Rosbier in his hand.

"I'm not calling any daughter of mine Sierra," said Meg. "Anyway, the McCollough children are all named for beers. I'm not a fan."

"You can call her by her middle name," Pete said. "Rose. Or, you could even combine it." He tried it out. "Sierrarose," then, "Nah, never mind. That's terrible."

I thought for a moment, then said, "I like Rose."

"Yes," said Meg, considering. "I like Rose, too. Maybe Rose for a middle name then. Not Sierra."

"Not Sierra," I agreed, and then that little thing in my brain started clicking for no good reason. I sat there for a moment, clicking away.

Rose for a middle name. Or maybe combine it.

Click, click.

We were fairly sure that Peggy Wist killed Ron Pigeon, but she would have had to find him, chat him up, get invited to his house, then talk him into taking that Viagra, which, admittedly, wouldn't have taken much doing. She could have done some of that on-line from Philadelphia, but it would still take some reconnaissance. She'd want to check out his living arrangements, his visitors, his situation. She would have had to have heard about the skeleton in the first place. No, I thought, she'd been in town, talked to him, flirted with him, probably for some time. I'd bet he hadn't known who she was.

"What?" said Meg.

I held up my hand for quiet and waded through my cerebral cortex like one of those cranberry farmers on that TV commercial, wearing brain waders and poking at my frontal lobe with a long stick.

"*What?*" said Meg again after a long minute.

Click.

"Holy smokes!" I said. "I looked right at it and it didn't even register."

"What didn't register?" said Nancy.

"I think I know who Ron's killer is."

"We already know that," said Nancy. "It's Peggy. Peggy Wist Young."

"Yes, it is," I said.

Chapter 29

Me and Pedro busted into the rehearsal hall like a couple of elephants into a peanut factory, not a factory that "makes" peanuts, because we know that only God can make a peanut, but the kind that puts them in the little cans and I don't know why the elephants would bust in except maybe they smelled those peanuts.

The Maestro was standing on the podium, her doctoral hood fashionably askew, a loaded baton in her hand. The NANNIEs were standing at attention, bleating out their coronation anthem, "Ein Feste Burgle ist unser Goat," specially commissioned for the occasion.

There was Adeline, Miss Mohair 2015, blinking her peepers in the soprano section, a terrified "maaa" uddering forth from her luscious lips. There was the Archbishop-Elect, cowering in the corner, fingering his Caprasian rosary and reciting the Confession of St. Jacques the Unstrapable.

"Well, at least we're all in the same room," I said.

If Father Walmsley and Kimberly Walnut were concerned for their careers, they gave no indication on Sunday morning. Both were in attendance, taking care of their regular duties, alongside the Rev. Dr. James Hook, who was celebrating the Eucharist and preaching the sermon. I had no doubt that Kimberly Walnut and Thomas Walmsley had talked after the fact, and Kimberly Walnut, in her usual state of denial, was sure that Joyce wouldn't spill the beans. To Kimberly Walnut's mind, that just left Axel Trimble, and no one had seen him since the incident. Baylee told me he had a cabin up in the woods where sometimes he'd go to cool off after a blowup. Nancy had been right. It was PTSD, Post Traumatic Stress Disorder, left over from his time in Iraq. Baylee assured me it was under control. They had been having problems, but they were working through them. She'd been very stressed, that's why she thought getting cuddled might be a good idea. Axel had a hard time with physical contact. He just needed a day or two, she said. He'd be back at school on Monday.

The service began as usual. We heard the collect, sang the processional hymn, then the *Gloria* (Glory be to God on High), and settled into the lessons. The church was full, chiefly because of Father Hook. His visit had been well-advertised and everyone wanted to see him for themselves. Moosey and Susan joined us in the choir loft, trumpets in hand, Susan planning to add descants to the hymns, and then, with Moosey, play the Purcell postlude. It promised to be a fine morning, worship-wise.

Kimberly Walnut was seated beside Father Hook on one side of the chancel. Father Walmsley had taken his customary seat on the other side next to the chair reserved for the bishop. Kimberly Walnut had decided that she should read the Old Testament and Epistle lessons, and the Gospel would be read by Father Walmsley, this in spite of the fact that Calvin Denton had been scheduled to read weeks ago. Kimberly Walnut was never one to miss an opportunity to show her worth to a potential boss. She read the first lesson, we sang the psalm, and then Kimberly Walnut began to read the Epistle lesson.

"Are any among you suffering?" she read. "They should pray. Are any cheerful? They should sing songs of praise."

Directly in front of Kimberly Walnut, four rows back, a woman got to her feet. It was Savannah Jean Butts.

"Heretic!" she proclaimed in a loud voice that caused every head to turn. She pointed a long accusing finger at Kimberly Walnut. "Let the women keep silence in the churches: for it is not permitted unto them to speak; but let them be in subjection, as also saith the law."

"Oh, no!" whispered Bev. "Savannah Jean. What is she doing here?"

"I guess she's here to put us back on the path to righteousness," Meg whispered back. "Maybe the Pentecostals are taking today off to visit other churches."

Kimberley Walnut, not a quick thinker, and certainly not good in a situation like this, stared directly at Savannah Jean. After an agonizing moment, she concluded there was only one way forward: to keep reading, but at a much higher volume, relying on the Word of God to silence her critic.

"Are any among you sick? They should call for the elders of the church and have them pray over them, anointing them with oil in the name of the Lord."

"Apostate!" called Larlene Hickey. She and her twin sister, Harmony, stood up next to Savannah Jean. "Hear the Word of the Lord. If women would learn anything, let them ask their own husbands at home: for it is shameful for a woman to speak in the church."

"Shameful," said Harmony, crossing her arms and glaring at Kimberly Walnut.

"Hey," said Moosey in a loud voice. "They're the ones that stole all our four-leaf clovers."

"I wonder," said Rhiza, "if they understand the irony of standing up in church and proclaiming the Word of the Lord, them being women, and all."

I looked at Jim Hook. He seemed to be mildly interested and attentive, but not in the least alarmed. Father Walmsley, on the other hand, looked panicked. He wrung his hands, stood, and walked up to the lectern behind Kimberly Walnut, who was determined to finish reading the lesson.

Calvin Denton, having been demoted from lay-reader to usher, and Joe Perry, the head usher, had gotten to either side of the pew, but Savannah Jean and the Hickey twins were planted right in the middle of the section, flanked by parishioners on both sides. If Calvin and Joe had been able to get to them, they might have dragged them from the service, but not without a lot of noise. These three weren't going to go quietly.

"Will you please *shut up?!*" hissed Kimberly Walnut. "You're ruining our service."

"First Corinthians 14, verses thirty-four and thirty-five," crowed Savannah Jean, with a smug smile. "Look it up yourself if you don't believe me."

"Shouldn't you do something?" Georgia asked me.

I shrugged and kept watching. There were at least thirty people now holding cell phones aloft, filming the festivities. Then, at the front of the church, coming through the side door just behind the chancel rail, I saw the familiar figure of Axel Trimble. He sat down in the bishop's chair, unnoticed, since all eyes were on Kimberly Walnut and Savannah Jean.

"Go back to your own church!" said Kimberly Walnut, nearing the end of her tether. "You bunch of Pentecostal hillbillies!"

"Hillbillies?" snarled Savannah Jean. "Hillbillies with the Word of God on their side, you Jezebel!"

"Jezebel? Who are you calling a Jezebel? I demand you leave this church this instant!"

"Now, now, now," said Father Walmsley, standing behind Kimberly Walnut. "Let's everyone stay calm. Remember the words of Jesus ..."

"We ain't leaving this church unless you drag us out," said Savannah Jean in a loud voice. "You hear that? You're gonna have to drag us out. We got just as much right as anybody to attend a church service and stand up and reproof you. 'All scripture is breathed out by God and profitable for teaching, for reproof, for correction, and for training in righteousness.' Second Timothy 3:16. Says so in the Bible and in the Bill of Rights."

"You don't know anything about the Bible!" yelled Kimberly Walnut. "*Or* the Bill of Rights!"

"Now, now, now," muttered Father Walmsley.

"I know enough to know my God-given right to free speech," said Savannah Jean, "and also my God-given right to bear arms." She pulled her jacket back revealing a holstered pistol on her hip.

"Uh, oh," I said, then to Meg, "Call Nancy. Tell her to get over here." I reached under the organ bench, pushed a hidden button and, when the drawer slid open, took my own pistol from its hiding place, and headed down the steps.

"I got me a carry permit," announced Savannah Jean. "I'm perfectly legal and within my rights. I could draw down on you before you can say another heathen word."

"You get out!" screamed Kimberly Walnut.

"Harlot!" Savannah Jean shouted back. "Thou shalt not commit fornication, nor adultery, nor lay with another woman's husband!"

"Harlot!" yelled Harmony Hickey, her arms still crossed in defiance.

I don't know if she had any knowledge of Saturday's exploits, I suspect not, but she hit Kimberly Walnut's last nerve.

"We never did!" shouted Kimberly Walnut, her eyes wild, then, "Who told you? I mean ... we never did!"

Father Walmsley bowed his head and shook it side to side.

Kimberly Walnut took a few seconds to rummage through the books and papers on the shelf beneath the lectern, then came up with her own pistol. She'd decided at some point that the Kentucky law allowing pastors to pack heat in church had merit in North Carolina, and had stashed a .38 automatic under her prayer book. Now she pointed it at Savannah Jean with both hands.

It was at this point that the congregation, including the Hickey twins, hit the floor, their iPhone videos forgotten. There was not a head to be seen, everyone taking shelter under and behind the heavy wood of the pews. I had a good view from the back, and saw Savannah Jean reach for her holster. I didn't know if either woman had been practicing, but bullets flying around in a church service is never a good thing. Luckily, we didn't have to worry about that. Before Savannah Jean could draw, from out of the corner of my eye, I saw a blur cross the chancel. Axel Trimble elbowed Father Walmsley backwards out of the way, and was on Kimberly Walnut in another half-second. It was like something out of an action movie. Axel, being a highly trained Navy SEAL dealing with some PTSD, went into attack mode. With a loud slap, the gun left her grip and fell harmlessly onto the floor. Two punches later, maybe three — it was hard to tell, they were so fast — Kimberly Walnut dropped to the floor in a heap, unconscious. I didn't know if she was dead. She very well could be. I'd seen her head snap back with the first punch. After that I didn't see where the blows landed.

I looked over at Father Jim Hook. He was sitting, looking around, concerned, but hadn't gotten up, nor made any move at all. Father Walmsley, though, looked as stunned as a man could look, his mouth hanging open. "Oh, no," he muttered, and flip-flopped his sandaled feet back toward his chair. Axel Trimble stood over Kimberly Walnut like a victorious gladiator waiting for the congregation to give the thumbs down sign so he could finish the job. I would have done it, but Savannah Jean was still trying to clear her holster. I was at the end of the pew in a heartbeat, my gun up.

"Savannah Jean," I said. "You pull that gun and I will shoot you."

She looked over at me and her anger turned to terror in a hot second. Both her hands flew into the air. "Don't shoot," she yelped. "Pentecostal lives matter!"

"Get out of that pew, and keep your hands where I can see them. You, too, Larlene, Harmony. This way. You other folks let them out."

The congregation was slowly getting back into their seats, not saying a word, wanting to hear and see everything.

Nancy came in the front doors and raced up the center aisle to where I was standing, her gun in her hand.

"Holy Mary, mother of Jesus," she said. "What on earth?"

"I'm going to let you take these three to the station and book them," I said, "then call Watauga County up and haul them to jail."

"Book us for what?" barked Savannah Jean as I relieved her of her weapon.

"Public endangerment, inciting a riot, and terrorism," I said. "For a start." I turned back to Nancy. "Call an ambulance first, will you? I don't know how bad Kimberly Walnut is hurt, but she isn't moving."

"Was she shot?" asked Nancy, pulling out her phone.

"Nope. Axel disarmed her."

"I already called," said Bert, appearing right behind Nancy. He was in his choir robe, but had his sheriff's uniform on underneath, and had pulled out two sets of cuffs.

"Snap 'em on," I said, with a growl. Nancy had her pair out in a flash and the three women were duly arrested, cuffed, and had turned to be marched down the aisle.

In the front, Axel Trimble seemed to be coming back from his brief visit to the killing fields of Iraq. He looked down at Kimberly Walnut and shook his head, as if trying to clear the cobwebs. Father Walmsley had gotten back to his chair and, wanting to take a moment to collect himself, flopped down on the cushion.

Snap!

I hadn't had a chance to wonder why Axel Trimble had appeared so fortuitously. As Father Walmsley danced across the chancel screaming, it became obvious. He'd been there to place a beaver trap on Father Walmsley's chair at some point during the service, covering it with a thin cloth to obscure it.

In my experience, if you want to do a beaver in, there are two kinds of traps. The one kind, a body-grip trap, is a set of rotating square jaws that a beaver, ideally, will walk into and be immediately dispatched. This style of trap was developed during the 1950s and is quite popular with modern day trappers, as it is considered the most humane. The second kind is the old-fashioned spring-foothold trap. It's the kind of trap that we're used to seeing in cartoons, with the jaws that spring shut, clamping on whatever happens to be between them. It has the added bonus of leaping into the air when sprung, thus assuring a solid "bite."

The trap that Axel selected was the second kind. Axel, being an outdoorsman, a hunter, and a collector of traps of all kinds, had chosen from his collection, an antique Newhouse trap, Number 14, circa 1870. The Newhouse traps were designed by Sewell Newhouse, a resident of Oneida, New York, sometime prior to the year 1840. The Number 14 had a jaw spread of six and one-half inches, stiff springs, and offset jaws. Also known as the "Oneida Jump," it came furnished with sharp teeth, six on a side, sufficiently close to prevent the animal from pulling its foot out. Axel kept all his traps in pristine condition, new and old.

It was a powerful trap, large enough for beaver, badgers, even a coyote. It was certainly large enough for Father Walmsley. The jaws clamped onto his backside and whatever else happened to be loose in the area. His fondness for not wearing pants under his alb did him no favors. There was one, maybe two thin layers of fabric between the Jaws of Death and Father Walmsley's altogether.

"Oh, my Sweet Jesus!" he screamed, leaping across the dais like a lemur with diaper rash. "Somebody help me!" Tears were in his eyes and both his hands tugged in vain at the metal torture device attached to his derrière. He was trying to remove it without doing any more damage to the tender flesh, but someone with some strength and a better angle would be needed to pry that trap back open. Axel looked at him for a long moment, then disappeared out the side door from which he'd entered. Father Walmsley finally lay down on his stomach beside the altar and whimpered. Jim Hook got to his feet, walked over to the unfortunate priest, and with considerable effort, pried the jaws apart, releasing Father Walmsley from their grip. The back of his cream-colored robe was turning red from the blood. Father Hook helped Father Walmsley to his feet and walked him back to the sacristy.

Our two EMTs arrived and came hustling down the center aisle with their gurney.

"We were just over at New Fellowship Baptist," Joe said. "An old guy thought he was having a heart attack. He's okay though. His wife is driving him over to the hospital."

I pointed at Kimberly Walnut puddled beside the lectern.

"Is she dead?" asked Mike, as we walked to the front.

"I don't know," I said. "Axel hit her mighty hard. Maybe two or three times. He went into some kind of PTSD flashback."

"Wow," said Mike.

"Hey," I said, "as far as I'm concerned, he's a hero. This could have ended very badly."

"Who's blood?" asked Joe.

"That'd be from the priest. He sat on a beaver trap. You need to take him with you as well. He's going to need stitches at the very least."

"Dare I ask?" said Mike.

"Axel set it. I suppose he's going to have to answer for that."

"I'm going to become an Episcopalian," said Joe. "We Lutherans hardly ever have this much going on."

Kimberly Walnut was not dead, as it turned out, and the EMTs strapped her to the gurney, collected Father Walmsley from the sacristy and headed for the hospital. I went back to the choir loft, still hearing quite a buzz from the congregation. They were all talking, trying to remember exactly what happened so they could, no doubt, tell their grandchildren. Finally Father Hook walked to the pulpit and raised his hands for silence. After a few moments, he had it.

"The service continues on page three hundred fifty-eight," he said.

The service had almost concluded when I got a text from Dave. He'd been doing background checks all morning, running down my hunch.

Chapter 30

Considering the morning's goings-on, the concert by the Mt. Basil University Concert Choir in the afternoon was refreshing and delightful.

Proceedings began with the concert goers being greeted at the door of the church by an army of miniature ushers. Meg and Bev had gathered their etiquette class, dressed them to the nines, and had them handing out programs and showing people to their seats. Moosey, Bernadette, Ashley and Christopher had all been in Sunday School since kindergarten. Dewey had joined them a few years ago. Samantha, Stuart, Addie, and Lily were all a year younger, but part of the etiquette group. Four tuxedoed boys, and five girls in their nicest dresses, all boutonnièred and corsaged.

Good evening, madam," Stuart said to Meg, with a small bow. "Would you care for a program?"

"I would, Stuart, thank you very much."

"My pleasure, madam," said Stuart, trying not to laugh. He handed Meg a program. "How about you, sir?" he said to me, holding another program aloft.

"Why, yes, please."

Moosey was working the next aisle over, Dewey and Christopher, the side doors up front. The girls were showing people to their seats.

"How many, please?" said Bernadette.

"Two down front," said Meg.

"Right this way," said Bernadette, with a soft wave of her arm. "Follow me, please."

"I'm impressed," I whispered to Meg as we followed Bernadette down the aisle.

"Of course you are," said Meg, smiling.

The other patrons were impressed as well, judging from the comments we heard. By concert time, the church was full.

I'd already seen the program, of course, and was looking forward to a fresh hearing of several of the works: Bach's *Singet dem Herrn ein neues Lied*; Mendelssohn's setting of Psalm 19, *Die Himmel erzählen die Ehre Gottes;* and three Poulenc sacred motets. A highlight was Monteverdi's *Laudate pueri Dominum* from the "1610 Vespers Service." Maestro Clochette had divided the eight-voice work between soloists and chorus and had a viol accompany the group. It was a stunning performance, achingly lovely.

We heard Vaughan William's *Shakespeare Songs*. Not pieces that I knew, and I would have not guessed them to be by that composer, but very enjoyable. There were other individual pieces, mostly by living composers, all well sung and expertly conducted, then the usual nod to the American Spiritual, always a crowd favorite. Maestro Clochette conducted most of the program, chatting to us occasionally between sections. The Mallarites each took their turn conducting a short work, Jeremy and Julia both choosing pieces by Eric Whitaker, Jenny, one by Egil Hovland, a Norwegian composer.

Father Walmsley and Kimberly Walnut were, understandably, nowhere to be seen, but the rest of us enjoyed the afternoon immensely. After a standing ovation and an encore, we adjourned to the parish hall where the church ladies had put out their finest spread of finger sandwiches and desserts. The singers dove in like only college kids on a choir tour can. The etiquette class walked around with their trays, picking up empty cups and used plates and napkins and whisking them off to the kitchen, all politeness and charm. As the event wound down and the choir got back onto their tour bus, followed by our good wishes and farewells, Meg, Bev, and the kids stayed in the parish hall to help the church ladies with the cleanup.

After the bus left, I found Mallary Clochette and her protégés back in the church picking up their scores and reviewing the concert.

"I thought that went very well," said the Maestro. "All of you pass."

All three laughed.

"Great concert," I said. "Do you guys have time for a beer before you take off for Asheville?"

Mallary looked at her watch. "We do. The bus is stopping for dinner somewhere along the way. A Cracker Barrel, I think. We don't have to be in Asheville till eight or so."

"Great! How about the Bear and Brew."

Mallary nodded. "We'll see you there in just a few minutes."

I'd gotten us a long table in the back and already had a Blue Moon in my hand by the time the four walked in. They sat down and ordered, three beers and a Chablis for Jeremy.

"Why don't we get a pizza?" I said, when the waitress showed up with the drinks. "That is, if you didn't fill up at the reception."

"I could eat," said Jeremy.

"That would be fine," said Mallary.

"What would you like?"

"I'm partial to the Black Bear," said Jenny.

"Seems like you've eaten here a time or two," I said with a grin. The Black Bear Special was a pizza topped with bear sausage, black truffles, mushrooms, a double helping of mozzarella cheese, and heirloom tomatoes.

"Too heavy for me," said Mallory.

"How about one Black Bear, and one artichoke and spinach," I said.

"Perfect," said Mallary. "I've had that one. It's delicious."

"Two mediums," I told the waitress, "and another beer for me."

"How's Thomas doing?" I asked Mallary.

"Oh, he's just ducky," she said sarcastically. "I already got the whole story. This isn't the first time, you know. I'm quite finished with Thomas Walmsley."

"I wonder," I said, after some discussion about the conducting of tone clusters, "if any of you knew a girl named Peggy Wist."

Silence and blank looks.

"I don't think so," said Jenny. "Does she go to Mt. Basil?"

"Nope. We found a skeleton of a girl earlier in the summer, and we're fairly sure it's her. It had been in the woods for thirty years or so."

"Well then, how in the world would we know her?" asked Jeremy.

I took a sip of my beer. "She was working at Camp Possumtickle in the summer of 1977. Someone killed her."

"Camp *Possumtickle*?" laughed Julia. "Really?"

"Well, you know how we bumpkins are, with our silly names and all." I looked at Jenny. "Anyway, I was wondering whether you might have attended the camp, maybe even worked at it when you were a girl. You did tell me you spent some summers up this way."

"Sure I did," said Jenny. "I even went to Camp Cheerio in Highpoint for a couple of summers, but I didn't go to Camp Possumtickle. I hadn't even heard of St. Germaine until I showed up for school this term."

"Is that the camp they're tearing down?" asked Jeremy.

"Yep," I said. "Sold to build a Renaissance Fair. See, here's the thing. We had a murder here in town three weeks ago, a man named Ron Pigeon."

"Thomas told me that was a suicide," said Mallary.

"It certainly looked like one," I said. "He was lying face down on the table, the gun on the floor, his right hand covered with gun shot residue. He was depressed, drinking, and self-medicating. He lost his business, his friends, his wife had left him — didn't even show up with his kids for the funeral. His bank account was empty. If anyone was going to commit suicide, it was probably him. Then, to top it off, he left a suicide note."

This isn't the way I wanted it to end.
Barbara, you were my first love and I am terribly sorry.

"And yet," said Mallary, disbelief clouding her voice, "you don't think it was suicide."

"Nope. He'd taken a couple of Viagras, and those pills, coupled with the heart medication he was taking, would have caused him to pass right out. He couldn't have shot himself if he'd passed out."

"Huh," said Jeremy, considering. He sipped his Chablis. "Well, what if he took Viagra and shot himself before they took effect."

"We thought about that," I said, "but why take Viagra if you're not planning on using it? They're not for shooting yourself in the head."

"So you think he was on a date," said Julia.

"I think so."

"And his date shot him?"

"Yep."

"I already told you," said Jenny, her face reddening, "I didn't go out with him. I'm married. Happily married."

I looked over at Julia.

194

"Absolutely not!" she said. "Okay, he asked me out for a drink, but why would I go out with him?" She gave a disgusted look. "Really? Me?"

"Hang on," said Jeremy. "What has this got to do with that dead girl?"

"Peggy Wist."

"Yeah, her."

"It's an interesting story," I said. "Camp Possumtickle, 1977. Ron Pigeon was a fifteen-year-old Counselor in Training that summer. Peggy Wist was a counselor at the girl's camp. She was nineteen. A music student at Stetson University in Florida."

"They have a good choral program," said Julia.

"I heard that," I said. "Anyway, Peggy was working as a counselor and the camp needed some help in the kitchen, so Peggy called her best friend Barbara McCuwen, also a music student at Stetson, and Barbara came up to the camp in July. You see, they'd been best friends for years. They grew up together at the Methodist Children's Home in Central Florida. So Barbara takes a bus up to Boone, gets over to the camp, and proceeds to start sleeping with all the boys she can find. We don't know if this was an ongoing pattern with her, or if she was acting out for some other reason, or what, but all the witnesses from that summer agree: she was available and willing."

"Well," said Jenny, "it was the '70s."

"It was. So Barbara and Ron eventually get together, probably sometime in early August. Then she broke up with him and moved on."

"How do you know that?" asked Mallary.

"Interesting thing. When they were tearing down the cabins to build the Renaissance Fair, they found a box of letters under the floor of the last one. Love letters from Ron to Barbara. Sixteen of them, to be exact, covering about ten days. Not mailed, delivered. They map out Ron's feelings pretty well. Who could blame him? Barbara was a twenty-year-old college girl, Ron was fifteen. He was smitten, first true love and all that, but here's something else."

I unrolled the Camp Possumtickle photo I'd brought with me and spread it across the table. I tapped on Ron's picture on the right.

"See here, that's Ron."

The group gathered around and peered intently at the picture.

"So that girl he has his arm around is Barbara?" asked Julia.

"No, that's Peggy Wist. We thought at first that it was Barbara McCuwen. We had the skull, you see, and our forensic artist gave us a drawing that looked awfully like this girl. When we talked to Ron Pigeon, he identified the girl as Barbara McCuwen. We had no reason to doubt him, but then he was killed. Someone else who'd been at the camp identified the girl as Peggy. Now why would Ron lie to us? Here's Barbara, over here." I pointed her out.

"They look a lot alike," said Jeremy, squinting at the figure. "*Most* of those girls look a lot alike."

Just then our waitress came up to the table with the Black Bear Special. A second waitress followed with the artichoke and spinach pizza.

"Can we just move that?" asked the first, nodding toward our picture.

"Sure," I said, sliding it to the end of the table. "Let's have some pizza."

We all helped ourselves and Nancy walked up to the table. "Sorry I'm late," she said. "Any of this for me?"

"Absolutely," I said. "There's plenty. You all know Nancy Parsky?"

Nods all around. I saw Julia and Jeremy flash a look. Nancy was wearing her uniform.

"I was telling them the story of Peggy and Barbara," I said.

"Please continue," said Nancy and took a piece of the artichoke pie.

"So, where was I?" I took a bite of pizza. The bear sausage was my favorite part. Delicious. "Oh, yeah," I said. "Barbara and Peggy both took off before their jobs were finished. Just a few days, but they disappeared at the same time. Barbara's foster parents, well ... ex-foster parents ... became concerned when they hadn't heard from her for weeks and couldn't contact her. The police talked to Peggy Wist, and she indicated that she gave Barbara a ride back to Florida, then went home for the Labor Day weekend. Peggy said she never saw Barbara again."

"Exactly right," said Nancy. "Hey! You mind if I get a beer? Be right back." She got up and headed to the bar.

"Hang on," said Jeremy. "You said that Peggy was dead."

"I know! Intriguing, isn't it? In 1977, Barbara disappeared and this Peggy Wist tells the police she gave her a ride home. Well, it turns out Peggy had lied to the police. She never gave

Barbara a ride home. We found her phone number, and when I called her, she said she'd just told the police that, that she was afraid to tell her parents that she'd gone to Daytona Beach and spent the week with her boyfriend."

"She was from the Children's Home," said Julia. "Did she even have parents?"

"No, she did not," I said. "She lied to me. Can you believe it? First Ron and now Peggy."

"How did you find her?" asked Jenny.

"That was Dave. Officer Dave Vance. He's good at that stuff. Social media, Linkedin, Facebook, social security, marriage records, real estate records, addresses, phone numbers. It's all out there if you know what you're looking for. We found her under the name Peggy Wist Young in Philadelphia."

All eyes went to Julia.

"What?" she said.

"Then we discovered that the skeleton wasn't Barbara at all. Whoever it was had suffered a bad leg break a few years before and guess what. Not Barbara. Peggy."

Everyone thought about that for a few moments.

"So if Peggy was dead," said Jenny, "who answered the phone when you called?"

"That would be Barbara McCuwen."

Just then, we heard a cell phone ringing under the table. No one moved, then Mallary Clochette got up, reached for her purse, and said, "I should probably take that. It might be about the choir."

"It's not," said Nancy, standing right behind her. "I was just calling Peggy."

"Once we knew where to start, Dave found out quite a lot," I said. "Peggy Wist finished college at the Curtis Institute in 1985. She'd transferred her credits from Stetson after withdrawing. There's a record of that, of course. She got married in 1987, divorced a year later, and entered graduate school at Westminster Choir College. More records. She finished her doctorate at Rutgers, then got a job at Temple University in Philadelphia. She married again, this time to a high school art teacher named Liam Clochette. They divorced after two years.

197

There's not much hiding you can do anymore. Not if you live a normal life."

"Wow," said Jeremy, his voice quiet. Mallary looked straight ahead, biting her lip.

"Margaret Hillary Wist," I said, looking at Mallary. "I read it on your high school report card. Peggy isn't a great name for a choral genius. Needs to have more panache. Why not combine your first and second names? Mallary. Mallary Clochette."

"So," said Mallary slowly. "Okay. I'm Peggy Wist. So what?"

"Yes," I said, "but Peggy's dead."

"You can't prove that."

"Actually, I can. I went down and visited the Children's Home. Talked to an old friend of yours, Beth Fountain, who works there as vice president of something-or-other. Anyway, she told me that all you kids went to Lakeside Dental Care — you remember, Dr. Gerard? They had an extensive set of Peggy's records which they were happy to provide. She'd had orthodonture work done when she was fourteen. It wasn't difficult to match the dental records."

"Oh."

"Here's what I think," I said, wiping my mouth with a napkin. "I think that Barbara killed Peggy Wist and Ron saw it. Somehow Barbara persuaded him to keep quiet about it. Maybe made him an accomplice."

"Why would Barbara do that?" asked Jenny. "You said they were best friends."

"Even best friends fall out," I said. "Our guess is jealousy, but we don't know. It doesn't really matter. There might have been drugs involved, that's what some of the counselors indicated. Barbara had brought pot with her to camp, pills, probably. She was sleeping around." I shrugged and drained my beer.

"So, you're saying that Dr. Clochette is Barbara?" asked Julia. All three students stared at their teacher with looks of disbelief.

"Yeah," I said, "I am."

"Don't you need a motive in a murder case?" asked Julia.

"Generally," I said, "and the prosecutor will come up with a good story, I'm sure. Barbara's main problem is going to be the trust fund."

"Trust fund?"

"When Peggy Wist turned twenty-one, she could claim her trust fund. It had been set up by the court, money paid on an accident claim that took the lives of her parents. The year after Peggy Wist withdrew from college and moved — no one knew where — she applied for the trust fund with her Social Security card, a Pennsylvania driver's license, and Florida birth certificate. They sent her a check for the entire amount: $62,347, including interest."

"How would she get a birth certificate?" asked Jeremy.

"Mailed away for it," I said. "Easy enough. According to Beth Fountain, Peggy and Barbara had been talking since they were kids about taking that trust fund money and moving up north. That's motive enough for any court. And then there's Ron."

"You can't prove any of this," said Mallary, desperation creeping into her voice. "You can't prove that I'm Barbara McCuwen."

"Well, I do have Barbara's dental records as well as Peggy's. So, unless you've had all your teeth replaced ..."

Nothing.

"Anyway," I continued, "we *can* prove Ron didn't kill himself. We just need to put someone else in the room, so now it's a matter of DNA." I stared at Mallary, the hard stare I got when contemplating murder done. "Now that we have a viable suspect, we'll get a court-ordered sample and check it against every loose strand of hair, the pizza box in the fridge, the unwashed glasses in the sink ... we'll find something."

"I ... uh ... I never said I wasn't in the house," Mallary said slowly. "Maybe we had a date. I might have had some pizza with him."

"Artichoke and spinach. We found half of it in the fridge. The receipt on the box says it was ordered the night Ron was shot."

"Wait a second," said Julia. "What about the suicide note?"

"It was one of the love notes that Ron wrote to Barbara back in 1977. She saved them all, left that one there, and put the rest of them under the cabin for us to find. Poor Ron, depressed, his family gone, and now the cops find the bones of his murdered lover in the woods. Why wouldn't he commit suicide? The box of letters confirms it."

"Wow," said Jeremy.

"Those letters probably have DNA on them as well," said Nancy. "We'll get them checked, of course. I'll bet that you read them quite a lot over the years."

"Oh, God," Mallary sobbed. She slumped deep into her chair and covered her face with both her hands. It seemed more like a sob of relief than a sob of anguish. "Oh, God," she said again, then straightened in her chair, dabbed her eyes with her napkin, and took a drink. "It was a horrible, horrible accident!"

I knew she was talking about Peggy. "You hit her in the head with a rock," I said. "You buried her in the woods. Doesn't sound like an accident."

"I didn't know what I was doing. I thought I was in love with Ron."

"You had sex with him," I said. "A fifteen-year-old kid. Then you moved on."

"I was a messed-up teenager back then, so sure, that's how it started. Then he started sending me those letters, those poems. No one had ever written me poems. I wanted him back. I told Peggy that."

"And she refused," said Nancy.

"She laughed, said it was her turn. We had a big fight. The first one we ever had."

"You followed them into the woods," I said.

Mallary nodded. "They were on a blanket, you know ... she was on top. I just lost it. I picked up a rock, came up behind them, and knocked her on the side of the head. I was so ... *mad!*"

We all stared at Mallary, nobody saying a word.

"I thought I'd just knocked her out, but she wouldn't wake up. Didn't wake up. After a few minutes, we knew she was dead. I told Ronald that it was his fault as much as mine, that we loved each other, that I had the letters. He helped me bury her and we swore never to mention it to anyone ever again. We wrote to each other for about four years after that — I was in Philadelphia by then — but he fell in love when he got to college, got married, everything else. I hadn't heard from him in twenty-five years." A blank expression crossed her face. "He didn't even recognize me."

"You dragged us here because they found the skeleton," said Jeremy.

Mallary nodded. "Thomas was already here. He told me about it. I don't know why he wanted to come here. I told him not to take the job. Then they find Peggy ... Ron's still living in the same town ... what are the chances?"

"Sometimes this is the way the universe works," I said. "Happens more times than I can tell you about."

"He was going to break down and spill everything. I could tell. He was at the end of his rope. All I worked for, gone."

"Yeah," I said. "That's tough."

Postlude

"It's over," I called to the Maestro. "Execute your cutoff and put down your baton."

"It's not over till I say it's over," growled the Maestro, in a voice much lower than any woman had the right to growl. "I can do anything I want. I'm the Maestro. Maybe I'll extend the coda. Maybe I'll even take it Molto Largo Espressivo."

"Maybe not," said Pedro, and his heater appeared in his hand: pow, it went. Pedro's motto was "Shoot first, then shoot one more time, then go have a drink." Pow, it went again, thus fulfilling two-thirds of Pedro's motto. I knew it wouldn't be long before he buttoned up the rest.

The NANNIEs brayed to a ragged cadence, then muddled to a stop.

"What's the meaning of this?" arfed one of the alto section leaders, a lady priest I knew named Gunner. Pedro walked to the podium and dragged the mohair wig from the Maestro's head.

"Dirk Knight," I said.

"Yep," said Pedro, "but her name's not Dirk. It's Pamela. She was pretending to be Dirk so she and Sarah could work the bar. They wanted info and Buxtehooters was the grapevine they needed. With the wig and enough makeup to clog a televangelista's drain, no one made the connection."

"She killed Sarah," I said, making sense of this whole plot, but not much.

"Sure she did." Pedro nudged her with the toe of one of his really expensive shoes. "Probably she was trying to finish me off since I'm the brains of this outfit, but Sarah was a loose cannon and she would have blabbed once you liquored her up."

"I do like to liquor them up," I admitted. "What about Adeline?"

"Just a nanny looking to have a little fun."

Mallary Clochette struck a deal with the prosecutor, and ended up with a sentence of twenty-five years to life for the murder of Ron Pigeon. They didn't prosecute her for the death of Peggy Wist. That was part of the deal. She'd be eligible for parole when she was seventy. Maybe, I thought, she'd start some kind of prison women's chorus and end up on *60 Minutes*. I didn't doubt it.

The three doctoral students finished their degrees with another professor, although it took them all an extra semester. They weren't happy about it, but there really wasn't anything they could do. Dr. Clochette's book, *LadySong: The Art of Conducting Women's Voices,* never made it past the publisher's editorial committee once her story was known. The entire episode was conveyed, via Jeremy and Julia, on the Choralwiki forum chatroom for months.

Savannah Jean Butts and the Hickey Twins, Larlene and Harmony, were convicted of public endangerment. Judge Adams fined them $300 each and sentenced them to forty hours of community service. He had them plant beds of four-leaf clovers all over town.

Axel Trimble decided to get professional help. He took the rest of the semester off from school and checked in with the Veteran's Administration in Asheville. He was never charged in the matter of the Jaws of Death versus Father Thomas Walmsley. Father Walmsley retired quietly back to Richmond. The Bishop of Virginia assured us he wouldn't be taking another pulpit.

Kimberly Walnut retired as well from mainline denominational ministry. She had needed some dental work and some speech therapy after Axel's not-so-gentle rebuke, but I thought she'd gotten off relatively easily. St. Barnabas generously offered to pay for the dentist and the therapist. She then tried to sue the church for damages — pain and suffering, and all that — but when the totality of her escapades were revealed, her lawyer dropped the suit, there not being much chance of a contingency fee to be had. The last we heard, her book deal was on hold, and she had applied to several non-denominational churches for positions in Christian Formation. We were not listed as a reference.

The Blessing of the Animals went wonderfully well. We held the service in the back garden and Father Tony Brown, our old priest, back in town for a few months, was happy to do the honors. Animals of all faiths ... Christian, Buddhist, Muslim ... all were blessed, and a good time was had by everyone. Seymour Krebbs' camel was there, some llamas, hedgehogs, dogs and cats of all descriptions. Helen brought her remaining fainting goat, which turned out to be a pregnant nanny. Sue Clark's dog, Bathsheba, did not bark at it. Even Rich Newport brought Luger the atheist German shepherd. One sniff of Bathsheba though, and that dog was saved, converted to the faith.

Penny Trice brought Pig Whistle, the famous groundhog, and her new baby possum, Terwilliger. Addie Buss had a cat named Princess Captain Hook. Jared Trimble showed up with a cigar box full of stink bugs.

Lena brought her ferret, Bert his coonhound. Meg was there with Baxter, Pete and Cynthia with Portia the Truffle Pig, and Moosey brought three little owlets, now named Wynken, Blynken, and Nod. Blynken was our favorite, and the one inclined to show up at our window most often. The pets of St. Germaine had a special place in our hearts, fainting goats aside.

I looked for the Archbishop, but he had disappeared. Pedro anticipated the question.

"He was here to lobby for liturgical codpiece retention. He's a traditionalist."

"Wrong crowd," I said, looking across the sea of unamused faces — the scowling countenances of women priests and the blank visages of Tennessee Kissing Goats. "No wonder he was cowering in the corner."

"No wonder," agreed Pedro.

"I guess you've wrapped it up," I said, "but I'm the boss and I'm keeping the two yards that Stormy paid us."

"Sure," said Pedro, lighting up a stogy. "You still owe me for the lugs."

"Hey!" yelled one of the sopranos contriving a fake little cough. "No smoking!" The choir all started hacking in sympathetic unison.

"Shaddap," said Pedro, disgustedly. He pulled his gun and shot the soprano to make his point, but not very much.

The Reverend Dr. James Hook was offered the position of rector, and to everyone's surprise, took it. His sermon on that fateful morning in September was fine, but, really, none of us in the congregation that morning paid much attention to it. The Spirit of Worship means different things to different people, but once the Minister of Christian Development and Ministry pulls a gun on a Pentecostal woman who's rebuking her, and is cold-cocked by an irate Navy SEAL who thinks the priest is sleeping with his wife, and then the priest sits on a beaver trap ... well ... even the Holy Spirit is apt to have trouble at that point. Dr. Hook would be joining us by Advent. The new church year. A new beginning.

The Etiquette Coterie, Moosey, Bernadette, and the rest, won a two-day pass to Carowinds, North Carolina's premiere amusement park, after graduation. The cost, including tickets, hotel rooms, transportation, and meals, was a little over $1,600. Money well spent.

Moosey continued his trumpet study with Susan Sievert at the university. His debut at church wasn't that great. He'd gotten lost a couple of times, but Susan was playing, and the organ was cranked up to three notches past *fortissimo*. No one noticed, and he was greeted with enough accolades and backslaps to keep him at it for the next few months. He'd be first chair in the band in no time.

Pete and Cynthia did get a black Labrador retriever puppy. Pete named her Fritzi.

The Renaissance Fair started going up in November, then the snows came in. In April, the crews were back and many St. Germaine residents made the trip out to Old Camp Possumtickle to watch the progress. They were constructing a sixteenth-century Medieval town, complete with shops, village lanes, outdoor theaters, an arts and crafts marketplace, a jousting ring, everything you might want for a complete Renaissance experience, but with time-warped plumbing included. They planned to be finished by July, up and running by late September. At the rate they were moving ahead, no one had reason to doubt it.

Lena Carver and Hollie Swofford practiced all year and their twosome, *Sapphire Lily*, was accepted for inclusion at the fair. They were thrilled. They would receive minimum wage and two turkey legs per shift.

Jeff Pigeon hired Brother Hog as his campaign manager. Why? We didn't know.

Meg decided on the name Abigail Rose, but only if the child looked like an Abigail Rose once we'd had the chance to meet her. We still had a few months yet.

"We'll need a nanny," I said one night, driving home from choir practice.

"All the best people have them," said Meg.

"How about an *au pair*? Someone French, or maybe Belgian. They can teach little Abishag another language."

"I wouldn't mind," said Meg, then looked at me with a grimace. "Abi*gail*, not Abi*shag*."

"I know," I said, "but it's hard to give up on my dreams."

"Oh, my dear," said Meg, smiling now and taking my free hand. We were in my pickup, the stars lighting up the sky like diamonds. The distinctive voice of Louis Armstrong was coming through the speakers and across the years ...

The colors of the rainbow so pretty in the sky,
Are also on the faces of people going by.
I see friends shaking hands saying, "How do you do?"
They're really saying, "I love you."

I hear babies cry, I watched them grow;
They'll learn much more than I'll ever know.
And I think to myself what a wonderful world.
Yes, I think to myself what a wonderful world.

"Oh, my dear," said Meg again. "Your dreams have not even begun ..."

"Another case solved," I said, "but, where's Marilyn?"

"She's down at Buxtehooters, waiting for you," said Pedro with a sly smirk. "There's a message on your machine. Something about a tenth anniversary. I guess you didn't hear it."

I smiled. Buxtehooters, eh? It's good to be a detective.

About the Author

In 1974, Mark Schweizer, a brand-new high school graduate, decided to eschew the family architectural business and become an opera singer. Against all prevailing wisdom and despite jokes from his peers such as "What does the music major say after his first job interview?" (answer: You want fries with that?), he enrolled in the Music School at Stetson University. To his father, the rationale was obvious. No math requirement.

Everything happens for a reason, however, and he now lives and works as a musician, composer, author and publisher in Tryon, North Carolina with his lovely wife, Donis. If anyone finds out what he's up to, he'll have to go back to work at Mr. Steak. He actually has a bunch of degrees, including a Doctor of Musical Arts from the University of Arizona. I know! What were they thinking?

Other books

The Alto Wore Tweed
Independent Mystery Booksellers Association "Killer Books" selection, 2004

The Baritone Wore Chiffon

The Tenor Wore Tapshoes
IMBA 2006 Dilys Award nominee

The Soprano Wore Falsettos
Southern Independent Booksellers Alliance 2007 Book Award Nominee

The Bass Wore Scales

The Mezzo Wore Mink

The Diva Wore Diamonds

The Organist Wore Pumps

The Countertenor Wore Garlic

The Christmas Cantata
(Okay - it's not a mystery, but you should read it anyway.)

The Treble Wore Trouble

The Cantor Wore Crinolines

The Maestro Wore Mohair

Dear Priscilla
A 1940s comic noir thriller!

Just A Note

If you've enjoyed this book — or any of the other mysteries in this series — please drop me a line. My e-mail address is mark@sjmp.com.

Also, don't forget to visit the website (sjmpbooks.com) for lots of fun stuff! You'll find the Hayden Konig blog, discounts on books, funny recordings, and "downloadable" music for many of the now-famous works mentioned in the Liturgical Mysteries including *The Pirate Eucharist, The Weasel Cantata, The Mouldy Cheese Madrigal, Elisha and the Two Bears, The Banjo Kyrie, Missa di Poli Woli Doodle,* and a lot more.